Praise for Molly Jong-Fast's *Normal Girl*

"*Normal Girl* is a searing, bitchy, funny novel about privilege in wretched excess and the accidental nature of grace. Molly Jong-Fast is a prodigy. Parents everywhere should be horrified by this deeply impressive debut."

—Jay McInerney

"Rich in dark comedy and sad pronouncements. The writing is always taut and effective, precise and assured."

—London *Times*

"[Molly Jong-Fast] has a great ear and a keen eye for the tired and tawdry world she describes here. . . . Obvious talent."

—*The Boston Globe*

"Already poised to be as talked-about as *Fear of Flying*."

—*Interview*

"An edgy comedy about a nineteen-year-old rich girl in New York who has 'more issues than Harper's Bazaar.' "

—*USA Today*

"So much talent, so young a writer! Hard-edged, savage, funny, brilliant."

—Fay Weldon

"If you want to know what goes on in the minds of New York's young, rich, and famous, read Molly Jong-Fast's hilarious novel, *Normal Girl*."

—Susan Cheever

ALSO BY MOLLY JONG–FAST

Normal Girl
Girl [Maladjusted]

The

SOCIAL CLIMBER'S

Handbook

The

SOCIAL CLIMBER'S

Handbook

A NOVEL

MOLLY JONG-FAST

VILLARD TRADE PAPERBACKS NEW YORK

2011 Villard Books Trade Paperback Original

Published in the United States by Villard Books, an imprint of The Random House Publishing Group, a division of Random House, Inc., New York.

VILLARD BOOKS and VILLARD & "V" CIRCLED Design are registered trademarks of Random House, Inc.

Library of Congress Cataloging-in-Publication Data
Jong-Fast, Molly.
   The social climber's handbook: a novel / Molly Jong-Fast.
     p. cm.
   ISBN 978-0-345-50189-9
   eBook ISBN 978-0-345-52633-5
   1. Upper East Side (New York, N.Y.)—Fiction. I. Title.
   PS3560.O57S63   2011
813'.54—dc22   0100495252

www.villard.com

Book design by Diane Hobbing

To my husband, Matt Greenfield,
who helped write this book. Really.

The

SOCIAL CLIMBER'S

Handbook

CHAPTER *One*

June 2, 2008

Dow closes down 134.50 points to 12,503.82

S&P closes down 14.71 points to 1,395.67

Daisy Greenbaum looked over at her husband, Dick, master of the universe. He was wearing one of those white strips on the bridge of his nose. He had a black mask on his eyes that read BRITISH AIRWAYS across it. Tucked neatly in his mouth was a custom-made mouth guard so he didn't grind his teeth, and looking at him across their California king-sized bed Daisy might have thought for a slip of a second (before she banished that thought away, like all her other vaguely communist urges) that this was a man on whom making money had taken its toll.

"I love you."

Dick kept snoring.

"I love you."

Through his mouth guard Dick Greenbaum squeezed out the

words: "I have to be at work in approximately seven hours and twenty-two minutes and eleven seconds. Go to sleep."

"I can't sleep."

"Take something."

"I said I love you."

Dick sat up with a start. He took off his eye mask and opened his eyes. "We are about to be faced with the biggest economic crisis of our lifetime. Next month you may see breadlines, a true unemployment rate of 22.1 percent. Never mind. I need to go to bed."

"You didn't say anything when I told you that I . . ."

"Imagine a world with no credit, no lending, imagine a world where you go into the Prada store on Madison and there is nothing on the shelves, and don't get me started on your precious Starbucks. Okay, now I need to be there in seven hours and twenty-one minutes"—he looked down at his expensive self-winding watch— "and thirty seconds, okay?"

$\mathcal{I}$n her infinite sadness, it seemed to Daisy Greenbaum that the loneliest time of the year on Manhattan's Upper East Side was the week between when the private schools let out and the social families packed up their Denalis and headed for the beach. The third week of June was the demarcation line: once it was crossed over, all of the apartments on Park Avenue would be dark, except for the flicker of the occasional husband enjoying a quiet tryst with a secretary or a nubile young associate.

Daisy Greenbaum hated summer. And perhaps this could have been traced back to a lifetime of summers spent at Camp Shane (or, as she called it, Camp Shame), a "loving, accepting, nurturing weight-loss invitational," which was known by people occupying the real world as "fatty camp."

Or maybe it was her hatred of sand, of heat, of sun, of wearing less clothing, of shedding her cavernous sweaters and her enormous winter coat. And maybe the rest of the world tacitly agreed. Summer was a time of mourning, a time to muse on various losses (real and imagined), a time when different layers of rarefied folks plunged through different layers of loss, all narrated by the constant zombifying hum of giant air conditioners. Loss affected everyone in every section of every gentrified neighborhood—the bookish Upper West Siders mourned the loss of their shrinks in August, the Brooklyn hipsters mourned the loss of their parents' ramshackle summer cottages on Fire island, the barely-getting-by working parents mourned the death of the school year. Yes, summer was the bleakest time of the year, and this summer was to be the last golden summer of the Dow at thirteen thousand.

Daisy was standing, feet on the cold white tile, in her gray linen pajamas (Daisy had seven identical pairs, all ironed by Nina, the long-suffering housekeeper, on Tuesdays, which was the day that Easton, the fancy twin, went riding in Manhasset and Avery, the funky twin, went to her acting class in the West Village). Daisy stared at herself in her enormous bathroom mirror. It was six A.M. and the sun was bright, or as bright as it could be, considering that she lived on the second floor. She squinted at herself. She didn't look like all the other mummies of the yummy variety. She had white skin that had never seen the inside of a tanning booth (spray or otherwise). She had regular features (her grandmother had always complimented her on her nonethnic nose, and she knew what this meant), pretty and appropriately sized for her slightly equine face, which was just slightly too long to be beautiful. Every time she looked in the mirror she remembered that she had been what had seemed (to her at the time) grotesquely fat in her youth. As a result she had never considered herself a pretty girl; hence she had developed a somewhat charming personality.

Having a good personality had served her—she had married up

(her husband had found her amusing), and she wasn't fat anymore, though she wasn't exactly thin; she was Banana Republic thin. Not truly thin, not thin like the other ladies on Park Avenue with their exposed vertebrae and their sharp, bony hips, but thin. Her Polish DNA, from her zaftig great-granny from the shtetl, would guarantee that she would never be Prada thin. But she didn't really care, and besides, she was funny. Maybe not laugh-out-loud funny, but ironic. And she was smart. Maybe not Ivy League smart, but Brandeis smart, which was still smarter than 99.99 percent of the yummy mummies on Manhattan's Upper East Side. And she was striking, with enormous blue eyes, which made her look like a model from the Eastern Bloc. A fat model from the Eastern Bloc.

She tweezed at a few stray chin hairs with her green metal tweezers. Soon Dick and the girls would be up, shattering the exquisite silence of morning. Soon she'd be burning waffles, and fighting with the extremely expensive espresso machine, and spilling orange juice on the floor. But for that slip of a second she was the last woman on earth, alone in the silence, alone enough to think. Daisy Greenbaum's brain was permanently awash in a sea of minutiae, constantly focused on trivialities, like who was the better dry cleaner and who made the best saddles. But Daisy had a secret, and it cut through the minutiae like a great white shark. Daisy knew what she was capable of. Daisy knew the animal that lurked inside of her, the one who could not be calmed by a million yoga lessons. She stared at her own eyes until the blue faded into itself, until her face faded into the mirror, until everything around her was smooth and blurry.

But there was trouble in the world of unfathomable wealth; Dick had passed down the edict—no more spending, no more car services, no Hampton house this summer, no more shopping, no more three-hundred-dollar dresses for the girls, no more trips to the Breakers, no more dinners at Per Se. Daisy looked back at her long face. She wasn't one of those airheaded trophy wives. She knew that one of two things had happened—one was that Dick had fucked up something big in whatever it was he did (she wasn't totally sure what he did, something with debt, something called credit default swaps), and the other was that what he had told her about the crumbling of the equities markets was actually true (but she couldn't quite wrap her head around this story).

After all, it was June 2008 and Barneys was still packed with ladies vying to buy thousand-dollar-a-pair lizard-skin platforms, condos and co-ops were still flying off the shelves, waiting lists for various gotta-have-it accessories were still snaking around the block, the culture of scarcity and panic among the wealthy was still going strong (not enough preschool spots, not enough Hampton houses, not enough Mandarin-speaking nannies, oh my). But some small men in large offices who worked for monstrous investment banks saw the writing on the wall, and the writing was recession, depression, end-of-the-world bad. One of these men was Dick Greenbaum, Daisy's small and vaguely simian husband.

Every night since March 14, when Morgan and the Fed had provided a twenty-eight-day emergency loan to Bear Stearns, he had suffered from some variation on the same nightmare. Somehow the collapse of Bear Stearns had made Dick realize that the whole system was intrinsically flawed. He wasn't stupid and he had known the system was truly fucked for a long time, but he kept thinking the debt wouldn't catch up with the bets. He thought it could keep going like this for years. But the crash of Bear was the death knell for the American economy. He saw it all very clearly. And in this clarity he realized his life was a house (or an apartment, as the case may be) of derivatives, and these derivatives (he was pretty sure) might well take down the American economy. And so suddenly he was panicked about the lack of derivatives regulation—where were the necessary derivatives clearinghouses? Who the hell was keeping track of all the little pieces of paper that were representing trillions of dollars of debt? It was as if one day Dick woke up and realized that bad math was going to eat up the entire world and that he somehow had to stop it.

The worst dream, the one that haunted him, the one that made him wonder what it was that he was doing on this earth, was this dream (it was a recurring dream but it always sort of went like this)— it started with him sitting there in his favorite brown pinstripe suit (the one that made him look five feet eight instead of five feet six, and tan instead of jaundiced) enjoying his strawberries and his champagne. Then a stewardess came out in her little blue frock. Usually in the dream it was one of two secretaries, neither of whom were in real life stewardesses: one was Maggie, the thick-calved Irish girl, but in some of the dreams it was Candice, the plucky-but-not-great-looking single mom. Everything would be going along just fine when all of a sudden there would be a popping sound, like someone making popcorn, and then the window next to him would pop open and then things would start getting sucked into the ether. Everything that was on the polished mahogany coffee table in front of him would go flying into the air. He would try to grab all these papers, all his careful, thoughtful documentation of his theorems. But it would be too late, the paper would melt through his hands and then he would wake up covered in sweat and gasping for breath. Sometimes Daisy would notice and volunteer a few semisoothing sentences (none of which really hit the right note with Dick), and sometimes she would pretend not to see him dripping in his own sweat, laboring to catch his breath.

$\mathcal{D}$ick walked on a path of golden speckled sunlight that penetrated through the space between the leaves and the smooth pavement under his feet. He mused on the restrained beauty of Park Avenue, as he did every morning. In one hand he carried his brown leather Ghurka briefcase (less showy than Hermès or Gucci, but still expen-

sive, unlike the standard Tumi briefcase, which he deemed too pro-
letarian in its proliferation) and in his other he held the small soft
porcelain hand of his daughter Easton. It was one of those perfect
early summer days, windy and warm. Easton's white skin glistened in
the sun and her dark hair magnified her beauty. How had his DNA
created something so intrinsically flawless? It almost made Dick forget about what was coming, but it was easy to love life (and parenting)
during a five-minute stretch on Park Avenue in beautiful weather.

Across the street, Dick saw a fellow father who was not loving life
or parenting—Bowdy Lodge was struggling with the youngest of his
three daughters from his current unhappy marriage, and he was, in
many ways, an advertisement for not having a third batch of children
at sixty. There was something so pathetic about this gray-haired man
leaning over precariously, liver-spotted arms filled with second-
grade textbooks. Bowdy had just bought a final resting place for family number three. Since two of the finest Park Avenue buildings were
already filled with his ex-wives (wife number one was comfortably
ensconced in 770 Park Avenue, while wife number two was living it
up at 730 Park Avenue), he was forced to seek asylum in a town house.
He found it humorous in the worst possible way that he now paid
maintenance at two of the best buildings in New York and had a $17-
million mortgage on his town house, and yet there was no one around
to get him a fucking taxi.

Ryland Lodge had a name that made her sound like a motel on the
side of the highway. And she would undoubtedly end up in one, perhaps after shooting a bag of dope. But that day all her ire was saved for
her beloved father, for whom she was pitching the fit to end all fits—
which Dick Greenbaum watched from across six lanes of traffic and a
grassy median, and one very large piece of modernist sculpture possibly created by Louise Bourgeois.

But back to his own delightful daughter: for the last few weeks
Easton had been pestering him about what it was, exactly, that he did.

Every day they would have what amounted to the same conversation and every day they would together come to the same conclusion, which was that Daddy couldn't explain it and Easton couldn't understand it. But somehow, every morning, like Groundhog Day, Easton would bring the whole thing up again. "Can't you just make it simmmple? I neeed to knowww wwwhat it is that you dooo, Daddy." Easton spoke in a kind of pseudo-Waspy whine that she had picked up from her better-born classmates. It made him feel bad that even at eight this daughter was all affectations, all style over substance. Where could a person possibly go from here?

Early that morning he had been thinking of a better, clearer way to clarify just what a derivative was, but ultimately every explanation came off seeming derivative. He couldn't stop thinking of the famous Sherman McCoy crumbs dissertation. But people understood bonds; bonds were simple, bonds were trusty, bonds made good northern sense. Sure, it was essentially a glorified sales job, but compared to the hocus-pocus of derivatives . . . "I make math problems to explain debt."

"Math problems like we do in school?" Easton looked at him like he was a moron, like he didn't have a Ph.D. from MIT, like he hadn't graduated cum laude from Harvard, like he wasn't a rocket scientist (and he wasn't technically a rocket scientist, though he had taken a bunch of "rocket scientist" classes at MIT). But she had stumbled onto an insecurity of his: he hadn't actually been a "big brain." He had been one of those kamikaze lunatics who had to work harder than everyone else to accomplish half as much. But it had just added to his drive, just made him harder, tougher, and slightly more insane. He hadn't been one of those guys that everything came to naturally. And perhaps Easton sensed (the way children often do) that her father had a tiny chip on his shoulder. He had never been good enough to win the prizes that some of his classmates had; he had never had "talent."

"Yes, but these math problems, they explain debt products, so say you have a bunch of stock in a company." Dick looked at his daughter hopefully. Maybe this would be the time when he would be able to explain it, maybe this would be the moment when it would all come together. "What's a company you like things from?"

Easton looked at him like she didn't totally trust where he was going with this.

"The Gap? Do you like the Gap?"

"Prada."

"Your mother doesn't take you shopping at Prada." Dick looked at his daughter, and then said quietly and in real, true utter horror, "Does she?"

Easton rolled her eyes.

"Okay, we'll say the Gap. So you buy bonds from the Gap, but you want to hedge your bonds, you're worried the Gap might default on their bonds, so you buy Daddy's product and then you have insurance against the Gap, in case they default or can't pay. It's what's called a credit default swap."

"Ugh, that's so dumb. Why would you swap default for . . ." Easton started to sound very confused. "Credit for shirts? Default? What's default? I don't understand. Why can't you do something cool like India's dad?"

"Well, what I do is cool." Dick looked at his little ERB-rocking genius child (or, as they called her with just the slightest bit of irony, the smart one). She was smart in a spectacularly uncomplicated way, the opposite of her twin, Avery, who seemed (to her parents anyway) more like a real person and less like something that sprung fully actualized from the pages of *Teen Vogue* at age eight. But Easton was the one who all the kindergartens had wanted. Easton was the one who would realize all her mother's secret social ambitions and none of her father's. "You see, honey, being good at math is cool. And Daddy was able to turn a love of math into an exciting, and . . ." He wanted to add the word *profitable* or *lucrative* to the end of his sentence, but he didn't like to talk about personal monies with the girls. Speaking about personal monies, like his staggering $12 million loan (a slightly illegal mortgage from his employer), or the monthly cost of garaging his SUV ($700 for oversized vehicles), or the $75,000 that he had to pay for private school every year, or the $27,000 he gave the New York Public Library every year so his wife could have something to do), was tacky, gaudy—of course, this was pretty ironic considering the fact that he spent much of his life talking about money, making it, losing it, hedging it.

"No, Dad. What you do is boring and dorky. India's dad has a house in the Maldives. He is BFF with Prince." What Easton wanted, of course, was a dad who was rich enough so he didn't have to work. Dick looked at his daughter. Easton was a vision of affluence, in a pressed gray jumper from the fanciest girls' school in Manhattan, long, skinny legs slightly toned from weekly jaunts riding a ridiculously expensive pony rented from Georgina Bloomberg on Long Island. The only thing that betrayed Easton Greenbaum was her "baum," her slightly out-of-shape nose, and her long jet-black hair.

India's dad was a lot of things (professional trust fund squanderer, aging granny defrauder, ski instructor screwer), but role model he was not. How could Dick say this in eight-year-old-speak? He committed himself to a fatherly sigh, reminiscent of his own father's disapproving sigh. What would his shrink scribble in his notebook about that sigh? Was it possible that he had become his father? It seemed impossible, but there it was—the sigh that hundreds of hours of analysis could not prevent.

"India's daddy got India another pony-y-y-y. She has six poniesss noooow. And I don't have any. Math is dumb—why can't you be friends with Prince?"

"Prince? The prince of where?"

"Dad, he's a musician. Ev-v-v-veryone knowsss that. India's dad is so cool."

"India's daddy doesn't . . . I mean to say that . . . he doesn't . . ." They were almost to the school. Easton had lost interest in whatever it was that they were talking about. Dick leaned over and gave her a kiss on the cheek. He put his hand on her head for a second. All this would slip away, all this would be gone soon, every second moved faster than the last, every minute more of his life was being used up, his life was being frittered away making up giant complicated math equations that no one could understand, and soon the bonds and equities would lose value, soon companies would default on their swaps and there would be no collateral, so the swaps would be worthless, billions of dollars of worthless paper and the markets would crash, and then it would be breadlines, and soup lines, and people with no shoes, and guys holding tin cups, and then who knows, socialism, the end of capitalism, not being able to get strawberries, melting polar ice caps, the end of the world. He shivered, but Easton had already slipped though his fingers into her fancy school where the girls wore little gray dresses just as they did a hundred years prior.

Meanwhile, a few blocks back uptown on Park Avenue, Daisy Greenbaum struggled with the taxi door as she held in one hand a sheet of sugar-free-wheat-free-peanut-free-tree-nut-free cupcakes, each decorated with a different ecological motif. Avery was the more "artistic" twin; her school was across town, and looked like a television. So every morning they did the same thing, committed themselves to the same roles: Daddy walked the perfect twin a few blocks down Park Avenue and Mommy took the "nontraditional" twin to her West Side "progressive" school. Often Daisy and Avery's taxi ride would become something slightly Bergmanesque, with daughter and mother staring into space, musing on their joint existential crises (sadly, none of this musing was in Swedish), but by the end of the taxi ride Daisy usually felt like she should get Dr. Mel to up her meds.

"I feel like there is a hole in my heart." Avery was sitting next to Daisy, staring out the window at the green trees that blurred past them outside the taxi.

"I know." Daisy looked over at Avery. She hadn't had enough espresso to deal with Avery's nihilistic crisis. She felt exhausted. And yet she completely understood her daughter's pain. Nothing came easily to Avery. Both parents related to this struggle. Dick and Daisy had been the types who were picked last for dodgeball.

"No, no, you don't know."

"You know, I know what it's like to feel bad." Daisy paused and tried to remember what it was that Avery's shrink had instructed her to respond with, but she couldn't remember. Avery's shrink, the illustrious Dr. Rose, believed Dick and Daisy were basically incompetent people-pleasers with no boundaries, hapless members of the "me generation" who had failed their daughter in a million different ways. It was up to Dr. Rose to instruct them in parenting, in loving their daughter, in keeping her from growing up and running a meth lab out of her basement. Daisy laughed to herself. It seemed impossible, the idea of Avery being organized enough to run a meth lab. Didn't meth require, like, eighty different ingredients?

"Really, Mommy? You know what it's like?" Avery just wanted love. Daisy wondered if she could solve all this if she just loved Avery a little more.

Daisy reached over and hugged her. "I love you, you know that, right, doll face? I love you so much."

"Ugh, you're smothering me."

Daisy looked at her daughter. Okay, so Avery didn't just want love. Luckily, Daisy was preoccupied with the possible end of the world. She thought back to right after September 11. Right after September 11 there had been crazy threat alerts nearly every week. Sometimes the whole city would close down for an hour or two: no bridges, no tunnels, no way out. But it turned out the big one had already happened, and all those color-classified alerts were just false alarms. They had never been forced into a 1950s fallout shelter like she had originally feared. And Daisy wondered intensely about these unloved spaces, these delicious corners of square footage that were just waiting for the worst-case scenario. What lurked in these basements? Were they filled with cobweb-covered supplies for surviving the fallout, with prehistoric first aid kits, with sixty-year-old cans of condensed milk? But the nuclear end of the world meant very different things to Daisy than the equity markets crumbling. It was one thing to die a horrible nuclear death, it was quite another to be . . . poor.

"I know what it's like. Did you know that your father and I were both not popular in school?" Daisy looked at Avery for a reaction.

Avery looked at Daisy like she was stupid, which in some profound ways she was. "Dad's a math dork and you were fat."

Daisy couldn't help but feel somewhat offended. She continued on. "It's very hard to be eight."

"Yeah? It's hard to be eight? Really?"

Daisy nodded. Now they were getting somewhere.

"That makes no sense."

"Why, lovely?"

"Because Easton is eight."

Daisy had gotten stuck in this trap by thinking that she (by virtue of the fact that she was almost thirty years older) was smarter. Parents who think they are smarter than their children always end up stuck in the mire of the impossible conversation. "Just because you two are twins doesn't mean that things are the same for both of you."

"Yes, that's right, because life is good for Easton because everyone loves Easton."

Daisy sighed. She was running out of things to say. "Well . . ."

"Everything is easy for Easton." And maybe Avery was right;

maybe everything *was* easy for Easton. It sure seemed that way. But Daisy wasn't eight. She had to act like a grown-up here.

Daisy didn't like to lie to her children. She did it, of course, but she didn't like to. "Easton has a hard time too. Things are hard for Easton too." Daisy hoped that Avery would get distracted and not ask anymore about it, because Daisy hadn't figured out a reasonable lie to go along with this line of thinking.

"And what about Walker?"

"What does Walker have to do with this?" As a parent Daisy knew that she was supposed to be above hating eight-year-olds. But weren't there exceptions for someone as spectacularly mean as Walker Stone? She certainly wasn't above hating her mother, Landon Stone, who had become famous in the annals of her very Waspy nursery school for Federal Expressing her cats down to St. Barts for vacation. Landon Stone, who believed that by virtue of the fact that she had her hair blown out every single morning and was squired everywhere by an ozone-eating Denali, she was truly better than other people. Landon had rebuffed Daisy's attempts at friendliness until someone had told her that Dick was very rich and would soon be very, very rich. Then Landon had decided Daisy Greenbaum was a truly wonderful human being. Even Daisy Greenbaum was not hapless enough to be seduced by someone as blatantly cash-loving as Landon Stone. That said, they served on the same very chic board at MoMA (which was a get-or-give commitment of fifty thousand dollars a year; Daisy would give forty-nine grand and then go around panhandling her friends to get someone to give the other thousand). She was truly afraid of the social power that Walker Stone wielded at Avery's school, so Daisy had obliged Landon. Daisy felt it was her job to use whatever social capital Dick's wealth provided to protect Avery.

"Walker told me that she is going to start the I Hate Avery Club."

Daisy looked back out the window. She felt so bad for her daughter, and watching her most beloved suffer through teasing and rejection, Daisy couldn't help but remember her own childhood. She looked at the trees and the traffic and the city that swirled around in front of them. "Really, Avery, she's not. I promise."

"How do you know?"

"I will talk to her mother."

"Thanks, Mommy, you are the best." Daisy felt she had been manipulated just a touch, but she always felt that way with Avery; it was as if her daughter were some kind of Svengali, a person with a Ph.D. in global parent positioning. None of that mattered now; she was committed (and breaking a promise to Avery would equal any number of mind-numbing lectures from Dr. Rose, shrink to the stars). And so it was onward to a whole other fresh hell: to a conversation with Landon Stone.

CHAPTER *Two*

Still June 2, 2008

Dow closes down 134.50 points to 12,503.82

S&P closes down 14.71 points to 1,395.67

Dick's car service car had neglected to show up on time for drop-off, prompting him to send an unusually snippy text message to his assistant that he was leaving "sans car." Luckily Bowdy was more than happy to give him a ride; after all, they were alpha dads—hunter-gatherer types had to stick together, especially in light of the growing number of fathers who (it seemed to Bowdy) were actually secretly supported by their wives.

Bowdy looked at Dick. "So I've bought my third house in Southampton. I'm hoping the third time's the charm. As you may or may not know, the last two houses went with ex-wives before I had even a summer in either one."

Dick smiled, looking up from his BlackBerry. "Whose fault is that?" Dick laughed.

Bowdy turned a bit pinkish. "I know, I know."

"But you're happy now." It was more like a question than a state-ment, and Dick paused as if there were a possibility that Bowdy might answer.

But instead Bowdy chuckled. "Yes, it's going to be a great summer if the dune erosion doesn't get us."

Dick smiled.

"Perhaps you saw *The Money Pit* with Tom Hanks."

Dick laughed, but then looked away from his BlackBerry and paused to really study Bowdy's face. He had not noticed how posi-tively stricken he looked. Was he a banker or was he a ghoul? Dick wondered if this man were like the Ghost of Christmas Future, sent to warn him of possible peril.

"Just listen to me. No matter how rich you are, you can never af-ford to get divorced. It doesn't matter if you are a billionaire and your wife is taking it up the ass from every NFL footballer in New York City. . . ."

"Lovely image, thank you."

"What I am trying to say is that the only thing more impossible than living in this city is living with ex-wives and numerous children in this city. And can I tell you one more thing?" Bowdy motioned for Dick to lean in. "No matter how unhappy you think you are, a new wife won't solve it. Because a new wife soon becomes an old wife."

"That should be in a fortune cookie or something." Dick had no interest in Bowdy's bad marriages, and since Bowdy had been ele-vated to the level of cautionary tale after marriage number two im-ploded, Dick sort of tuned out when Bowdy tried to give advice, which he often did. Besides, Dick had a math mind: every problem laid it-self out like a quadratic equation, and he was not moved by the left brain at all (this meant that while he might cheat, he would never partake in something as fortune-halving as divorcing a perfectly good wife: it served no purpose, and ultimately it made no mathematical sense). Slightly revolted, he changed the subject: "Wachovia, what a nightmare that company is."

"There's a value play there."

"That's insane."

"Why do you say that? I always like to think of you as a value investor."

"Yes, Bowdy, I am a value investor"—Dick looked up—"but only when there is value there." Of course Dick wasn't a value investor really, he was actually a quantitative arbitrage guy, but when there was a pun to be had he was happy to volunteer the verbiage, besides which Bowdy was kind of a jockish idiot who didn't really understand the type of nuanced trading that Dick did.

Bowdy had become even grayer as the conversation turned to inverse ETFs and mall REITs, and as the car continued through traffic, the two men left their unhappy home lives back in Carnegie Hill and became absorbed with forecasting the future.

$\mathcal{D}$ick often congratulated himself for the fact that he had slept with his old assistant only once. He hated his new assistant so much that he promised himself that no matter how drunk he got he would never ever sleep with her. She was a young Indian woman whose efficacy and intelligence made her totally repulsive. He wasn't normally a psychopath, and he wasn't really a cheater, but the prop desk was like another world where normal morals and values never entered. Like being high on crack, the land of proprietary trading was a world where reason and virtue were considered to be the worst sins of mortals. Of course, Dick wasn't a trader. The traders were the people who ran up thirty-thousand-dollar hotel bills, smoking crack with hookers. The traders were the guys who totaled hundred-thousand-dollar sports cars, drank fifty-year-old scotch, snorted blow off the fake breasts of strippers, and ended up in rehab multiple times. No, Dick wasn't a trader: he was a dork, he was a quant. But it didn't matter: the testosterone leaked everywhere. It was like Chernobyl: the traders affected everything within thirty kilometers.

The prop desk was not a "desk" per se, but a whole floor filled with large men who used The Bank's glorious money to make more glorious money. There were a few prop desks housed in the offices at 27 Wall, but this one was the best, the most profitable, the one that Luke Brinkover spent the most time gloating about. This was the prop desk that everyone wanted to be on, and Dick was its king, well, almost its king.

This is the way in which the prop desk differed from a hedge fund: in a hedge fund the money belonged to millionaires or billionaires or pension funds, whereas the money Dick played with belonged to The Bank, or, rather, to the people who owned the stock and the bonds of The Bank and who so generously provided the raw material out of which the employees of The Bank created their magnificent bonuses.

Dick was number two on the desk. It was unprecedented for a quant to rise so high in prop. But this particular prop desk was heavy in quantitative-related trading, things like index arbitrage, volatility arbitrage, macro trading. So Dick had become number two because of his mad math skills, because of his big brain (big for i-banking, smaller for a quant fund, and positively minuscule for the academy). But Dick had been smart and he had leveraged his people skills (relatively average, but impressive compared to his fellow quants, most of whom were on the spectrum somewhere between Asperger's and full-blown autism), his mathematical talents, and his whining into a position of power. And so Dick was happy with his enormous office, his huge paycheck, and his use of one of the company's wonderful G5s. Or, rather, Dick had been happy until he realized that his peers, mathematically inclined and otherwise, had spent the last fifteen years gnawing away at the foundations of the American economy.

And even before his (apocalyptic) epiphany, Dick had resented many things, one of which was that there were very few actually talented people around him. He had always thought that traders who made money in a bull market were not talented but lucky. Some people just had their jobs because of their last names or because their fathers had played golf with Gus Levy. As someone from the second least desirable block in Roslyn, Dick had never had much love for the Wasp mafia (or the even more subtle, the even more annoying, German Jewish mafia). Pitiful as these two groups had become over the years, they still raised Dick's ire.

Dick also knew it was a truth universally acknowledged that he could really be making more money at a hedge fund. But as Dick arrived at his office, and smoothed out his call sheet, he remembered why The Bank was something that people didn't just walk away from.

Raja, his efficient assistant, was standing at his door, waiting for a sign that she could cross the threshold and annoy him. Everything about her drove him up the wall. She looked like she was fifteen, yet had an MBA from Hofstra (who knew Hofstra even gave MBAs?). She also always smelled like a sickening mix of car air freshener and ambition. "What?"

"Ken Griffin called. He is hoping you'll return before the end of the market today." She frowned.

"Fine, what else?" He didn't want to be so unfriendly but he did sort of despise her. She was so competent, he didn't doubt that if he dropped dead tomorrow, she would have no problem stepping calmly over his smoldering corpse and sitting down at his desk and continuing business as usual. Of course, his corpse wasn't smoldering . . . yet.

"Well, also you said you had some memo that you wanted distributed. Now, are you going to want that sent out as an email or as a printed letter?" But before she could finish her question, she was interrupted by his boss, a rather fat, rather red-faced, rather talentless, rather Waspy man, who stormed in waving a piece of paper furiously.

Dick looked up from his call sheet, from his huge Italian desk, from his enormous blotter, from all his beautiful papers. "Why, hello there, John." Raja scurried off.

John was even more puffy and flushed than usual. And Dick's smooth salutation seemed to inflate him even more. John looked like a giant malformed hot-air balloon. "I'd like to speak to you about something."

"Why don't you sit down?"

"I'd rather stand."

"Okay." Dick smiled coolly and installed himself in his gigantic leather desk chair. "So, what's going on?"

John looked like he was going to have a heart attack right there. He blustered, stammered, and seemed as if he were going to convulse. "Let me just get to it, shall I?"

Dick nodded.

"I'm going to start taking the steps toward terminating you."

Dick grimaced. "Why?"

"I think you know why."

"We have a responsibility to the world . . ."

"Dick, everything you're saying in this memo, everything you are saying is . . ." John started stammering. He looked like he could pop. Dick wondered, if John popped, whether his head would fly off or his eyes would just burst from their sockets. "Well, it's nothing short of libelous. You're saying that this is the end of everything."

"Just think how upset I was when I realized the larger implications of my life's work. I believed in this more than anyone. For God's sake, I discovered it. I was the first person to ever write a derivative of this nature. I was the father of this. This is my child. This is everything to me. Try to understand how much worse this is for me."

John paused. "A little grandiose, don't you think?"

Dick frowned and said nothing.

"So." John looked out the window. The sun sparkled against the Jersey City skyscrapers. John had always loved the word *skyscrapers;* he always loved the idea that these huge pieces of metal could touch the heavens, could use their enormous metal points to scrape the sky. "What are you hoping for here? Let's be honest. How long have we known each other?"

Dick said quietly, "Fifteen years?"

"And in that time have I ever been less than candid with you?"

Dick looked at the mountains of papers dealing with bureaucracy on his desk. Dick wasted so much time on dumb bureaucracy, useless minutiae, things that did not directly involve making *money.*

John asked it again, as if Dick hadn't heard it the first time. "Have I ever been less than candid with you?"

It was a dumb-boss question, the kind of question a dumb boss asked, and it fit because John was, more than anything, a dumb boss, a bad manager, a hapless nepotistic Wasp, a . . . "What are you saying?"

"I'm saying, I'm asking, what do you want? More money?"

Of course Dick wanted more money, but what he really in his heart of hearts wanted was to fix things before they spiraled out of control. This kind of thing John didn't get, and he never would. John had never had an original thought in his entire life. "I'm saying we have to fix this before it blows up."

"You can't distribute this. This is going to turn into a self-fulfilling prophecy."

"Look, John." Dick paused, looking down at his call sheet. He could get a better job at a hedge fund, he could make more money, he could stop having to deal with stupid crap like who gets to fly business class and who has to fly coach, like who gets a 10 percent raise and who gets a 5 percent raise. But one didn't work at The Bank solely for money: after all, The Bank ruled the world. "This is the right thing to do. We can, if we start now, we can fix a lot of stuff, make a suggestion to the SEC to regulate the derivatives trade, we can keep this whole thing from blowing up and we must, it's our responsibility to ourselves, to our children, to our legacy." Dick stopped and looked at John. He was particularly pleased with this soliloquy. It felt very Shakespearean, very polished.

"You had no authority to do this, and not only am I going to get rid of you . . ." John paused and looked at the shiny buildings, at the blue, blue sky. There was no space in John's world for acts of heroism, not that this was particularly heroic. John really wanted to fire Dick. Something about this memo filled with incomprehensible math equations and rantings about level 3 capital, something about Dick had always rubbed him the wrong way. John had always hated Dick, so small and slimy and slithering and simian. So what if he had a Ph.D. in some kind of stupid math that no one cared about or under-stood. He was such a show-off, and besides . . .

"And . . ."

Besides, Dick was fat. Well, just a little, but in the wrong places. He had love handles. "And then I am going to ruin you. You won't just slip into some hedge fund by the time I'm done with you; you'll be lucky if you can be a fry chef."

"Why, because I want to fix a broken system? Because I see a chance to fix everything or at least try to before this whole thing blows up in our faces?"

"Because this is not up to you, because you do not have the author-ity to do something like this. And if you do, if you do this, I promise you—I swear to you—I'm going to ruin you." And both Dick and John knew this was true because John had ruined people before. He had destroyed his last protégé, who had ended up in Moscow, and then, through a series of really bad coincidences, was murdered by a prominent Russian billionaire-slash-politico.

"Well . . ."

"Well, what?"

Dick felt sheepish. "What if I want to stay."

"Make this"—John took the memo and ripped it in half; it was such a tacky move, and so classic John—"make this go away forever. And let's forget that"—John spread his hands up in the air—"that any of this ever happened."

Dick could feel the rage burn in him. John was a sales guy, a front man, a hairpiece, and not much else. A guy who had risen to power on all sorts of shady crap—things like front running his trades (a slightly illegal move when the brokerage gets a big order and the prop desk buys the stock first and then resells it to the brokerage client at a higher price, taking advantage of the knowledge that the client's big order will drive the price up). Dick doubted that he had even understood the memo. Dick wondered if John even knew what a synthetic CDO was. But it didn't matter. John was a master of politics, of reputation ruining, of all the things one needed to be good at to achieve success in i-banking. "Okay." Dick looked back down at this desk, at his call sheet. "Okay, let's just say I get it, I understand. I get what I need to do here and I will do it."

"I don't want to hear about this again, okay?"

Dick frowned. Now it was time for the mandatory shaming, another great management tool that John employed.

"And if I hear about this again, do you know what I will do?" Ah, the rhetorical question, another one of John's fabulous people-managing moves.

"Yes, yes, yes."

John cleared his throat. "You sound a bit flippant about this." Of course, John didn't really have the authority to get rid of Dick. He would have to get together a consensus. But John had done it before.

"No, I understand." Dick hated this conversation. But he did have a $12-million mortgage. What kind of person had a $12-million mortgage? And since 740 was (like any good building) an ALL-CASH building, which meant you had to plunk down the entire cost of the thing (plus show you had millions and millions more), the mortgage loan had been through The Bank. He had thought his parents were rich; they lived in a $200,000 house, the second least nice house on the second least nice block on the second least nice street in the least nice section of the least nice of the five towns. Now he had a mortgage that was forty times larger than the cost of his childhood home. What kind of human being needs to live in a house that is $12 million more than he can afford?

"Do you? Do you understand what an honor it is to work at The Bank?"

Ugh, the rhetorical questions, the shaming. Dick frowned. "You know I am as committed to this place as anyone."

As John left, he slammed Dick's door, shaking the desk. Dick watched the waves in his coffee reverberate against the sides of its little paper-cupped home. For a minute there was no sound. The trading day hadn't started yet and the phone hadn't started ringing. It was another day—another day of rallies, another day of the Dow above twelve thousand, another day of inconceivable oil prices, another day of low interest rates, another day of money to be grabbed off the money tree.

$\mathcal{D}$aisy had been at the Heavenly Rest soup kitchen cutting carrots when he had called. They weren't supposed to use cell phones in the basement (perhaps the three-hundred-year-old ladies who worked there worried that the cell phone signal might have produced a repercussion that could have interfered with the delicious smell of the place, a potpourri of stale Chanel No. 5, mold, kasha, and dandruff). Daisy could feel the other volunteers giving her dirty looks. They treated her as if she were the new girl, even though she had been working there three days a week for the last five years. But she was new to them—she was new, flashy ethnic money, and she always would be, even if she worked at the Heavenly Rest every day for the rest of her life. She would still be the girl who carried the Hermès Garden Party tote, the girl who tried just a little too hard to look like she belonged. "I'm so sorry," she said, and smiled apologetically. "I'll be right back," she said to no one in particular.

"Dick, I'm at the soup kitchen. I can't really talk."

"Look." She could feel something in his voice. Did she know that the power balance was shifting, did she know that Daisy Greenbaum was about to become the hero of her own life?

"Yes?"

"I did what I thought was right and it might be that I am about to lose my job."

Daisy suddenly felt detached, like she was watching herself in the movie version of her life. "What the fuck?"

"The system is going to crash, it's started already. It's going to be the biggest global catastrophe ever. Anyway, I wanted to try to salvage the system and I wrote this memo about how everything can be fixed, because, you know, Daisy, it can all be fixed."

"Dick, if you lose your job . . ." Daisy looked down the street. There was no one around but she still felt vaguely panicked by the possibility of someone hearing her. She spoke in a hushed whisper filled with rage. "If you . . ." Making threats was not going to help anyone; she needed to not be divisive. "Okay, how can we fix this?"

Dick sighed and ran his fingers through his hair. "Well, why do I even want to stay? I mean, the man is an idiot. Maybe I can destroy the memo, forget everything I know to be true and become a protector of the status quo." Dick paused. There was probably some kind of huge upside to elevating this level 2 capital to level 3 capital, pretending that it was still worth face value, lying about there not being a market price available. The market price was readily available, but if they marked all of that toxic crap to market, the firm would have a negative book value and be out of business within twenty-four hours. Dick wondered if it was possible that John knew about this all along and that perhaps his bonus was tied to his ability to hide the problems in level 3 capital. Was that possible? Dick wondered how big his bonus could possibly be. Three million? Four? No, probably a lot more. Thirty million. Enough for several houses in the Hamptons and a yacht. He hated water but surely he could get someone else to sail it, right?

"Hello!! Are you there?"

"Sorry, anyway, he wants me to lick his ass for the rest of eternity and then I get to stay."

It was clear to Daisy that her husband was far too angry to be able to do this, to be able to keep his job, to eat his rage. "So?"

"So?"

"So, what the fuck do you want me to do about it?"

"Daisy, I don't know what the fuck to do. I don't know if I can do it." He sounded so desperate. It was so awful to hear him so exposed, so vulnerable. She would fix this. Suddenly she knew what she had to do.

"Okay, look, just do your work today, avoid John, and I'll be home later, much later." Daisy took a long and deep breath in. "Much later."

$\mathcal{A}$ few hours later, Daisy was walking with the long-suffering mother of India. It turned out that India's playboy father was not the greatest husband. Shocking. They had just finished yet another meeting of their parenting book club, where they read different books on parenting and discussed them endlessly. It was one of the many ways that Daisy was a better parent than her own parents—not because she read the books, but because she could endure mind-destroying semantic quibbles about how hard it was to parent children of privilege. (Yes, it was obviously much easier to be poor; everyone knows food stamps equal fun.) She had even said that once in the discussion, and then everyone had stared at her blankly. Daisy's phone started buzzing and she excused herself.

She sat on a bench on Fifth Avenue, trying to pull something sticky out from in between the grommets of her Italian driving loafers. "Look, I'm not telling you to tell Walker what to do . . ." The wind was blowing and it was causing loud static on the cell phone.

Landon Stone's voice dripped hostility. "Is this about Walker's party?"

"Is Walker having a party?" Daisy's heart sank. This would kill Avery. Unless maybe Landon was inviting her. Maybe there had been some kind of mistake with the invitations, or the mailing address, or postage. Maybe it had been the postage. Maybe she had blocked on the fact that Daisy lived at 740 Park Avenue.

"Yes, at the grand ballroom of the Plaza."

Daisy started laughing because she thought Landon Stone was kidding. "Right, right, of course. That's why we couldn't get it for Avery's party."

Landon Stone was stony as she stared into the air shaft that her huge prewar living room faced into. Sure, it was a good building, but it was on a side street filled with other people who used to live in better, fancier buildings, and all the "public" rooms faced air shafts, and the bedrooms faced brick walls. Her stepmother had gotten her custom window treatments but they could not hide the downward mobility, the building itself a testament to downward mobility—filled with people who had grown up in better buildings, filled with people who had apologetically "downsized."

It had become impossible just to maintain the lifestyle in which Landon Stone was raised, and she struggled by with handouts from her parents and his to keep up appearances. The party had been gotten as a freebie, the space anyway. Her rich stepfather was paying for the catering. Landon Stone's mother, Lily Stone, felt it was very important that her daughter projected an image of wealth, so that maybe Landon could divorce up. After the accident, after her mother left her father and took Landon to New York City, and married Landon's rich stepfather, after she had forgotten that she came from Roslyn Estates, after that, Landon Stone had been bred to marry a millionaire (or, better still, a billionaire). She had gone to the school that guaranteed it. Of course, she was always considered a new girl because she hadn't been a student since birth. After graduating, Landon had gotten the fake job at Sotheby's. She had it all, the lanky limbs, the stick-straight long hair blonded within an inch of its life, the blue eyes, the white creamy skin, the long, thick nails, the shockingly white teeth. If she had been a racehorse she would have won the Kentucky Derby.

But sadly, unlike races, life couldn't be fixed, and Landon Stone had never landed the billionaire. She had married for love, or perhaps some other equally confusing reason. The husband had great breeding too. His ancestors had come over on the *Nina* or the *Pinta* or the *Mayflower* or something—and that was worth exactly nothing, it turned out. And so her parents had stayed saddled with her as if she were a stone. Daisy had studied this case with fascination because she thought of herself as a social satirist, perhaps a sociologist of the very rich. Of course, all social climbers hide behind the mantle of sociologist.

Daisy Greenbaum knew Landon Stone hated her but she was not totally sure why. She guessed it was because Landon had gone to all these schools and she looked at people like Daisy as immigrants fresh off the Long Island Expressway. Daisy thought Landon thought of her as a migrant worker desperate to take private school spots and gotta-have-it accessories away from citizens. But the real reason that Landon hated her was much more complicated than that, and it was a secret suspicion Landon had kept hidden almost her whole life.

"Anyway, Avery is not invited, because it's just a small group of Walker's best friends."

"Oh." Daisy paused.

"Yes, well, I'm sorry that Avery couldn't be mature enough to handle things, but you know she is a very emotional child. That said, I am happy to drive the girls to the barn. You know, Walker loves Easton. And of course Easton is invited to the party."

Daisy was about to say something about how cruel it was to invite one sister and not the other, but she couldn't stand to extend the conversation any longer. So she summoned her best Stepford and wished Landon a good day, and then she hung up the phone.

$\mathcal{D}$aisy had slept with her husband's boss, but only once. She had hoped it would become more. When replaying the event and its aftermath she imagined it as one of the cruel rejections that shaped her life. Daisy was uniquely talented at seeing everything that way, of telling her story of rejection and ignoring the less interesting things, the things that normal people call facts. Yes, Daisy believed that John had dumped her, when in actuality the story was far more complicated than that.

John was, though he didn't admit this, even to himself, a kept man. His less than lovely wife was the boss's daughter. Of course, he had gotten himself into this whole stupid marriage nightmare, and this was a leitmotif in his life: he had enough (breeding, wealth, some talent), and then, greedy for more, he had screwed himself by doing something that he thought would help him but instead hurt him ten times more. It always shocked him that he could be so spectacularly unself-aware until months, sometimes years, later. He wondered if his father's legacy to the three brothers (he was the most successful, though of course his youngest brother wasn't really even in the competition: he was a hapless drunk who had recently crushed to death an eighteen-year-old dilettante with his father's Bentley) was this bottomless pit of greed, this desire, this obsession for more. It was stupid on John's part. He had never needed to marry her. He could have gotten along just fine on the clout of his own prominent family, and he had really, truly screwed himself, because, shockingly, the boss's daughter is never as charming as she seems when you first meet her.

Daisy had visited her husband's boss in his office before, late at night, only a few times. They had slept together only once, but the flirtation had dragged on, had taken months. And even after, she would show up sometimes, if she had been out drinking with girl-friends, if she had been drunk enough to have forgotten all the rejection he had heaped upon her, she might show up there, eye makeup down her face, pretending to look for her husband, who never stayed past seven ever in his life, who was on the road at least two weeks a month. She hadn't shown up totally blitzed in a while. The last time she did, she ended up crying in his lap, and then she had given him a blow job, which he had sheepishly accepted.

But most nights John was a sure thing. He was always at the office because he was one of those people who truly despised his eight-thousand-square-foot duplex on the corner of Fifth Avenue and Eighty-first Street. Well, not the apartment, he loved the apartment—the horrible wife was a good decorator, he would give her that. Those people, the children of the very rich, they knew how to spend it. It was making money that the second generation had a problem with. But it wasn't the apartment he despised, and he didn't even hate his children, even though they were fat and dark and looked nothing like his beloved maternal grandmother, who had been one of the ladies who shaped the old club on Park Avenue. No, there was one person who made it totally untenable to come home, and that was the boss's daughter, the woman he had married to get ahead, Piper Strauss.

Daisy knew the drill. She knew how to get to his office without being seen, she knew how to skip in and out of the shadows, to go up the back stairs, to head through the hall that didn't have the cameras, to slip by the guy who washed the front hall on the fifth floor. It was, it could be said, an old building, the kind that did not have the newer security. The prop desk was there just temporarily until they finished renovating their new offices, which included a seventy-three-thousand-dollar Oriental rug à la John Thain.

When he came back from the bathroom she was sitting in his desk chair, one of his contraband cigarettes between her lips.

"You're not allowed to smoke in here, you know that, right?"

There was something so appealing about this Daisy Greenbaum—not quite attractive, but appealing, with her thick, lustrous hair and her neediness. Sure, there were more beautiful women—models, actresses, the girl who worked in the Starbucks on Lexington Avenue—and he had slept with all these women multiple times, but there was something compelling about Daisy Greenbaum.

"I'm not smoking."

"It looks like you're smoking."

"Nope." Daisy smiled. She was funny. She was always game. Dick liked her. He did, right? She almost couldn't remember. Their lives had grown so complicated and distracting. Everything had moved so far away from when it was just the two of them in that studio apartment in Tudor City, the one with the horrible Murphy bed, which looked stupid when it was up and was uncomfortable when it was down. She wondered who lived in the tiny lightless space now, who had claimed those 341 square feet. Was it another couple longing to break free, longing to save every penny so they could live on Park Avenue? Yes, the American Dream: a huge apartment on Park Avenue, a $12-million mortgage, and a house in the Hamptons. Although they really didn't have a house in the Hamptons. They rented, which made Daisy resentful. Dick said it made more financial sense. Daisy hated Dick when he said things like that. No one else worried about things making financial sense; in fact, most of their friends were so overextended they absolutely lived life in the red.

"What are you doing here anyway?"

"That's not much of a welcome, is it?"

John looked at her. She was right, and honestly, he was happy, maybe even thrilled, to see her. There was something slightly thrilling about her, even though he found her fat, deliciously fat in all the right places, with luscious thighs and gloriously floppy breasts. There was something beyond enchanting about her, something charming, hapless, slightly vulgar, and shockingly naïve. "No, you're right." He still held back a little. He hadn't invited her and he was, after all, a married man. She couldn't just go showing up all the time at places; he needed to be firm, like with his zaftig daughters. What kind of Wasp has fat children? It killed him.

"You don't ever think about me, do you?"

John looked down. This was such a female conversation, such a bore, such a waste. If you could make money having this conversation, well, then, maybe, maybe, he might engage. Otherwise, not so interesting.

"I thought so."

"No." John looked out his huge window. All the skyscrapers were lit up, scraping the sky, yellow lights in the otherwise black night. You could never see the stars in Manhattan and that made him sad. He had loved his summers in Rockport because you could see stars and planets. Had he felt he had a choice maybe he would have done some-thing different with his life, something meaningful, something real. But he didn't even know what other careers there were. Sure, he had a vague, nagging sense that one could be something other than an in-vestment banker, perhaps a lawyer. Maybe he could have been a doctor, or a senator? Politicians always seemed helpless and dim-witted to him, like Dan Quayle. "No, I'm happy to see you," he admitted. Why lie when the truth gets you as much?

"Really?" Daisy was thrilled. And in that thrilled-ness she started to puff herself up into a prideful balloon. She was beautiful, sensuous, and appealing. She walked over to him and slid her hands up and down his chest. There was something slightly lyrical about the way the two of them moved together.

"I like coming here at night, sneaking out, coming to see you." It was so typical of Daisy: her husband was the smart one, the big-brained quant who made the trains run on time, and here she was with the dumb drunk salesman.

John needed a drink for this conversation, a scotch. A big scotch, a huge scotch, a scotch in a vase.

"Can I get you a drink?" He thought about his brother. It was impossible to mutter a phrase like that and not think about his brother, his drunk brother, who crushed a girl with his car. So far they had done a pretty good job of keeping the whole thing covered, quiet, on the down low. But once the trial started, once he went before a judge in Palm Beach, the family would be tarnished forever. They would become a caricature of themselves. They would become the worst cliché of Wasp life.

Daisy smiled. "No, I'll get you a drink. Let me get you a drink."

Most women kill with poison, and why wouldn't they? Poison is a thinking person's tool. And poison is, of course, all about premeditation. Nobody walks around with a bottle of red gentian capsules of Triclofos in their 25-cm gray ostrich Hermès Birkin bag (a bag that Daisy might have languished on a waiting list for, a bag that she might have been obsessed with, a bag that she might have paid slightly more than the list price for, a bag for which she might have bought tons of ugly patterned sweaters in order to achieve "preferred customer" status for), and certainly not a mother of small children. But Daisy did carry this brand of chloral hydrate in her Birkin, and maybe that was one of the ways in which she was different from all the other yummy mummies, for Daisy was always ready for whatever problem might present itself, because deep down, below her lust for social prominence and her lust for her husband's slightly slow boss, deep deep down beneath her insecurity, her need to be liked, her obsession with her twelve-room apartment on Park Avenue that was tragically on the second floor, deep deep deep deep down at her core, Daisy was a murderer in the best possible way.

Premeditation—a word that rolls off the tongue, that sounds deceptively like some kind of Zen ritual. Daisy often thought about premeditation. It was in many ways the demarcation line in the criminal justice system. On one side of it lay the death penalty and on the other such seemingly lightweight things as manslaughter (it hardly sounded like a crime, though the word did have *slaughter* in it; *slaughter* sounded bad). But manslaughter often led to very little jail time. Manslaughter was what happened when rich or famous people killed someone; they got convicted of manslaughter. They didn't murder people; that was something vulgar, like wearing white shoes after Labor Day.

She thought about premeditation that day as she emptied two capsules of the Triclofos into the lead crystal glass, as she watched the crystals disperse in the slightly viscous, slightly yellowish scotch, as she encouraged him to drink, as she fixed him another drink, this one even more filled with poison (three capsules this time). She thought about the word *premeditation.* She thought about it as she brought the garbage cans and placed them under his wrists, as she slid the razor up and down the insides of his wrists. It was a common misunderstanding about suicide, the idea that one was supposed to slice left to right and not up and down, one that she would someday rectify in her prison memoir, a book she felt someday she would inevitably write and call something to the effect of *The Social*

Climber's Handbook. It was an ironic title, for sure, but Daisy Green-baum was all about irony. Anyway, it is a common misconception about suicide—horizontal slices did nothing. Under the armpits was best. There was a big, juicy vein under the armpits. Was it called the carotid? She didn't know. A close second was vertical slices along the veins in the wrists. She did, however, want this to look like a sui-cide, and since nobody ever killed himself by slicing his armpits, it was better to do the wrists. She promised herself that if she were ever to kill herself (she wouldn't, of course, because she had young chil-dren), she would be original and pathbreaking and go for under the armpits. As she put the bottle of pills back in her purse she thought about her choice of poison. It had been the poison that Agatha Christie had used to murder Emily Brent in *And Then There Were None;* it had provided the bee sting mark. Daisy had an appreciation for a murder that had literary undertones. Perhaps she did harbor bits of pretention under her faux anti-intellectualism.

She thought about the word *premeditation* as she held each wrist, angling the blood directly into the two small brown Italian leather garbage cans (with gold leafing) and not onto the rug. Because Daisy knew someone would have to clean that rug and it would be some poor, long-suffering cleaning lady who had worked for The Bank for 105 years and always had to clean up after rich guys who flicked their cigar butts onto it. Daisy always thought about the cleaning ladies.

CHAPTER *Three*

June 6, 2008

Dow closes down 394 points to 12,209

S&P closes down 43.37 points to 1,360.68

$\mathcal{D}aisy\ had$ dressed silently that morning in black. Avery had gone to school with Nina, and Easton had walked with Bowdy and Ryland Lodge. Dick had had to run into the office that morning before the funeral. And so he had, and when he had gotten into the office his assistant had been waiting for him. She handed him an enormous stack of papers.

"My God, what time did you get here?" He frowned at her.

"Four-thirty."

Dick was bleary from a night spent looking at the numbers (the GDP, the debt ratios) for Iceland. It had occurred to him casually around 1:42 A.M. as he was drifting in and out of sleep that it looked as if Iceland would go broke, but it seemed (even as he looked at such indisputable facts) impossible. It was unprecedented. First

World countries don't go broke. People go broke. People with $12-million mortgages go broke, but countries don't go broke. It had unnerved him, and in the end he had admitted defeat and taken a Tylenol PM, thus falling asleep sans mouth guard on the sofa in his home office, the room that the decorator had called his study.

That night he had the same dream. He was sitting in the G5, looking out the window. A thick fog blurred his view, so he could only slightly make out the buildings. Was it Copenhagen or was it Geneva? One of those ambiguous European cities, and it didn't matter much at that moment because he was leaving it. The stewardess was someone he had never met before who looked a lot like a young Margaret Thatcher. (He had admired Margaret Thatcher during his youth, finding her surprisingly charming though politically repugnant. Not that he was a dreaded liberal—no, he had not grown up rich enough to be willing to surrender more of his plunder than was absolutely necessary.) The stewardess was saying something to him but he couldn't hear her and he kept staring at her, hoping that maybe he might be able to read her lips, but it was too hard. Finally she said he was able to turn up her volume using a little dial on her neck that looked like an old cable box dial from the early eighties when cable was in its most barbaric stages. He turned her knob all the way up, and she was of course in midsentence. "... and so we were fighting, you know about that, obviously. You know that Bank of America is about to buy Countrywide? It seemed impossible that B of A would buy something so inherently worthless, but you know the head of B of A tans with that Countrywide idiot. Isn't tanning great? You know you can't get cancer from tanning." And as she was speaking her skin was going from normal white to bizarre orange just like the CEO of Countrywide.

He woke to find that he had drooled all over his deranged decorator's beloved custom twenty-seven-thousand-dollar suede sofa. As he tried to wipe the drool into the suede so that it might be absorbed, he thought about what twenty-seven thousand dollars could do. It could probably feed an African village of a hundred people for twenty-five years (perhaps that was a stretch), it could buy a street of modest homes in India (Dick was pretty sure that was possible), it could pay for City College for ten kids for one year (or for one kid for ten years), it could pay for twenty-seven hundred women to have mammograms, it could pay for twenty-seven thousand children to have vitamin E drops to prevent blindness . . . or it could buy one (now drool-covered) sofa.

Dick glared at his assistant. What was it that sparked so much rage in him? He had to wonder if it was racism rearing its ugly head. "Can you get me a latte?" Raja frowned. She did not like to be asked to get coffee. To Raja (who was an obsessive television watcher) it felt very *Mad Men* to be asked to get coffee. Meanwhile, the movie she should have been worrying about was *Wall Street*.

But he didn't have time to worry about the emotional state of his assistant now. He sat down in John's office, which was now his office, and turned on both monitors (his and John's). As the screen lit up, Dick noticed a folder that he had not seen before. He opened the file and started to read. The folder described a play on the mortgage-backed securities market. John had placed a bet against some pools of subprime mortgages using credit default swaps. Every month, The Bank had to pay AIG $50 million for insurance on those subprime mortgages. If those mortgage-backed bonds defaulted, then AIG had to pay The Bank the full face value of the bonds: $12 billion. The Bank had bought insurance on bonds it didn't own. And that insurance was going to pay out as subprime borrowers all over America stopped paying their mortgages—all those busboys and strippers who bought six houses each using loans where their incomes never got verified. The credit default swaps were a good investment, even a brilliant one, as long as AIG didn't go bankrupt because it had written too many contracts like this one. Unfortunately, John had gotten more and more heat for spending $50 million a month of the profits made by the hardworking traders in other divisions of The Bank. So John had done something that seemed totally risk-free and prudent to offset that big monthly expense: he had used a big chunk of the firm's capital and leveraged it up fifty times to buy a different type of mortgage-backed security, bonds backed by Alt-A mortgages, which were a little less trashy than subprime mortgages but still had something a little wrong with them—like, for instance, the income of the borrower was never verified, the loan required repayment of only interest but not principal, the borrower started with a loan worth more than the value of the house, or the borrower started off with a low, low interest rate of 1 percent and the unpaid interest got added to the already excessive principal amount of the loan. So The Bank owned, or sort of owned, $80 billion worth of these Alt-A bonds. That is how many of these higher-quality bonds it took to pay for the insurance on the $12 billion worth of subprime bonds. Fortunately, The Bank paid only a negligible interest rate on the $78 billion it borrowed to buy the Alt-A bonds. But somewhat less fortunately, it now looked likely that those Alt-A bonds would also end up defaulting. So The Bank had bought insurance on $12 billion worth of trashy bonds but paid for it by buying $80 billion worth of almost equally trashy bonds.

John had started to see the steamroller barreling toward him, about to crush his head into a puddle of slime, and he had done the only thing he could think of: he had buried his head in the sand like an ostrich and pretended nothing was happening. More specifically, he had moved the Alt-A bonds into level 3 capital. The stuff in level 3 capital was stuff for which no ready market existed, so you couldn't determine what the fair price for it was. When The Bank made a venture capital investment in a wind farm, if the stock was not publicly listed, that went into level 3 capital. Now John had put the $80 billion worth of Alt-A mortgage-backed bonds into level 3 capital as well. Of course, The Bank could sell those securities anytime it wanted to. But the price was now a not very gratifying fifty cents on the dollar, meaning The Bank had lost $40 billion. How much more pleasant to tuck it all away in level 3 capital and say it was still worth $80 billion. And hey, maybe the federal government or the Federal Reserve, which was not exactly part of the government, would someday decide to pay the full $80 billion for those securities and rescue The Bank. It made sense. It was almost smart. That said, there were lots of things wrong with shoving worthless trash into level 3 capital, and saying there was no market for the stuff was technically lying. But now one person stood to benefit, one person would get the biggest rewards for all of this stuff, and that person had died, so it made logical mathematical sense that Dick would be next in line.

$\mathcal{D}$ick arrived at 7:40 in a low-level panic. Was he going to turn John in, and who was there to turn him in to? After all, there was nothing that he had been doing that was technically wrong. And he would surely be fired, and besides, he was making tons of money for the desk, and what if he couldn't deliver those returns if he wasn't doing this kind of stuff? What if his best numbers were behind him? Besides which, there were fewer and fewer arbitrage opportunities. Maybe he could just keep all the balls in the air, keep writing off the debt, until the media forgot and then everyone started rambling about "green shoots." No, that would never happen. Would it?

He sat in the car service car in front of the building. He kept calling up on his cell phone. Daisy wasn't answering. Finally he deigned to get out of the car and told the doorman, "Go up and fucking get my wife." It was one of those buildings where you could say things like that. The very rich buildings had no rules and the doormen were used to the Ronald Perelmans of the world. They were used to the type of people who called their ten-year-old daughters "motherfucker" in front of their schools.

She got in the car.

She frowned. "I'm sorry."

"We are going to be late to my own boss's funeral. If there ever were a time not to be fucking late it would be now." He cackled with a kind of brittleness.

The car snaked off into double-parked traffic on Seventy-first Street.

Right before they got to Frankie Campbell's (funeral home to the great and the near great and also the merely very rich), Dick's Black-Berry started buzzing. He looked down at the CNN Alert emails, which were almost always minor events of no relevance to him or anyone else at 740 Park Avenue: a 3.5-magnitude earthquake in Jaipur, an outbreak of mumps in Uganda, a helicopter down in Honduras. But today the news was almost laughable. It said, "Bear market of 2008 declared." He looked at his wife's six-hundred-dollar shoes. Something a lot worse than a mere bear market was about to happen and he was the only one who knew it.

They slid into the row behind a huge drunken racehorse of a woman, who was midsentence and stopped for half a second to ignore Dick and Daisy and then continued loudly: "Personally, I wanted St. Thomas More. In my mind a church is always always better for this type of thing, and since there was something slightly suspicious about the nature of his death, I say just do it in a church, have five people, get the whole thing taken care of. . . ." There was a pause. "Fast, like the Jews. I love the Jews for that."

Daisy froze. Her blood ran frosty though her veins. Could Daisy survive in prison? Could she live in a five-foot-by-seven-foot cell, with one small opening of sky?

"Suspicious?" coaxed the friend (fat little Magee Pink, always a bridesmaid, never a bride—of course never a maid, Daddy had taken care of that with his giant oil fields; not a bad life, but Magee would still have liked to have found someone to marry, even someone much older, even someone with no money, one of those marriages where everyone knows what he's up to but it doesn't matter).

"Well, I mean, I don't believe that heart attack story for a minute. I mean, come on . . ."

Magee Pink seemed embarrassed (as if she knew that it was a suicide). "Shush."

"What?"

"Let's just not raise our voices."

"I mean, it doesn't matter anyway. St. Thomas More wasn't going to go for it anyway, because of the brother and the car accidents and then the father remarried that much younger girl and they don't even really live here anymore, they live out in Jupiter, much more understanding out there."

Magee frowned. "Wow, that family has taken a beating. Poor them."

"Poor me."

Magee laughed softly. "More money, more problems."

"I feel bad for my mother-in-law. Anyway, the family is a little on the outs with Father Blanchard right now, as you can imagine. It's such a nightmare. I have to tell you. When I married into this family, I had—" The lanky wife, Alix, stopped talking for a moment to dab at her long black lashes. Daisy watched in quasi-awe, quasi-horror, unable to take her eyes off her long elegant fingers covered in enormous stones of various varieties, including a diamond as big as the Ritz, and her thick head full of white-blond ironed hair. Daisy was no fool; she quickly picked up that this was the wife of the middle brother, or, perhaps more apropos, the middling brother. "I had no idea it would all turn out this way. Of course, I had known Rick my whole life from Piping and I knew that no family was perfect. I was not one of those women who marries for anything else but love, but you know there was a family legacy there, a legacy. Sometimes those kinds of things are hard to break, you know. That said . . . I had no idea."

"No idea?" Magee was always pushing.

"No idea that things could turn quite so profoundly pear-shaped."

"You know, personally I just really feel for his wife."

"Don't. Look at her," Alix said. "She is trying . . ."

"To? To what? To?"

Alix had lost her train of thought. "To contain her enthusiasm."

Daisy looked over at Dick and smiled, and then mouthed the words "Are you listening to this?"

Dick frowned at Daisy. Of course he was listening to this: everyone within a three-mile radius was listening to this; it was impossible to shield oneself from this awfulness. But Dick was distracted. He was playing with his BlackBerry. Fighting, actually, with his ex-mistress. Who was at that very moment sitting two pews in front of them, one pew in front of Rick's drunk wife. Yes, in spite of Dick's morality, in spite of his enormous brain, in spite of his various Ivy League degrees, in spite of his giant paycheck, his enormous mortgage, and the fact that he was allowed to use the company's G5, Dick had had a mistress. At least he had thought to put his coat between the two of them this time so that Daisy couldn't read over his shoulder, as she often did.

"You know he was a total cheater. It must be hereditary," Alix said loud enough for Sir Smith Kingly to turn about, head tilted back to them ever so slightly, as if to say, "I hear you but am too polite to acknowledge this infraction."

Magee tried to soothe. "I know, I know, it's upsetting. Would you like a Life Saver? Or some gum, maybe?" Magee had also noticed that Alix seemed to be trampling all over funeral etiquette, especially such a Waspy and understated one, in such a profoundly fancy funeral home on Madison Avenue, sandwiched right between a store that sold $250 floral men's bathing suits and a store that sold $17 chicken salad sandwiches. It was arguably the finest funeral home in Manhattan. Rising majestically from the limestone sidewalk brownstone, built originally in 1867, it had been one of the first buildings to venture so far north, to disturb the farmland. Ahh, to have lived in 1867, to be Dutch and wear funny hats and raise ducks. Daisy could have been a good Dutch duck farmer's wife, couldn't she? Daisy wondered what the building's original purpose was. Could it have been some kind of brothel? A Dutch duck farmer brothel filled with ducks and people with funny hats? All buildings had originally (or sometime in the economically bleak seventies) been something seedy, except for the very good buildings, like Dick and Daisy's building, which had been built by a Locust Valley socialite to house her friends in a tasteful and Jew-free environment.

"B-but, I never thought that the family was really cursed. Which now it seems like they are."

"Shush." Magee was panicking. People were looking at Rick's wife. Her words had hit a loud enough decibel level to be heard by other people in other rows, on other pews in the venerable halls of Frankie Campbell's. "I understand how times like this make people so upset, make people so crazy."

Daisy looked over at Dick. She wanted to touch him, to say something to him about how she had done something huge for him, as a favor, as a token of her love for him, and now, in spite of everything she had done for him, in spite of this, he had his thick black Burberry raincoat (purchased in an outlet) between them, which meant only one thing: he was emailing with the mistress, Petra Smith Kingly, who was in fact two pews in front of them with her husband, the elderly and infirm Sir Smith Kingly, British aristocrat. Daisy knew about Petra but was pretty sure he had ended it, though she knew that he still emailed with her every once in a while. It filled her with rage that he still had any kind of contact with her, but Daisy had only so much power in her marriage.

"It's the curse. If I had just known that it would end like this." Alix paused. "And they say it's all about family. Everything with these people is about the family, family first. They say family first when they're suing to take your children away, when they're trying to get at your trust fund, when they are trying to make sure that your son will get less inheritance than his drunk uncle's illegitimate daughter whom he had with a stripper, who's already hooked on meth at the tender age of . . ."

"Shush, let's go." She started pulling at Alix. "Not here, not now."

But Daisy wasn't interested in the ruckus. She was thinking about her marriage. Daisy looked over at Dick—his shiny skull, his rounded head, his short legs, his fat little calves covered in pink socks—and thought about what had brought them together in the first place. They had met in high school when they had been in the same AP art history class. She had loved being so close to so much beauty and so had he, though he had told her he was taking it so that colleges would think he was well rounded.

Besides, pictures made sense to him. Even they could be explained by math equations. Beautiful pictures usually had perfect equations, usually could be seen as triumphs of proportions, of mathematical elements combined. At first he had needed her to teach him about how society worked, how to interact with people, how to be places on time, how to get up at six. But since they had become rich, since he had become a master of the universe, since the earth had shifted, so had the power structure in their marriage. Now she needed him more, much more than he needed her. After all, the world was filled with pretty (not beautiful) women who could make babies and pick out furniture and supervise renovations. But she would show him, she would prove her use to him. After all, she had done things for him, fixed things, people, wrists, blood, garbage cans . . . and there was that word again, *premeditation*. "I love you," Daisy said, looking over the coat at Dick.

Dick pretended not to hear her. Daisy looked down at the pebbled leather of her gray Hermès handbag. It was so smooth and supple.

She loved owning something so beautifully made, so well crafted. It felt wrong to love a material possession so much—deeply wrong. Incredibly wrong. "I said I love you. Did you not hear me?"

Dick frowned. "I am in the middle of a crisis."

"Existential or otherwise?"

Just then Landon Stone interrupted them. "Hello, Daisy," she said flatly, as if it were hardly worth the trouble.

They hadn't known each other long, a few years. They had met when the girls had been in nursery school together. But she always gave Daisy a bad feeling, something she couldn't quite put her finger on. And now the girls rode together, and of course she saw Landon everywhere, but the Upper East Side was just that way—when you didn't want to see someone, that was when you saw them everywhere, in the next taxi, on the next bike at Soul Cycle, next to you on the bar at Exhale.

Daisy smiled. "Hi."

"I didn't know that you knew . . ." Landon smiled, then looked over at Dick. "Is this your husband?"

Dick looked up crankily. "Dick Greenbaum, sorry for your loss." Wan, slightly green, slightly deflated-looking, profoundly elflike, Dick put out his hand while still looking at his BlackBerry.

"Actually, honey, this is Landon," she said, as if that were supposed to mean something.

Dick looked at her, puzzled.

"The mother of Walker?"

Dick vaguely remembered one of the girls complaining about Walker. Or was she complaining about walking? He didn't know. He felt he had already spent way too much psychic energy on this already.

Landon looked coldly at Dick. "Nice to meet you."

Dick ignored her and choked out his own well-practiced epithet: "John was my boss." Could he do this, could he lie this much? Sure, he lied all the time, and now, now his job was one big lie. He knew the whole thing was going to blow up. And then there was the lie of his mistresses. But this seemed so much worse, so much more blatant.

Landon looked puzzled at Daisy. Daisy looked puzzled at Dick.

"What can a person say about John? He was a good man." Dick paused. "No, no, a great man." Daisy looked back at Dick as if to say she hardly knew him.

"I didn't know you were friends with John." Daisy smiled.

Landon looked caught off guard. "Well, you know, we know the family from Palm Beach."

And then Daisy realized that Landon didn't know John at all and she was filled with a kind of quiet glee. Landon was funeral climbing (attending the funeral of someone she didn't know in the hopes of being seen by the right people). "Right, of course." Daisy smiled, as if to remind Landon that she was, in fact, an asshole.

Landon then wandered off, to what looked like her mother, a round old doyenne wearing polyester pants and a black floral Hermès scarf.

Dick looked over at Petra, his favorite immoral act. That was over now, had been for a year. But that didn't mean he couldn't remember. He could remember Petra's incredibly smooth skin—mistress skin, unmarked by years of childbearing and nagging. Petra was only a year or two younger than Daisy, but she was much less worn down by life than his wife. She had a kind of elasticity, a kind of buoyancy, which seemed to match her poreless and supremely soft superhuman skin.

"I said I love you. Did you not hear me?" Daisy looked over at Dick looking over at Petra. Petra turned to wave and smile at Dick. Daisy caught all of this—she caught the look in their eyes, she caught the curl of their lips. The two of them smiling at each other, as if Daisy were invisible, as if she did not exist, as if she did not almost bleed to death eight years ago delivering twins—and not any twins but Dick's

THE SOCIAL CLIMBER'S HANDBOOK 51

beloved twin daughters, one of whom went to the fanciest, most in-sider, most venerable girls' school in Manhattan.

Dick was slightly startled by the look in his wife's eyes. He realized she was watching him, recognizing his happiness as something sin-ister. Why did all these delicious immoral acts have to be contra-band? Why couldn't she just let him do these things? Why did every marriage have to be this 1950s construct? Didn't people have open marriages anymore? Petra had an open marriage, or at least her hus-band was just too senile to notice. "I'm sorry, darling. I was just dis-tracted." And then he added quickly, as a way of confusing her, "Did you see Sir Smith Kingly is here?"

"Yes, I see all of it." She held her eyes in his for a moment too long, as if she were trying to hypnotize him. "You realize that I see EVERY-THING. Don't you?"

Dick had never thought of Daisy as a scary person. In fact, if he had to choose two words to describe his wife, he would say *hapless* and *helpless,* and these were the things that had originally drawn him to her. But now, seemingly out of nowhere, Dick started to wonder if Daisy was hiding something under the haplessness.

The service ran a scant twenty-one minutes. It was an incredibly restrained affair. Not once did anyone utter anything that would lead a person to think that this death had been anything but a totally nat-ural occurrence. No family members spoke. A gray-looking Episco-pal priest muttered a few prayers, lit a candle, ended the service with the usual schtick—"Life is a journey, and death a destination"—and then everyone filed out into the overcast summer day and it was over.

$\mathcal{I}$t was an office that was meant to lull the patient into calmness: calming paintings, calming sound machine in the corner of the wait-ing room humming white noise to all who might otherwise start screaming, calming herbal soap in the small white bathroom.

But Daisy did not find herself calm as she sat across from Dr. Rose in her office.

"It's all about listening," Avery's shrink, Dr. Rose, mused. It was an ironic soliloquy, because at that moment there was someone who was listening who was not supposed to be, through a tiny hole in the wall obscured on Dr. Rose's side by a large Mondrian-esque painting. She had come by the idea honestly. She had seen the movie *Everyone Says I Love You* (in it a daughter listens in on her psychoanalyst mother's sessions). She promptly returned home with a drill and proceeded to drill a hole in the wall that separated her mother's office from her broom closet. So there she was, sitting only a few feet away in the "office" that her mother had set up for her after she was fired from The Famous Media Blog.

Candy Ross Rose never thought she would be fired from anything. After all, she had gone to the smart fancy girls' school, then to Harvard, then to get an MA in journalism at Columbia, and yet she had been fired from The Famous Media Blog. She had gotten a perfect SAT score, she had been the editor of the school paper, she had learned to make herself throw up three years before her friends had even realized that anorexically thin was in, and yet she had been fired from The Famous Media Blog (perhaps for calling people "gay" as an insult; possibly for spelling Rick Moody's name wrong; or possibly, most possibly, for writing obsessive fan letters to Jerry Stahl, one of which she posted on the blog along with a picture of her naked breasts). Also, she did accept huge quantities of free swag for mentions of said swag in the blog. For example, she was constantly touting five-hundred-dollar custom tie-dyed dresses festooned with pictures of Elvis while musing on Jon Stewart's newest bon mot.

Now she was working on a novel called *WEB of Love* about a girl who falls in love with a guy who exists only on her BlackBerry (it turns out he is God, in a post-post-post-postmodern twist). And then there was her blog, where she posted half-naked photos of herself with various hats on her small, slightly rounded head, along with some vaguely autobiographical interviews. But what she really wanted to do was get involved with a particular financial blog, which was written by this guy who had once been an analyst at The Bank. A man who had been fired from The Bank for perpetrating a rather complicated pumping-and-dumping insider-trading drama that had involved his father's mutual fund.

But in spite of his distinctly criminal leanings, Trip McAllister was still gorgeous. He was also a Harvard alum, he had gone to a very fancy Boston boys' school, his mother had been a famous Boston socialite (which is almost an oxymoron), and he wrote a blog that, well, let's just say had a bit of an ax to grind with The Bank, which is why Candy was listening to her mother and one of her mother's dumb mummy-daddy combos. But she knew that this guy was some bigwig at The Bank, and a story that spread a little egg on the face of The Bank would play big, would make Trip love her, and then she could post half-naked photos of their honeymoon on the blog, and then half-naked photos of their wedding, and then half-naked photos of their baby.

"Sometimes—" Dr. Rose pushed her glasses up and looked down at her notes. "Sometimes, Avery says she feels you don't hear her."

Daisy nodded frantically. She wanted so badly to be the parent Avery needed her to be. "Did you hear that, Dick? All that time you spend multitasking."

Dick looked up from his BlackBerry and at Daisy, eyes full of fury. It was two P.M. on a trading day, *a trading day*. The markets were open, and oil had just gone past $140 a barrel, a number he thought he would never see in *his lifetime*. His firm was either losing or making millions of dollars, and here he was being lectured on the fine art of child rearing by a woman who needed to look at *notes* to tell them that their daughter was unhappy, that their daughter had no friends, that their daughter had not been invited to Walker Stone's birthday party in the grand ballroom of the Plaza Hotel.

And he was not an unsympathetic father. Dick understood that Avery was unhappy. He understood that Daisy was also unhappy. He even understood that deep down (below the riding and the perfectionism) Easton was also unhappy. But they would all be a lot more unhappy if they were poor. Dick seethed. "You know, you understand that I have a very big job."

Dr. Rose smiled patronizingly. "You have three very big jobs: father to Avery, father to Easton, and husband to Daisy."

Dick turned slightly greener than usual. "There is no way you say that to Rupert Murdoch."

"Richard," Daisy gasped in horror.

"No, it's okay, Mrs. Greenawitz, I am used to some level of parental defiance. After all, I understand this is hard to hear."

"I am sure that's not what he meant, right, darling?" Daisy nudged him.

"First of all, it's *Greenbaum! Greenbaum! Not Greenberg! Not Greenstone! Not Greenfield! Not Greenberger!* And secondly, I am the head of the prop desk, the head, *the head.*" A seismic shift had occurred. The world had moved on its axis and Dick Greenbaum had (due to unfortunate circumstances and perhaps a little help from his wife) been anointed head of the proprietary trading desk. Head. He was a master of the universe times a million, times a trillion; he made Sherman McCoy look like a fry chef, and yet the only time he could get to meet with Dr. Rose (Dr. Rose was, of course, the most famous, most prominent, most intelligent, most fancy, most impressive, most decorated, most chronicled in *New York* magazine, most revered by directors of private schools, most referred by anyone fancy and fabulous child psychiatrist in town) was at two P.M. during a trading day.

That's because the better times, the times that would not totally

THE SOCIAL CLIMBER'S HANDBOOK 55

screw up his day, were taken by people who had more juice, the children of the people who ran New York and possibly the world. They got the coveted six P.M. time slot, right before dinner, or the equally wonderful eight-thirty A.M. slot. But you know who did not get a good time slot? Dick and Daisy. Even though next year, if he continued to do well, he would get a $15-million bonus.

"It's all about love. I write about this a lot in my book, my book about love and parenting and eating disorders. It's called *Loving the Pain Away*, and I really think you should buy a copy. It's great for parents. The truth is that you don't even need to be a parent to use this book. It's for everyone really."

"I'm not sure what your book has to do with anything, but"—Dick frowned—"I hope you understand this is a very inconvenient time for me."

"I am trying to slot you a more workable time, but you must understand..." To Dr. Rose, Dick was just another faceless investment-banking asshole. She had originally put Avery on her waitlist. Eventually he had gotten his boss's boss to call for him. The boss had better things to do than call a shrink for one of his employees, but Daisy had said it was superimportant. This in itself would not have been enough; after all, Daisy deemed many things to be of the utmost importance. But then she nagged him and nagged him and emailed him and threatened him and held him hostage in a million different ways until he cried uncle. And did the kid need therapy? Not really. But Dr. Rose had used this as an opportunity to have the child teach the parents the meaning of life in a totally unsophisticated and heavy-handed way, all for $15.50 a minute.

Dick's BlackBerry started vibrating like crazy. He smiled to himself and looked at Dr. Rose, who was still musing on. "I have to take this."

Daisy felt the rage rise up inside of her. "We are talking about listening and then you are not listening."

"Daisy, I am head of the prop desk. Do you understand what it means for me to disappear for an hour?" He looked at Dr. Rose with the meanest eyes he could possibly muster. "I am in charge of 451 people. I'm no Woody Allen, but still, two P.M. on a trading day is not for me the best time."

"I'm not so knowledgeable about this investment banking thing." Dr. Rose said "investment banking" as if she were saying "child molester."

"I just got made head of the proprietary trading desk at The Bank."

For someone who had so much contact with so many socially prominent people, Dr. Rose didn't have a really sophisticated sense of who went where. Sure, she knew the big names. She recognized and she understood the importance of the Manhattan caste system staying in place, but she could not make heads or tails of the people one level down. If you were famous, that was one thing, but the nuances of the hierarchy of wealthy investment bankers were lost on her.

Dick leaned in, so close he could see her enormous pores, her lined face, and the few stray gray facial hairs that lurked around her mouth. It had been a long time since he had seen a woman that age who wasn't Botoxed to the hilt—his own mother had had her eyes pulled so tightly that the first time he had seen her postlift, he wasn't sure it was her. He mused on this for a second. A world where one could not recognize one's own mother was a brave new world. He leaned in, so close he could hear and feel as well as smell her fishy breath, and he literally looked down his nose at her and said, "Look at it this way. I am the head of the most important, most profitable division of the most important, most profitable investment bank in the world."

Daisy looked at Dick in horror. "It's enough. You're not here to talk about you. We are here to save Avery. You remember Avery—your daughter, the one you don't like as much, the one who's more like her mother, the imperfect one. The one who couldn't get into SPENCE!"

"You mean the actress? The one who goes to the British dramatic center for children's arts, ten grand a semester, so she can express herself? Well, I'd like to express myself."

"Drama is Avery's passion!"

"Easy to spend it when you don't have to make it." He looked at her eyes filled with rage.

"I am not going to justify my existence to you."

"Why not?"

Daisy looked away, her eyes filled with tears.

"What the fuck do you do anyway? I know you have a very busy napping schedule, but otherwise . . ."

"I think we are getting away from the point here. I think we are getting away from the main thing, which is that Avery . . ."

Daisy looked at the framed needlepoint on the wall, a picture of a sailboat. They had taken a sailboat on their honeymoon. They had both gotten really seasick but they had been happy. Well, maybe not happy, but at least life had been small and uncomplicated. Daisy wondered if they would ever be able to go back there. "At least I am not cheating on you."

"I'm not . . ."

Daisy could not stand another second of it. "You told me you ended it and then I see you practically drooling on Lady Petra. It's disgusting."

Dick looked down at the floor. Dr. Rose looked at Dick with her large patronizing eyes. "Perhaps this is why . . ."

"Can we not do this now?" Dick hissed.

"Why? For God's sake, she is a shrink!"

Dick's BlackBerry kept going off. It was now vibrating like an irritated rattlesnake. "This is not appropriate. We're not here to talk about this."

Dr. Rose could hardly contain her giddy enthusiasm. So many hours of rich children complaining about their nannies, teachers, tutors, trainers, and various other god-awful handlers. Most of Upper East Side life was a sea of minutiae, punctuated every once in a while with fabulous drama, and here was some. Dr. Rose loved the big, dramatic *Days of Our Lives*–style problems. It was wonderful to get something juicy like this. This kind of thing was actually why she had become a shrink in the first place, to get to experience other people's drama. And did she say *Lady Petra*? Was this woman a royal? Dr. Rose loved a good story, and one that involved the famous or a royal was even better. "No, it's okay, let's talk about this. I am more than happy to talk about whatever you want to talk about."

"Yes, so I'd like to know what it is about me that is so disgusting and vile, that makes me so revolting to you, that you can no longer stand to stick your dick in me."

Dick was shocked. "Daisy!"

"Not genteel enough for you? Not something that Lady Petra would say?"

"Daisy, I will not do this here." Dick stood up and looked at his BlackBerry. There were a few messages from Lady Petra and a few from the office, some from his assistant, one from Blankfein, nothing urgent with a capital *U*. "I'm leaving. Since some of us have to earn all this money for these $15.50-a-minute sessions in the middle of the trading day."

Daisy looked at Dr. Rose in desperation. She would not cry. No matter what, she was not going to cry. No, no, no. Daisy tried to swallow the tears back down, but they would not go. The air conditioner hummed, and she looked up at the old dried-flower arrangement. For someone who made so much money, Dr. Rose had a fairly crappy office (like all the other Upper East Side shrinks: they were, of course, shrinks and not plastic surgeons), ground level. Sure, it was on Park Avenue, but in one of the more dreary white-bricks in the noisiest corner of the sixties. "Dick . . ." But it was too late, he was through the door, gone.

"Well . . ." Daisy paused, listening to his footsteps. Then all of a sudden he was back. Maybe he wanted to talk to her, maybe he was going to remember her worth to him, maybe they could work this all out.

"Actually—" Dick poked his head back in the office, oddly cheerful. "Actually, I was thinking about something."

Daisy's face was filled with hope; Dr. Rose noted this on her large yellow legal pad. Dr. Rose never referred to her notes, and in fact at the end of every year she would throw them out, but she still took them. Why? She wasn't sure. She also never felt there was anything worth writing about these oddly tragic people, these small, unfamous, unfabulous people. Why did people like this come to New York? Dr. Rose wondered. The city was filled with them. Half her practice consisted of them (though she would never admit it to herself or to others). She questioned the existence of these small, unfabulous people. They were never going to be truly accepted. They would never be insiders. They would never be at one of Woody Allen's dinner parties. Sure, they were rich, but they would never be famous, they would never be able to wow her with stories of the Cannes Film Festival. She was (by virtue of the fact that she held the power to heal, and heal not just anyone but children) worshipped by the famous. They all wanted her; she had to turn down famous people because she had so many. Well, not really, but she liked to tell herself that. And she had become friends with some of them. Of course, you weren't supposed to, but it was impossible not to—here were these people, famous people, courting her, calling her. She had been at one of Woody Allen's dinner parties when he had had the town house on Ninety-second Street, and what a dinner party it had been—filled with famous people and their authentically witty banter. "Why, Dick, thank you for coming back, we would love to know what you were thinking about."

"Yes, darling. Please, darling." Dr. Rose noted the pathetic tone of

Daisy Greenbaum's voice. Dr. Rose was able to muster something like sympathy for the woman, but then her eyes traveled down to Daisy's hideous quilted shiny Chanel flats. There was something slightly appalling about Daisy Greenbaum, something about her that prevented Dr. Rose from fully pitying her.

"I was thinking that in the end this whole debacle costs me more than $15.50 a minute, because—" Dick paused and looked over at his wife. There was something compelling and powerful in her eyes. For a minute he did not know how to qualify it. What was it? And then he realized what it was. It was pain, and he wanted to say something kind to her, but then all of a sudden he was gripped again by rage. After all, he had wanted to be taken seriously, he had wanted to teach at MIT, or solve the climate crisis, and instead he worked as a banker, a glorified bank teller counting the cash. He had sold out and she had encouraged him; well, maybe not encouraged him, but she had let him—let him sell out. At least, sometimes he felt like that. Sometimes he loved his glorious money. What about his dreams, what about what he wanted? Where did he fit into this life? "There is the cost of the town car getting all the way back uptown, then there is the cost to my employers of my missed hour and fifteen minutes of time, that includes travel time, of course . . ."

And he got up, he put on his gray jacket, and walked out of the room. Silence, and then she heard his footsteps grow softer and softer until they disappeared. She could imagine his small feet pacing through the waiting room, and out into the waiting town car. The front door slammed and he was gone, leaving Daisy seven very expensive minutes of crying in front of Dr. Rose.

CHAPTER *Four*

Still June 6, 2008

Dow closes down 394 points to 12,209

S&P closes down 43.37 points to 1,360.68

Later that same afternoon Daisy found herself standing in a black T-shirt and ninety-dollar Lululemon yoga pants next to the woman she suspected to have been at one time (and perhaps still was): her husband's mistress, Lady Petra.

Going to Exhale, the spa/gym housed a floor below the Gagosian Gallery on Madison Avenue, had not been the plan. She had thought the day would have been eaten up with activities in preparation for Avery's school's Friendship dinner, which she chaired.

But she had finished early, and had run out of activities to ease the guilt. The soup kitchen was closed that day, she had already finished the crossing guard schedule for the next year for Easton's fancy school, and she had spent three hours volunteering at a school in Harlem sorting books in their library. There was nothing left to do, and she felt that if she went back to her large dark apartment she would scream so loudly that her ears would bleed, and Avery would find her in a pool of blood, and then she would really need therapy. So there Daisy Greenbaum found herself, sucking it in with the mon-eyed elite.

Daisy Greenbaum tried never to exercise; she found herself dia-metrically opposed to it on the grounds that she did not need another leisure activity. And since Daisy Greenbaum spent much of her time trying to prove to herself, her husband, and her daughters that she was not one of *those* women, she tried to stay away from the activities that *those* women are famous for—manicures, pedicures, trainers, hair blowouts, Botox, spa trips, diet doctors, and personal shoppers. Though sometimes she succumbed.

But both girls were off doing after-school activities. Easton was riding on Long Island with the other gray-uniformed, *Vogue*-aspiring daughters of privilege, and Avery was doing her photography class (which Dick had worked out came to $137 a class, not to mention the taxi). So here she was.

Petra smiled at Daisy. She felt sheepish and bad for her. Not that she would ever give up Dick—in fact, quite the opposite. Of course, technically Dick had dumped her, but she was convinced that when her husband finally kicked it and the girls got older, then she would run off with Dick and they could be together forever and she would never have to worry about money again. Not bad for a girl from Queens. Yes, Lady Petra was from Queens. She had married an old Brit with a title and not much else. She could someday perhaps be the first queen from Queens. Of course, for that to happen, half of En-gland would have to die, as her husband was number 712 in the line of succession. But at least he was in the line of succession.

They found themselves putting their shoes on together, sitting right next to each other, so close their thighs were touching. Daisy turned her head to look at Petra. She wanted to say something to her, to bridge the gap, to make peace, to connect with someone. After all, Petra had at one time had a level of intimacy with Dick that Daisy might never have had. Was it possible that she had never been as intimate with her own husband as his mistress had been? "Hello, Petra." Daisy's voice sounded angry and hollow, as well it should.

"Oh hi, Daisy." Petra's voice sounded happy and casual, as well it should.

"I know what you're doing," Daisy said in a hushed whisper. The other ladies from the class had already moved on, and it was almost as if Petra had lingered on purpose, with the hopes of a confrontation, with the hopes of fresh drama.

"And what's that?" Petra smiled. Daisy thought about all the things she had done to prove to her husband and children that she was better than those women, and yet her husband had preferred the company of the queen of those women. Petra Smith, who was so tan and so anorexic she looked like a stick of beef jerky.

"You can't sit here and be all sweetness and light when I know the truth about you."

Petra smiled. "Which is?"

"I know what you did."

"I don't know what you're talking about."

"Of course you do." Daisy felt the rage bubble up in her as she struggled with her shoes. Daisy had giant bunion-covered feet that she had to wedge into her enormous, shockingly stinky sneakers. Petra had tiny feet that easily slid into her Tod's loafers.

"No, I'm sorry. It sounds like you have some problems with your marriage and for that I am very sorry for you and very sorry about the situation. Perhaps we can talk about it sometime soon, or maybe you'd like the name of a good shrink."

Daisy frowned. "Think of this as a shot across the bow of your ship."

"Oh, darling, I don't have any idea what you mean. Our ship is on the Italian Riviera for the summer months, so you must be confused or confabulating or something."

Daisy could feel her face growing red.

"It's funny." Petra smiled. "Dickey said that you had a tendency to get confused. This must be the sort of thing he meant. Pity, though. Both of us married to people so profoundly confused and out of it."

Daisy felt again totally hopeless, like she had against Landon Stone. What could she say, what was there to do? Her only consolation was that he had dumped her. He had stopped seeing her, he had told her that, and she believed him. Well, she sort of believed him.

"Great to see you."

Daisy looked at the floor.

"Take care. Have a great day."

Daisy started to walk off. As she got to the door, she turned around. "Look," she said softly, so softly that Petra had to lean in toward her to hear her words. "Look, I don't want any trouble."

"Nor do I." Petra smiled.

Daisy felt oddly exposed, skinless.

Petra almost felt bad for fat little Daisy Greenbaum, with her classless accent and her fat little fingers and her small, realistic breasts and her many, many un-Botoxed wrinkles. "See you around town." She waved and continued, "And I am sure I will." Both ladies knew this was true; they would see each other everywhere, as was the law of Upper East Side quantum partial affluence physics.

As Daisy got into the gray steel and glass elevator, she paused for a minute and looked down at her clownlike feet in their long gray sneakers. She felt small and helpless and awful.

Then, all of a sudden, the elevator slowed, and she remembered the truest fact about herself. She didn't need luck, which in itself was lucky because she wasn't a lucky type of person. She paused to study the eyes of a murderer in the polished steel. Luck was for those who neglected to make their own.

———————

$\mathcal{T}$hat night when Dick got home, the large master bedroom suite was empty and dark. He found his wife curled up in the fetal position on the small twin bed pressed up against the wall in the maid's room. Since the girls had turned five, Nina had stopped sleeping in. She now slept over only when both parents went on a trip together, which was never. He tried to wake her, not because he really had anything to say to her, but because he hated the girls to see their parents in different beds. His parents had always hated each other and had horrible screaming fights that brought the house down, which he felt had made him capable of what had happened that afternoon at the shrink. Eventually his parents did get divorced, but by then the damage was done. Whatever it was, the fighting, the separation, the divorce, it was impossible to know, but either way it had made him a cruel person, to his wife anyway. He was removed from his cruelty by his emotional emptiness, and he hated this about himself, although not, of course, enough to change it. He was not sure how he would change it if he wanted to, which he did not.

After making a few small and unsuccessful attempts to wake her, he decided to go to bed alone. It was the first time he had ever slept alone in the king-sized bed in the master bedroom, and it felt oddly luxurious. He piled all six pillows behind his head. He was, after all, the head of the prop desk. He could use six pillows if he wanted to.

He fell asleep before he could masturbate, and in that sleep more ghosts visited him—his wife and Raja, his evil associate. Of course, this was not his usual anxiety dream, with the papers being sucked out the window. This dream was different; it had a much more sinister tone. He was wearing a pinkish-gray suit, one he had tried on but decided not to buy at Ralph Lauren. He had decided, with the help of Lady Petra, whom he relied on for all shopping decisions (or had before they had broken up), that the pinkish gray made him look slightly fatter than usual. He was, of course, in the company's G5 again, heading to Davos to meet with some of the European foreign wealthy idiots, and the plane was filled with other prop desk guys. John was there, and so were a few guys whom he knew only slightly.

They were arguing about the coming crash. "It's going to be the end of everything we've made!" Dick screamed. He was, for some reason, smoking an enormous joint, and there were dogs running around, and coming out of the cockpit was the pony that Easton had been begging for, a fifty-thousand-dollar animal that had been sired by one of Christina Onassis's ponies. He made the joke that for that price it should have been sired by Aristotle.

"Shut up, that's bully shitty," John said.

"I think you mean bullshit," Dick said in his usual patronizing way.

"That's what I said, bully shitty." John smiled. Dogs passed by them, walking in between their feet. John was eating strawberries. Dick was drinking scotch. Classical music was playing.

Of course Raja was on the plane, looking all efficient and irritating in her little sweater set. Someone must have told her that sweater sets would make her look softer—maybe she had gone to an image consultant; that seemed like something she would do. "What the fuck do you want?" he said.

"I just wanted to say that hiding the debt, and then having your bonus based on profit that isn't really profit but debt, it's stealing."

"Ugh!" Dick threw up his hands.

"And you know what's going to happen?"

"No."

"The American taxpayers are going to end up footing the bill for this whole scheme. Little grannies in nursing homes won't get their medicine, poor kids won't get rubella shots, because you hate flying commercial."

Dick felt nervous, but then his subconscious reminded him that this was only a dream. There was no possible way that the American taxpayers would be footing the bill for the debt on the balance sheet of a bank. It was impossible. "What even is rubella? Is that a real thing? I don't think it is."

But there was no time for musing on vaccines for children, because just then Dick grabbed John and pushed him out the door of the plane into the howling slipstream and John plummeted to the ground and died.

A second later, they were in the small grassy yard of the house they used to rent in Westhampton when they were normal, before they had become rich enough to have a $12-million mortgage. It was a tiny house with two tiny bedrooms on a tiny unfashionable block filled with share houses and townies. Dick tried to remember if they had been happy there. It would have been easy and simple to say that they were happy there. It would have been the kind of moralistic answer that someone with a logical math mind like his would have liked. But the reality was, the truth was, they hadn't been happy there. Every single night he had lain in that hot little bedroom obsessing about a deal he was trying to get done, and she had wondered about the girls from high school, where had they gone. If they had married better, happier. And both of them had dreamed of the day that they would be able to rent a hundred-thousand-dollar house, one on the right side of the highway, on the ocean, closer to the Bronfmans, the Tisches, and God.

And Daisy was standing in front of the grill in an apron that said in big red letters KISS THE COOK. Dick looked at Daisy, whose black hair had been blow-dried, and something seemed slightly off about her, though he could not place what it was. It took him a minute to realize that her apron was covered in blood.

"Why are you covered in blood?" he asked.

"I've been doing my own . . ." But before she could answer, he had interrupted her.

"Oh, what are you making? It smells delicious." Dick wondered to himself in his wonderful anxiety dream if his wife was pregnant, because she had only ever cooked when she was pregnant with the twins.

Daisy smiled. "Doesn't it smell good?"

"Yes."

"Do you know what it is?"

"No."

"It's human toes."

"Daisy!"

"They are, like, the new Kobe beef."

Dick frowned. For some reason, finding out his wife was a murdering cannibal was not such a horrible shock. He felt the same level of displeasure as he would have if she had spent a few thousand dollars too many on her American Express card. "Whose toes? It's not Petra's toes. Are they Petra's toes?"

"No, silly, I would never murder your mistress. I know how much she means to you." Daisy paused, then stuck her metal barbecue fork into a piece of the meat and raised it to the sky. "They're very juicy." It was a big toe and the hair on it was burned. The toenail was blackened too. The rest of the toe was a pinkish color.

"Whose toes are they, Daisy?"

"Whose do you think?"

"Petra?" He grabbed her and examined the blackened toe, but he could tell almost immediately that they were men's toes. "They aren't Petra's toes. Are they?"

"No!" Daisy laughed and laughed and laughed. "They're John's toes and there are ten of them, ten toes for dinner! Ten! But I'm saving the fingers for lunch tomorrow."

Dick shook himself—somewhere deep within his subconscious mind, he knew he was having another in his long string of nightmares. It's a dream, he told himself, a dream.

And eventually he did wake up, covered in sweat. Every part of him hurt and felt awful. And standing over him was his loving wife, Daisy Greenbaum. "I have to tell you something and I don't want to upset you, but since our marriage is clearly in dire straits . . ." She enjoyed saying "dire straits"; she knew how much Dick prided himself on his "wonderful" marriage, on the fact that he was one of the few managing directors to still be on his first wife. Of course, he had cheated on her and that had almost destroyed their marriage, but he had placed that firmly in the past.

Dick was still slightly asleep and everything still had a dreamlike quality. "Is our marriage in dire straits?" Dick rolled over and looked at the clock next to the bed. It was three minutes after five A.M., and the sky was grayish blue; the sun was slipping up. Soon another day would be upon them, another day of incredible rallies and enormous money to be made, another day of false economy, another day of wealth before the fall. It was all slipping away. Time was moving faster and faster and soon it would all be over. Soon Countrywide would go under, then Lehman Brothers, then GM, then inflation, then Treasury auctions where nobody bids, and eventually the currency would crash, then it would be breadlines and soup lines and cloned sheep and environmental catastrophe. And now, as the head of the prop desk, now he really was part of the problem, one of the power brokers who was steering the American people toward a horrible end.

"Were you there today or was that someone else?"

Dick tried to remember the answer to this question. "Where?"

"At Dr. Rose's."

For a minute, Daisy felt something stir in her chest for Dick. He was the man she had married, confused and slightly vulnerable, defenseless against his nightmares. And then he sort of snapped to attention, he kind of woke up. And his eyes changed toward her and he looked at her in his usual cynical way.

"Dr. Rose is an asshole."

"She can help Avery."

"How?"

"She helped Ryland Lodge and Ryland Lodge's older sister; she saved her life."

Dick thought about the scene he had witnessed with Bowdy and Ryland, the one that he had been able to observe through six lanes of traffic and a modernist sculpture. In his mind he replayed the movie, the image of the little blond-haired girl in her gray pinafore throwing herself on the sidewalk. Daisy thought about the elder Lodge girl, who had just returned from Circle Lodge with Lindsay Lohan. It didn't seem like she was doing all that well. He shook his head at her. "You know it's five A.M.? Right? I have to leave for work in one hour and twenty-seven minutes."

"Can we be friends?" Daisy said in a slightly patronizing way. This was something that Dick was very sensitive to.

"Why are you patronizing me?"

"I'm not."

"If I got to spend all day shopping and getting massages, then personally I would feel that I had nothing to complain about."

"I want you to stop with Petra." But he had stopped with Petra almost a year ago. He had told her he would and he had. He wasn't a bad guy. But he was still angry. He hated to be nagged. Why couldn't she just trust him? Why did she have to grill him?

"So my word means nothing to you."

"You promised me!" She felt small and helpless.

He felt angry at her. "What do you even do all day? Hermès? The gym?"

"Stop it."

"Why? I have the fucking weight of the world on my shoulders and all you do is shop."

Daisy's eyes started to fill with tears. She hoped he could see her tears in the blackness. "I volunteer at the soup kitchen, work with the storefront school in Harlem, read to the blind, am Friendship chair at Avery's school, am crossing guard chair at Easton's school. I am not going to justify my existence to you."

"They have a crossing guard chair?"

"It's a lot of time, these things."

"Ladies and gentlemen, my most expensive employee."

"Why are you being like this?" Daisy's face was now wet with tears. Her nose was running. She was all curled over in her gray crumpled pajamas. And as he looked at her, he felt for her. She wasn't like the other wives. She had married him because she had loved him, deeply, and it hadn't been her fault that they had been catapulted into this world—the wacky world of wealth.

He started to soften. She was not the enemy. He had loved this woman at one point, and he might well again, possibly, someday. He didn't need to be as cruel as he was being.

"I want you to know something, I want to tell . . ."

"Daisy, let's talk later. I know you're tired. I'm sorry I've been such an asshole. This new job is insane and there are so many bad problems with the system and so many things that we are going to need to fix and it's just a nightmare, but I love you and I want you to know that and that I'm sorry that I was such a horse's ass to you. I will fix this. We can fix this. I am sorry." He hugged her. It felt wonderful to be kind to her, and he realized in that moment how weak she was and how much she suffered. He had hurt her and he now realized just how profoundly.

"John didn't die of a heart attack, you know that, right?"

"A lot of people around the office are speculating it's a suicide." Why was he pretending to be politic with his own wife? "We all think he killed himself. Raja is sure of it, but what does she know? She feels we missed the signs. But she's such a pill, so moralistic."

"He didn't kill himself." Daisy looked at Dick. She couldn't believe she was going to tell him. He had given her no reason to trust him and yet she felt the need to unburden herself greater than her fear of getting caught. Part of her didn't want to tell him. For a minute or two she played with the idea of not telling him, of keeping this one all for herself. But she had done this for him, to help him, to save him. The truth could destroy their marriage, but part of Daisy trusted her husband's bloodthirstiness, knew that that was what had sealed them together in the first place. They were cannibals, Darwinian to the core.

He had been most impressed when occasionally Daisy had a piece of gossip that was totally shocking to him, when it was completely inconceivable as to how she had gotten it and yet totally accurate. It had happened only a few times in their marriage, but when it had, he had found it totally disarming. So when she said that, he stopped in his tracks. "What do you know?"

"Well . . ."

"Wait, Daisy. No, not possible. He killed himself. He definitely killed himself. He hated that wife, was pretty tormented about that thing with the brother, and he came from one of those great big Wasp families that was spiraling to a tragic conclusion. Also, all the men in that family are alcoholics." Dick found alcoholism a real sign of weakness. He never drank more than three glasses of scotch in an evening, and never more than a drink an hour. Dick was all about control, about measure. "Like the Kennedys."

"He didn't kill himself."

"Okay." He rolled his eyes. He didn't have time for the dramatic buildup. "Okay, how do you know that he didn't kill himself?" He paused for effect. "How do you know?"

She didn't like it when he patronized her. Fuck him. "Because I did."

Dick started rubbing his eyes. He could be sleeping! He should be sleeping! But he was also slightly aroused by the idea that maybe Daisy was crazy. In some ways he might love her more if she possessed depths. Craziness would not be his first choice, but he would be impressed if she were doing something totally outside of shopping and various trendy exercise classes. And, of course, the volunteering, she was like Mia Farrow, enough with the volunteering. Have a Coke, wear a fur, get over yourself, he thought. "Right, of course, it all makes sense now."

"I'm not kidding. I murdered him."

"Sure." He sighed. "Look, I need sleep and I am exhausted and I realize I have been a total asshole and I am very sorry and I will stop being one. So here's what I will do. We can skip whatever thousand-dollar-a-plate rubber chicken dinner we have tonight and instead we can just have dinner, the two of us, and we can talk about everything and work everything out. What do you think?"

Daisy took a giant slug out of her green-glass Italian water bottle. "You're going to Davos tomorrow for a week."

"Oh, shit, Davos!" Some of his dream started to come back to him, the cooking and the toes, and the house in Westhampton. He wondered who lived in that house now, who slept in that old tiny double bed in the master bedroom. Were those people as burning with ambition and greed as Dick and Daisy had been, or were they happy with the little house and the little bed?

"But, Dick, I have to tell you something. I did murder John, you know that." It actually felt pretty great to say it, liberating, oddly wonderful. It wasn't a perfect crime, because she felt that ultimately he hadn't really deserved it. He wasn't, after all, a pedophile or a rapist or a serial killer or Hitler or Pinochet. But she had done it and she had done it for love, or whatever it was that they had.

"Will you stop saying that?"

"But it's the truth. I did it. I murdered John."

Daisy had been nagging Dick for a long time to go to couples therapy. He had resisted. He was already being lectured by some patronizing schmuck about how to be a father, and he did not also need to be lectured on how to be a husband. But at the same time, here was his insane wife telling him that she had murdered his boss. It would certainly be an easy way to get the last hour and a half of sleep that he would get in his own bed before a week with the pompous morons in Davos. "Okay, we can go to couples therapy."

Daisy knew he didn't believe her, which was fine. But it irritated her (though only slightly) that the reason he didn't believe her was not because he thought she was too kind to murder but more because he thought she was too incompetent to murder, incapable of dealing with all the moving parts of murdering someone. "I want you to stop with Petra."

"I stopped the first time you asked me, a year ago. God." But she could see in his eyes, in the way he averted his eyes, that she still had a hold over him, that ultimately he didn't have the power to say no to Petra. He had sustained his promise until now, but it was only a matter of time until he relapsed.

"I need to go back to bed." He looked up at her. She was kind of lovely in her own way, and she was the mother of his children. And he did love her. He knew that. He knew he loved her. But he needed sleep.

"Can we work this out?"

Dick grabbed Daisy. He didn't believe that she had murdered John, but he loved her for wanting him to think that she did. "Of course we can work this out. I love you." He kissed her passionately. They had sex, real passionate sex, slightly better than the standard married sex. Afterward they fell asleep and slept through their alarm. The twins had to wake them up, both of them, snuggling, in the same bed, her head nestled in his shoulder, like nothing was ever wrong, like they were the perfect family, the family that deserved to inhabit their perfect Park Avenue apartment.

*I*n the taxi on the way to school, Avery complained about Walker. Walker had told Avery she was her secret best friend at first-period knitting, but by third-period interpretive dance, Walker had started the I Hate Avery Club. At lunch Walker wouldn't let Avery sit with her, and at transcendental meditation Walker told Charlotte Jones not to let Avery sit next to her and not to talk to her. At mini golf, Walker hit Avery over the head with an umbrella. And that night was the cruelest cruelty of all: Walker's birthday party, which Avery hadn't been invited to. Out the window a homeless man was pissing on a big green leafy oak tree, but Daisy couldn't hear any of it, because she was thinking back to her first time.

By the late eighties people had stopped calling it fatty camp. It was no longer chic to blatantly shame people for being fat. So that meant that all the shaming was couched in a kind of awful thera-talk that made fatty camp even more horrific. The only thing worse than being forced to spend a miserable summer humiliating yourself in the name of losing weight so that you didn't embarrass your parents by being fat was being forced to pretend that you enjoyed it, that in fact you wanted to go to fatty camp because you wanted to "feel good about yourself."

Camp Shame was, ironically, filled with everything a fat kid loathed about camp and so much more—the horrible zip line across the lake (perfect for falling off and getting soaked), the aggressive fly-eaten ponies (perfect for getting bucked off), the giant ATVs (perfect for getting run over), the high ropes course (does this even need an explanation?), the gymnastics studio (nothing a fat kid loves more than a tight leotard), the dance hall (for rejection from members of the opposite sex), the healthy-eating hall (for being forced to eat in front of other people), and the farm (where a child could learn responsibility by taking care of an actual live pig).

But shockingly, Daisy Greenbaum had actually been popular at fatty camp—she had been queen of the dorks, because in her own way she was a social animal, someone who could follow the cues. And fatty camp had been such a pleasure, a wonderful rest from the constant teasing that she endured at Roslyn Elementary School, where all the girls were stick-skinny and played field hockey.

But there was one dark cloud at fatty camp, one thorn in Daisy Greenbaum's side: Hayden Rosenberg. Hayden Rosenberg had been Daisy Greenbaum's Walker Stone. Hayden Rosenberg had been Daisy Greenbaum's best frenemy. Five years of teasing, five years of emotional blackmail, of pseudo-friendship, of the Daisy Greenbaum Is a Fat Idiot Club, of stealing her mother's meticulously packed "food-free" care packages, of making other girls hate her and convincing the boy she liked to hate her, and various other forms of adolescent torture.

And every year Daisy Greenbaum did nothing. She took the high road, going back to her bunk and crying into her pillow, or she wrote angry poetry, or she went to the cantina and ate her allotment of fat-free treats in silent agony. The other thing Daisy Greenbaum never did was tell her mother. Daisy's mother thought Hayden Rosenberg was Daisy's best friend. Daisy knew that her mother needed Daisy to be normal, needed her to have friends. She knew that her mother would feel worse about her social ineptitude than Daisy did. Grown-up Daisy respected adolescent Daisy for hiding her pain. There was something very grown-up and mature about dealing with your problems yourself. Avery told Daisy everything. It was what Dr. Rose had instructed, and Dr. Rose knew best, right? Daisy wondered about that. But surely Dr. Rose's own daughter was a model of mental health? Candy Ross Rose went to Harvard, after all. But Dr. Rose wasn't there to talk about her own family, as she reminded Daisy the one time she had asked. This wasn't about her. No, this was about the Greenbaums' parental incompetence.

But Daisy wasn't thinking about the patronizing shrink anymore;

her thoughts had lulled her back to her first murder. It had played out much more perfectly than she could have even dreamed of, with the two girls sitting by the lake, sipping Diet Cokes and smoking cigarettes. It was the last night of fatty camp, forever.

"I am so glad we met each other," Hayden had said. Daisy could still remember many of the elements of that day as if it were yesterday: the fake sand running through her fingers, the cool breeze blowing a handful of black bugs her way. The way her waistband made it impossible to breathe. She was still somewhat fat, and she would remain that way until she got to college. The sky was black except for a few small stars. Hayden wasn't fat anymore, she was thin, but she had cheated. Not that the world cared, of course. It mattered to no one but Daisy that Hayden's mom had gotten her hooked on diet pills. "I feel like I should apologize to you."

"Why?"

"Well, sometimes I might have done things, back when we had just started, things that I didn't mean. I told people things about you that weren't true. And do you remember James?"

Did she remember the first boy she had ever loved? "Yes."

"I told him you didn't like him."

"But I did. I did like him." Daisy paused, slightly indignant. "I loved him."

Hayden took a deep breath. "I know"—she smiled slightly—"but I liked him too, and, I mean, let's be honest..." Daisy remembered how it had smelled that night, like a snuffed-out fire. She would smell something similar years later on a horseback-riding vacation in the Southwest, and it would stop her dead in her tracks, would remind her of the night she entered the realm of the impossible, the night she crossed the Rubicon, the night she had fulfilled what she now considered her destiny.

"I don't understand." Daisy pretended. She always pretended. She was never as naïve as she pretended to be, never. She just took advantage of her status as a fat girl, took advantage of the haplessness that other people saw in her. "I told you I liked him."

Hayden looked at Daisy, eyes still so filled with malice, even after all this time, all these many years. "But it made no sense, someone like you with someone like him. No one would believe it. No one would understand it. You and James made no sense. I made more sense with him." Hayden could see that Daisy was upset. "What does it matter? It was so many years ago."

"But I told you I liked him." It was at that moment that Daisy knew everything she had planned—the large sharp rock she had placed right near where she knew they would be sitting, the rumors she had started about Hayden's drinking problem—was right, was necessary. And she knew that what she was doing was, well, perhaps not divinely inspired, but inspired nonetheless.

"He was a popular boy. You know how they are. Sooner or later he would have figured out that you were, well, just because you are popular at fatty camp doesn't mean that he wouldn't have figured out that you were a dork. After all, the queen of the dorks is still deep down a dork."

Daisy smiled. "I guess you are right. I guess the queen of the dorks is still deep down a dork."

For a second they both sat quietly, the murderer and her victim—both of them staring at the kidney-shaped man-made pond. Man-made ponds always looked so ugly to Daisy, so profoundly fake. But it was also sort of apropos because few people were as fake as Hayden Rosenberg.

In the last moments of her life, Hayden Rosenberg was thinking about college tours, about taking the SATs again, about her love of chic Freelance shoes. Profound thoughts did not spin around the brain of Hayden Rosenberg that evening and perhaps they never would have.

As Daisy lifted the enormous rock, the one that she had placed there, and as she brought it down with enormous force on Hayden's small, blond sixteen-year-old head, a few thoughts occurred to her.

Head wounds bleed a lot and Hayden Rosenberg was no exception. As Daisy rolled the girl off the dock (with a rope tied around her waist, of course) and into the hideous kidney-shaped pond, she mused on all the blood—she had not imagined that Hayden could have so much blood inside her. Daisy had learned the first rule of murder: It's always messier than one thinks it will be.

The days that followed were spent searching the woods and surrounding areas for Hayden Rosenberg, *runaway*. Daisy had refused to go home until Hayden was found, which her mother had found very moving. Hayden's parents were also profoundly affected by Daisy's friendship to their dearly departed daughter. Finally, Daisy was sent home, and the camp was officially closed for the winter. The assumption was that Hayden had run off, or perhaps she had hitchhiked; she might have gotten lost, fallen into a ravine, encountered a coyote, or some other outdoor tragedy. Hayden's mother was convinced that she was just living in some other state and one day would show up at her door. Perhaps she would have by that time become a doctor. But most sane people believed that Hayden had slipped away into the night, down into the earth, and beyond.

The next summer, a cloud would cover Camp Shame. Later the Rosenbergs would sue the camp for $27 million. Daisy was never sure how the family landed on the figure. It seemed slightly insane that Hayden Rosenberg's life would be worth $27 million and not a more rounded number like $25 million or $30 million. Eventually the camp settled and soon after that it was forced to close. The owners (a couple in their sixties who were devoted Pritikins and had run the camp for thirty years) had to sell their home and move into a trailer.

The camp site was eventually (after passing though a few owners and being rezoned, in spite of negative town sentiment toward the developers) turned into high-end vacation condos, all of which were built to resemble barns. The developers were forced to drain the hideous kidney-shaped pond in order to put in an enormous golf course, and there, ten years later, they finally found the body of Hayden Rosenberg. Conveniently, her skull had subsequently been mashed by a giant underwater piece of dredging equipment, so it was totally impossible to tell if there had been any damage to the body that might have caused the drowning.

No one ever linked Daisy in any way to the "accident," which was of course now totally classified as such. Hayden Rosenberg ended up in an urn on her mother's mantel in the Hamptons house. And, actually, the settlement financed Hayden's mom's month-long trip to Canyon Ranch, where she met husband number two, a billionaire hair-plug king with low self-esteem and a weight problem. The hair-plug king subsequently subsidized the lifestyle of her younger sister. And so, though her sister (now Landon Stone) actually owed a debt of gratitude to Daisy Greenbaum, sadly, she didn't think of it that way.

Though she didn't know it, there was one person who had a burning hatred in her heart toward Daisy Greenbaum. There was one person who did not believe that Hayden's death was an accident, one person who was sure that Daisy Greenbaum had had something to do with the disappearance of her sister. She was a little girl called Landon Rosenberg, and though she had never met Daisy Greenbaum, she had seen her from afar one day when her parents had come to camp to pick up the belongings of her dead sister, and since then, that face, something in Daisy's expression—something proud and guilty at the same time—had been etched in her brain, and she had been sure, looking at fat little Daisy Greenbaum (and remembering what her sister had told her of the girl); she had pieced these things *together* and become convinced over time that this fat little girl had done something to her sister. She was sure of it.

CHAPTER *Five*

August 10, 2008

Dow closes down 32.12 points to 9,337.95

S&P closes down 3.38 points to 1,007.10

Being the chair of the Friendship Committee at the school where her daughter had no friends was one of the many unhappy ironies of Daisy Greenbaum's life. She always felt like a fraud, and she had even mentioned this to the director of development, who had offered her the opportunity, which was considered to be one of the plum volunteer assignments. But Daisy was not head of the committee because of her daughter's social life and she knew this. Daisy mused on this as she sat with a few other graying Upper West Side mothers cutting red construction paper into large misshapen hearts.

The conversation at Avery's school was always radically different from the conversation at the gray-pinafore girls' school. The West Side moms did not readily admit to the decorating and vacation lifestyle that the East Side moms relished. Since West Side moms "weren't really like that," their committees met on the occasional summer Saturday instead of just during the year, the expectation being that these moms were so "down to earth," they did not have a summer home. It was one of those West Side gestures calculated to project humility.

In the hopes of appearing more down to earth than the other millionaires today, the ladies were talking about the tick problem on Fire Island (Fire Island was considered less fancy by virtue of the fact that the average Fire Island home was less expensive than the average Southampton home) and Daisy was staring into outer space, trying to think of something to add. And then she realized that she could top all of them. She had done the most unpretentious thing ever: she had decided to stay in the city. Sure, it was because her husband was convinced that they were poor now, but did she need to add that? Maybe not; after all, this modesty was largely faux. No one these ladies knew was anywhere near falling off the grid. "We didn't get a house this summer, we're doing weekends in the city. It's been really fun."

There was a pause. Had Daisy been a normal mummy, this nugget of information would have been met with the usual cheerful schadenfreude, but since Daisy was known as the very, very rich mummy who lived at 740 Park Avenue, the idea that she had not rented a $200,000 summer behemoth seemed inconceivable. Jane, the grayest and most hip of the moms (an overachieving mummy who was a Ph.D. candidate at Columbia but also made time for volunteering at the kids' schools, all three of them), paused, trying to fight her shock, to say something nice and not too barbed, but before she could get a word in Faye spoke.

"So, are times tough at The Bank? Does this mean you're going to be giving up your membership at the Century?" Faye was the meanest, coolest Upper West Side mom. She lived in the Beresford with the Seinfelds, Vikram Pandit, Glenn Close, and God. Faye was famous for being fancier than even the fanciest East Side mummy, but was able to maintain her smugness because she was, after all, down to earth, due to her West Side status. Shockingly, Faye was the mummy who always wanted to be chair of the Friendship Committee.

"Not at all," Daisy answered. Daisy was visibly wounded, and Jane wondered how she survived at the fanciest, most venerable girls' school when she had such a profoundly thin skin.

"Faye." Jane frowned at Faye. Jane was the daughter of a Ruden and a Rose (two of the most venerable Manhattan real estate families). She carried this honor in a quiet and dignified way, sending her children to progressive schools and silently giving money to Democrats. She was a rich liberal (like everyone else), but she was one of the dying breed of quiet billionaires, as opposed to noisy dollaraires—people living their lives in the red, spending everything on coats (like a J. Mendel fur) that cost more than houses, all in the hopes of keeping up with the Falcones (hedge fund manager Philip Falcone, who in 2007 made $1.7 billion).

Jane had no time for other people's meanness. And so it was with glee that she remembered a hushed rumor that she had heard about Daisy Greenbaum. "How are things at the Heavenly Rest soup kitchen?"

Daisy looked slightly embarrassed (and slightly thrilled). Daisy was not someone who dined out on her volunteer work (but if someone else outed her, well, then). "Oh, okay. You guys should come. It's really fun and the work is sort of mindless and hypnotic. And then there are the church ladies. I love the church ladies, they are totally fascinating." Faye was looking at her BlackBerry. Two of the other women had started talking loudly. Daisy could tell she had lost her audience.

Just then a rather ashen lady came down into the basement looking pained and agitated. She was one of the many school administrators and she looked anxious. "Mrs. Greenbaum, there is someone who needs to talk to you urgently. Can you come with me upstairs?"

A chill ran down Daisy's back. Was it something with the children? It must be something with Avery. She followed the administrator into the tinny and terrifying elevator that jerked back and forth as they went up to the first floor. "I told her to wait outside. She seemed upset."

Daisy realized that this was possibly not Avery. What was it? Could something have happened to Dick? Nah. What about her mother? No, she had very mixed feelings about her mother. What about her sister? No, there would have been a million people who would have come to her. It had to have been her father. Something horrible must have happened to her beloved father.

She could feel her heart beating out of her chest. She could hear the pounding ring in her ears. She ran out of the building and onto the street. Sure, she had loved her father, but she had lost touch with her family since she had crossed into the territory of the "fabulously wealthy." She had been a bad daughter these last few years, helping the homeless but ignoring her parents. But they had been cruel to her too. They had blamed her for Dick's wealth, hated her for it, felt that she was no longer one of them. There had been an ugly scene at her father's birthday party (it was hazy in her memory and she didn't remember how long ago it had been, but she knew there had been a Christmas or two that had passed them by), and then later there had been angry emails back and forth, and since then radio silence.

She thought about the complexity of these things, of fathers and daughters, as she walked down the long, long hallway. Would her daughters lose interest in her someday, perhaps after she had been convicted, or when she was on trial? Would Easton still visit her when she was locked up in Bedford Hills? Would Easton remind Avery that their mother loved them very much, that she had done this for them, or would both girls turn their backs on their disgraced mother? Would Dick remarry someone lovely and would they start calling her Mummy? Maybe first as a joke and then it would catch on and soon Easton and Avery would have to think really, really hard to conjure up a picture of their mother, and often Daisy would appear to them as an amalgam of Betty Ford and Betty Crocker—neither of whom she particularly looked like. No, she couldn't think like that, could she?

As she rounded the corner she expected to see her older sister, Jenny, with her enormous ass protruding from her St. John Knits suit, eyes filled with tears, but instead she was met with the not totally unfamiliar sight of her husband's hopefully ex-mistress. This was both good news and bad. It meant that her father was still alive. It meant she still had time to make up for her derelictions. But it was hard to be happy to see your husband's mistress, even if she was his ex-mistress.

"What are you doing at my daughter's school?" Daisy was angry. Not as angry as she should have been, not as angry as a normal person would be, but angry. She was less angry than normal people because she had a wonderful outlet for her rage, something that worked much better than bargello, something that worked much better than needlepoint or spinning or even smoking. Yes, Daisy found that murdering people really cut down on her rage.

"I have been trying to get your attention. I have been following you all day but you are so totally clueless and unobservant that you totally haven't noticed. I was standing behind you at Starbucks, my taxi followed yours through the park. I waited for you outside your shrink." She had noticed her at Starbucks, but assumed that Petra was just getting a coffee. And she had seen her at the shrink but she thought it was possible that they saw the same shrink (after all, it was a very small upper class; they all saw the same doctors, shrinks, trainers, etc).

"Okay, so now you have it. What do you want?"

Petra had not planned for this. She had not planned to actually get Daisy's attention. Now that she had her attention, she seemed flummoxed. She smoothed her blond hair. She wasn't that much more beautiful than the wife, but she knew how to use what she had in a way the wife did not. Petra was all Jessica Rabbit with enormous boobs and giant hips and a skinny waist. Sure, Daisy was sexy too, but Petra had her outsexed. Petra wore a push-up bra every single day of her life. She even had push-up workout bras for when she went to the gym. But no bra could help her figure out what to say to Daisy, who was standing there looking both bored and slightly confused.

Would she try to convince Daisy that Dick loved her, even though Dick hadn't returned her calls for going on a year, or would she try to convince Daisy that she could ruin them? "Dick loves me."

Daisy wondered if Dick was still screwing Petra. For a minute the whole thing could have gone either way, but Daisy trusted Dick, and something about their recent conversation had felt very real and true to her. The sex had seemed sincere too. She believed him, or she at least believed in his remorse. Daisy was also weirdly canny, and she did believe that Petra's showing up at school smacked of a kind of desperation that was really truly totally hopeless, which meant that Dick was sticking to his word. "Well, that sounds like it has nothing to do with me, so I am not sure what you would like me to do about it."

This was not the response Petra was hoping for. "Dick loves me."

Daisy had to remind herself not to engage. "Perhaps..."

"No, not perhaps." Petra could feel the fire in her. "He does."

"Maybe." Daisy could feel herself getting sucked in. "Maybe, but I am the mother of his children and he is staying with me." There was a kind of banal tragedy in this statement, and Daisy mused on this for a second. But American life was filled with compromises, filled with undramatic truths, filled with choices that were chockablock with banality. Grown-up life wasn't supposed to be fun; it was supposed to be reasonable, measured, filled with responsible actions and moral high roads taken, passions ignored until they were snuffed out (leaving the victims to wonder if their passions were ever really passions at all or merely manifestations of some kind of dysfunctional longing). And so Dick was doing what he should. He was doing the right thing.

"Your husband may be back to you right now, but sooner or later he will go back to me. Because he loves me." But Petra's statement rang hollow to both women. The truth was, if he was going to cheat again, why would he maintain loyalty to a lover he had already gotten sick of? If he was going to cheat again, he was going to cheat with someone younger, better, faster, and both women sort of knew this. There was no honor among thieves, and this was clear to both women, as they were both thieves—or, more precisely, Daisy was a murderer and Petra a husband stealer.

"Okay, now it's my turn to ask a question."

"Fine."

"Why now?" Daisy could feel tears forming in her eyes. She was angry. She could feel her angry self rising from her little Jewish-princess-slash-church-volunteer-lady self.

Petra paused.

"Why after a year? Why do you come now? Why are you so interested in ruining my marriage? Why now?"

Petra blushed. She couldn't tell her why. She couldn't tell Daisy that she was quickly running out of options, that her husband's Ponzi scheme was unraveling, that her credit cards were being declined, that the automated phone calls had started, the people named "Mrs. Johnson" were calling, asking to speak to the cardholder and explaining why there was a freeze on that account.

"Yes, why now?" Daisy could see her pain, as much as she didn't want to. She could see it in the furrow of her brow, in the way her eyes squinted. This was not a happy woman. But that certainly wasn't Daisy's fault or responsibility.

Petra couldn't tell Daisy the truth. She couldn't tell Daisy that she was seriously considering going to the FBI. That everything they had worked so hard to build, that the wealth that they had assumed they would always have, was gone. That Dick was her last resort. "Because, because . . ." But before she could say anything Daisy was gone. She had turned on her heel and taken off, leaving Petra totally deflated, alone on the West Side sidewalk a whole park away from her home.

On Seventy-ninth Street and Madison there is a restaurant on the second floor of a nondescript Italian-looking building where a pizza for one can cost upward of forty-seven dollars, which is pretty spectacular if you think about it. But this is neither here nor there, because at that moment (as at many other moments) no one was thinking about the cost of their meal. No, Easton and Avery and their mother were sitting having a "relaxed" girls' lunch at one of the most overpriced Italian restaurants in the city. Did I mention the service is awful and the food is mediocre?

"I was thinnnnking about what I want to be when I grow up."

Both Avery and Daisy sort of wanted to roll their eyes, but neither did.

"That's wonderful," Daisy said, trying to sound chipper, as she imagined someone from Darien who wore Lilly Pulitzer might say it.

Avery gave her mother a weary look.

"I thinkkkkkkkkk I want to be a mathematician." It was one of those restaurants frequented by girls and their mothers from the gray-pinafore girls' school, one of those places that the mothers took their daughters for an early dinner, genteel but still faux casual.

"A what?" Avery said. She was trying not to crack up. Daisy gave her a look that sort of said, "Don't you dare."

"A mathematician." Sure, Easton was smart, she had rocked the standardized tests she had had to take, and at her competitive school she got mostly As. But even at eight it seemed clear to all who knew her that the chances of the popular, beautiful gossip-girl-esque horseback-riding twin someday graduating from MIT seemed unlikely. Harvard, sure. Princeton, like the smart Bush girls, seemed totally right. But MIT? Nope.

Neither wanted to make Easton feel bad, so both tried to say something encouraging but not too encouraging about something they didn't quite think would ever happen.

"So you're liking math, that is wonderful. Math is a wonderful thing. You know, it is so useful."

Avery rolled her eyes at her mother. Daisy frowned. "Well, I want to be an actress," Avery said with great zeal and gusto.

"That's great, Avery, an actress," Daisy said dismissively. Daisy knew Avery wanted to be an actress, because she had been schlepping the kid to acting and singing lessons in the West Village, and there Daisy had learned that Avery was gifted at neither acting nor singing. But modern parenting was about encouraging your child's passions, right? Even if they were god-awful? Even if they were setting themselves up for a lifetime of rejection and hardship, even then? She could never tell her daughter the truth, that she was pretty enough for a happy life and a career in investment banking but not to be able to play Matt Damon's love interest—no, that was considered child abuse.

"I want to star in movies and maybe someday direct."

"Wonderful." Daisy gently shifted the conversation to something more realistic, more lucrative. "But Easton, why do you want to be a mathematician? What has brought this sudden love of math on? Not that I am complaining. I love the idea of you being a math whiz and you know who will love it even more. . . ." Now the wheels were turning for Daisy. Now she was getting ideas. For a second she saw Easton at MIT, Easton as a math genius, Easton surpassing her father. Easton taking over for Jamie Dimon at JPMorgan Chase. She could feel her heart beating in her chest. She was suddenly so proud of her little math whiz. She had been so worried about these girls being a disappointment to Dick. And now . . .

"Daddy." Easton smiled, like this had been her plan all along, to figure out a way to really upstage Avery once and for all.

"Why do you want to be a math whiz?" Avery smiled at her mother. "Tell Mommy why you want to do it."

Easton paused. "Well, India's dad said that my daddy makes a ton of dough and is so rich and that's because he is a Jew, and all Jews are good at math, and if I want to be rich I should get to be good at math, and besides, India says no one from a good family will ever want to marry me because I'm not a good kind of Jew. She says the good kind of Jews are called . . ."

Daisy cringed; Avery tried to keep from laughing.

"Are we German Jews? India says the only kind of Jews that are good Jews are German Jews. Is that true?"

Daisy put her head in her hands. Easton stared out into the darkness.

"Darling, that's very anti-Semitic." Daisy mulled this over in her head for a minute. Was it actually anti-Semitic? She didn't know. It seemed anti-Semitic to say something bad about the Jews, but she wasn't sure. After all, they were saying something good about a small group of Jews. God, it was such an arcane notion, the idea that German Jews were better than Russian Jews or Polish Jews.

"But"—Avery smiled—"he's saying he likes Jews."

Daisy frowned at Avery. "Thank you, Avery, very helpful, really."

Easton chirped up again. "I don't understand, Mom. Where does our family come from? I told India's dad that I thought we were German Jews, but I was lying because I knew we weren't and he said we could probably get a full membership at the club if that was true."

The club. Of course this was all about the club. Since Easton was such a rider, she had persuaded her parents to join a restricted riding club so that she could ride with people who came over on the *Mayflower*. It happened to be that being a "riding" member and not a "full glorious member" with access to the golf and tennis and glorious swimming pool was actually a kind of torture.

Avery was looking at the floor. She enjoyed looking at the floor. It was a good way not to offend anyone, and as her eyes traveled the floor they picked up a pair of Tod's loafers attached to the legs of Landon Stone. "Mom, it's Landon Stone and Fizzy!"

Daisy looked up, slightly irritated already. Landon was chatting happily, gesticulating like mad, with Fizzy Tisch. Fizzy Tisch was a friend everyone claimed to have but no one did. She was a mummy in demand. Daisy couldn't help but feel a bit left out. After all, Fizzy was her friend. Daisy had introduced Fizzy to Landon and now they were carrying on without her.

Daisy frowned and then pushed her lips into a smile. The girls didn't see her, so she waved.

"I think it is, Mom." Easton was chewing on a lettuce leaf. She didn't eat pizza or carbohydrates of any kind. She was doing a self-proclaimed cleanse, so she now ate only single-ingredient foods. Daisy had run out of arguments, since food also tormented her. That said, it was absolutely heartbreaking to see her daughter struggle to be something she was not.

"Easton, will you please eat something, please, anything?"

"Mom, I am doing a cleanse."

"You're an idiot," said Avery.

"Don't call your sister an idiot."

"Why?" Avery took another bite of pizza. Avery wasn't fat but she also wasn't particularly thin. She probably would be going through an awkward chunky stage if she lived anywhere else in the country, but since she lived at the center of the juggernaut of thin, she could not be anything but. "She is an idiot." For a few seconds Daisy agreed. It was disarming having a child who was so profoundly style over substance, but it was still rude.

"First of all, Avery, your sister is not an idiot." Daisy looked over at Easton. Easton was looking at her watch, thinking about riding or boys, or about blowing out her hair or not eating or something. "And second of all, it is not okay to say it. Even if she was, which she is not."

"They're coming over here," Avery said.

Daisy looked up, then stood up, knocking a bottle of Pellegrino all over the table, which was typical.

"Fizzy! Landon!" Daisy seemed a little too happy to see them. This happiness betrayed her, made her seem overly anxious, like she needed something. It wasn't good to need something from these ladies. That was how they got you. You didn't *ever* want to need something from them.

Fizzy and Landon were friendly but not too friendly. They both smiled at her and air-kissed her, but they obviously had been talking about her during their lunch. Both ladies smiled and greeted the girls. The girls looked at each other and rolled their eyes. "It's so nice to see you both." Daisy couldn't think of anything else to say.

But Fizzy was obviously feeling guilty because she said, "So the girls are riding tomorrow, yes?"

Daisy nodded. Easton looked up from her lettuce. "Can't wait."

"Walker's going to come ride too. Isn't that great?" Landon smiled.

Daisy was annoyed. For years it had been just Fizzy's spawn and Easton, and now stupid Walker Stone was going to horn in on their time together. "Just great. Really."

"Isn't it?" Landon smiled, and Daisy couldn't place it but there was something in her eyes. Something that looked like malice.

———

$\mathcal{T}$rip McAllister had one goal in life now, and it was to bring down The Bank. He wanted to watch blood gush from the doors, to see the headquarters for sale, to see the company G5s on the block. He wanted to kill all the sacred cows. So far all the cows he could find had killed themselves. He had wanted to get the head of the prop desk, that incredibly smug asshole, but John had killed himself, and now Trip had become distracted by a potential Ponzi scheme he was investigating.

Sure, he hated Dick Greenbaum, but Trip was a Wasp, and he felt that going after Dick Greenbaum was slightly anti-Semitic (he was very paranoid about anti-Semitism). Also, he respected Dick for being a math brain, a real quant. Everyone knew that John was a glorified salesman, whereas Dick Greenbaum did something that not every other asshole out of B-school could do. That said, he hated all those fuckers.

Trip was sitting in his loft in Brooklyn, which was five thousand raw square feet, and it had views of the bridge and the fucking Jehovah's Witnesses from every window. But he had to take a subway to the city, to the real city, to the city where the people who worked at the company that had destroyed his life lived.

"Come back to bed," Candy Ross Rose called. She was naked except for her tattoos.

"Give me a minute." Trip thought about Dick Greenbaum, sitting in his huge office on the fifty-seventh floor of millionaire's plaza getting a blow job from his secretary, and suddenly hated him as much as he had hated the asshole before him.

"Come on . . . I want you to do that thing you did last night."

"Don't you have to get up and start posting?"

"I'm getting material for posting."

Trip McAllister got up from his desk and walked over to the bed. Candy exposed her huge breasts to him. "You know you can't keep doing that."

She batted her eyelashes at him. "Why?"

"You just need to add new things to your repertoire."

"I'm going to."

"Oh, yeah?" He smiled. She was fun, not the kind of girl you marry, not the kind of girl you settle down with, not the kind of girl you bring back to Boston to meet the Cabots, to play tennis with the Lodges, to talk to God, but she was fun.

"I'm going to start posting on your blog."

"Oh, yeah?" He laughed. "What are you going to post, half-naked pictures of you?" But before the words had escaped his lips, he realized he had gone too far with this. Shit, she was going to get all feminist movement on his ass. Why did he do things like that?

"*Fuck you.* You are such an incredible asshole."

"Ugh." Trip sighed. "That's not what I meant."

"You know, I went to Harvard too."

"Really?" Trip was being sarcastic. Candy had slept with all his friends. In fact, she had slept with everyone from Adams House. It actually made him slightly dizzy to think of all the men Candy had slept with.

"It doesn't matter. You be the asshole you want to be, because I am working on something, something huge, something that will make you know that I am more than just an incredible piece of ass with phenomenal tits."

Trip thought about Candy's breasts. They were huge, enormous really. But were they phenomenal? Not really, just huge; it's not like they were filled with money or candy or state secrets or something. "Oh, yeah?" He was slightly shocked that she was letting him off so easily. Why was that? She had to be up to something.

"Yes."

"What?"

She started rubbing him. "Something fabulous."

He started to get turned on. "Yes, what?"

"Dick." She said it slowly, like she was talking about his dick.

"Greenbaum?"

"Of course."

Now, this was a woman. "I love . . ."

She paused. He had never said he loved her before; perhaps this was the moment he would do it. "Yes?" She batted her eyelashes.

"I love this idea."

Candy was pissed. "And . . ."

"And I think you will be a great contributor to the blog?"

"And?"

Trip was quickly getting un-turned-on.

"And what?"

"Where do you see this relationship going, Trip? Where?"

Trip felt exhausted. Life was too short to have these kinds of conversations with a woman he would never in a million years get serious with. Didn't she understand that in his social class men didn't marry until they were in their thirties or forties? But he didn't want to say anything nasty. Correction—he didn't want to have to apologize for saying anything nasty. So he did what he had seen his father do many times with his mother. He just wandered off as if their conversation were over. And then it was.

$\mathcal{D}$ick was standing on line at Starbucks watching the news on the little TV against the wall. President Bush was sitting at a giant desk signing his name on a stupid piece of crap called The Housing and Economic Recovery Act of 2008. Dick frowned. It would keep things going for a little while longer. Then he smiled. He had had fun with Daisy that morning; they had lain in each other's arms and told stupid jokes. She was a fun person to be married to and life was good, and things would be fine. And he had these great daughters, Easton and Avery, who were pretty and intelligent. And things would be okay. He ordered his drink and then looked behind him, and all his happy thoughts went right away because behind him was a person who was not fun, who did not make him happy.

The person behind him was Lady Petra. She put her hands on his shoulders.

"What are you doing here?"

"Getting a latte."

"This isn't funny," he whispered. He did not even turn around because there was nothing to see, or nothing he hadn't already seen many times.

"What isn't funny?"

"I'm married."

Her hands rested closer to his neck. "You never used to think that way."

"Well, now I do."

"But Dickey, I love you. And you love me and you asked me to marry you. Don't you remember? And now—" Her voice started to get raspy, like she was about to tap into the enormous reservoir of pain that lurked beneath her affectations. Each affectation masked a different painful reality from her childhood—the fake British accent masked the alcoholic machinist father who often cashed his paychecks at Mulligan's Irish pub; the way she called everyone "darling" hid the mother who instructed her to pray for every sin (real or imagined). And then there were other pains: there was the reality of her husband, Lord Kingly, and there was the bombed-out town house they lived in. It was, or had been, one of the finest town houses (a twenty-five-foot-wide brownstone with huge windows) on one of the finest blocks in Manhattan. But things had gone horribly wrong with all of Lord Kingly's fake investments, and no one knew it yet except her and him (and an "auditor" in a strip mall in west New Jersey who possessed a rubber stamp that he used freely), but things were going to be very bad for all of them. It was called a Ponzi scheme, named after some guy named Ponzi, but soon it would be called a Kingly scheme, named after them (she had hoped for a museum or a wing at a hospital, not a crime). How had she done this? She had married her father again. And somehow they had run out of money first. What little that was left from the scheme was now being put directly into keeping the offices running, with the hopes that they could find some more people with more money to pour into the sinking ship.

And so they had had to stop renovating the palace on Seventy-eighth Street between Fifth and Madison, the enormous brownstone with a double-height living room, from which now hung, instead of chandeliers, bare lightbulbs. Luckily she had installed huge thick curtains, and no one could see behind them.

"Yes, but now I am focusing on my marriage." Dick thought back to last summer. They had been in Paris for two weeks, Lady Petra and he, in the George V, just the two of them, like married people. Had he proposed to her? He thought back. Well, he might have. He might have asked her if she might want to, someday, after both of their spouses had been done away with—maybe after hers had died and his had been sent off to an eternal summer of living full-time in the Hamptons, married to a gardener. But now that would never be.

Meanwhile Sir Smith Kingly was looking for money in the couch cushions, change to pay the deliveryman and then also money, big money, to keep everything going for just one more month. The deliveryman kept ringing the bell, ring ring ring. He just needed some cash. "Yes, yes, I'll hold." He lifted off one of the pillows; in the fold of the couch he saw an enormous pile of silver coins (he hoped they were quarters and not some weird valueless European coins). It was a seventeen-thousand-dollar couch (perhaps he could pay with one of the pillows), but it was purchased before. He could now divide his life into before and after, and for a moment he was struck by an un-believable wave of self-pity. But that thought was immediately dis-placed by insane optimism. After all, the man was a gambler and he did believe that he had once been on top and so he could be again, and perhaps this was true, and perhaps not.

The change in the sofa turned out to be lire and not quarters. The deliveryman kept ringing. *Ring. Ring. Ring.* He was hungry and he wanted that egg sandwich so badly he could all but taste its gooey cholesterol-laden goodness, but then he couldn't very well tell the guy that he'd pay him some other day, that he used to be rich and so he should trust him. He couldn't do that with the guy from the Greek diner on the corner. No, but he could do that with his investors; he could do that for now.

Finally he remembered he had seen change in the kitchen cabinet. One of the contractors had left it. He grabbed it and counted it. Just enough. He ran to the door. The young Mexican man looked despon-dent. Sir Kingly handed him the change. The man peeked inside the door; he could see boxes, some dust, and a giant hole in the ceiling.

"No tip?" He looked even more despondent.

Sir Kingly wanted to say he was sorry, that he was poor now, that there wasn't money for that kind of thing. But he had not gotten rich being kind. He thought of the maxim that behind every great fortune there is a great crime, and for a minute he mulled this as he slammed the door on the deliveryman.

$\mathcal{D}$ick and Daisy could not stop talking to each other, and neither could remember a time when they weren't blissfully happy. They had laughed throughout dinner, as she had regaled him with stories of Avery's drama camp friends. He had laughed so hard that tears had formed in the corners of his eyes and he had congratulated himself for marrying someone so witty. They had shared pasta and fish at San

Ambroeus and then walked home through the deliciously empty summer streets. They were among the four remaining families at 740 Park that summer. And they were finding that the poverty of not having a Hampton house was truly enjoyable. Sure, the girls had complained bitterly (or Easton had whined, rolling her consonants, and looking generally miserable, but in the end she had spent her weekdays at field hockey camp and her weekends with more socially prominent friends in Southampton, and she was now well on her way to becoming a junior member of the Southampton Bathing Club).

It was a cool July night and a soft breeze was blowing. They turned the corner off Seventy-first Street and onto Park Avenue, her sharp heels tapping on the smooth gray concrete sidewalks. The air smelled vaguely burned and her mind flashed briefly to fatty camp, to the fake lake, to the dock, to the blood on her arms and the cold fake lake water. Then her mind went back to Dick, to her perfect husband, to the perfect night, cool, summery, filled with hope. Arm in arm, they were the couple who deserved their Park Avenue lives. And maybe things would be okay for Lehman Brothers, for the equity markets, for the GM bondholders, and for them.

Augustus Malmot was standing outside the building smoking a cigar and wearing a funny hat. At first it appeared that he was alone, but as they walked closer they could see her in the shadows. Daisy was struck by how much her husband's mistress had aged in a few days. Her skin was sagging around her eyes and her face had a positively ghoulish quality to it. Daisy was overcome by sadness for this fragile slip of a person. Being a mistress seemed to her for that moment the worst of all possible worlds, the monotony of marriage with none of the stability.

"What are you doing here?" Dick hissed. Daisy was shocked at how cruel the timbre of his voice was. He had loved that woman, and now all she could hear was hate.

Dick looked at Augustus. "I'm sorry, would you excuse me?" Augustus wanted no part in any of this; he would have his own excite-ment to deal with in a few short months. He quickly faded off back into the blue velvet lobby.

"What the hell are you doing here?"

Petra was clearly shocked by his tone and it took all three of them a minute or two to regain composure. Daisy looked up and down Park Avenue; there was not a car in sight, and New York felt like the loneli-est city in the world. Daisy looked at both of them. This had nothing to do with her, not really, and she was glad of that. "Perhaps I'll go upstairs and relieve Nina."

Dick looked at Daisy helplessly. It was as if he thought Daisy could fix this. But why did he think she could fix this? Had she fixed some-thing else for him? His mind flashed back to the dream, and to a con-versation that he thought that he had had in real life but more likely had in the dream. It went something like this:

"You told me that you would never murder my mistress, remem-ber? When you were cooking my boss's toes."

After this sentence floated around his brain for a second or two, his mind flashed to Daisy's "confession." She had told him that she had murdered his boss, but he hadn't believed her. Now, as she walked calmly upstairs, Dick wondered if he had underestimated her. "How could you possibly think showing up in front of my house was okay?"

Petra had hoped he would have been slightly happier than this to see her. "You don't return my calls."

"Why would I?" he hissed. He had been surprised that Daisy had been so apathetic to the whole thing; she had not attacked Petra or him. She had just acknowledged the whole situation and then dis-missed it. It was as if she felt the whole situation was none of her business. And this worried him, because Daisy Greenbaum had gone from his most expensive employee to his most capable.

"It isn't over just because *you say it's over.*" She had started to raise her voice, and Dick could feel the eyes of a few Park Avenue doormen on him and her and the developing drama. They were bored, it had been a long, empty summer (most of which had taken place in the Hamptons), and here was finally something interesting.

"Not so loud."

"Why the fuck not? I can be as loud as I want. What do I have to lose?"

He grabbed her arm. "It's been a year. A *year*! Why now? Why do you want me now?"

She looked utterly surprised, speechless almost. It hadn't been a year. It had been more recently than that, but what did it matter? She needed him now, for love and for money, and she had no more options. She had no answer for his questions, so instead she just ignored him and continued. *"I will not be ignored."*

He started to get furious. He hated scenes. "You are making a scene. We are both married people with spouses who could be hurt by this and I think it is important that we respect the fact that we had a good time but now it is over and we both need to try to make it work with the people we are married to." Both of them could hear it in his voice, the timbre: it was desperation in its basest form. He was desperate—desperate for this drama to be over, desperate to make it work with his wife, desperate to be happy, desperate to be the better man that he now thought he could be. "Our lives together are over. I am done with the double life. I don't think you understand. I need all my psychic energy focused on my job, which is right now minimizing the amount of damage the American economy will sustain."

Petra smiled; she thought back to all the wounded mistresses she had seen in the cinema throughout time (and there had been many). She would not become a cliché, and yet she would not slip into the background. He owed her an explanation; he owed her some kind of emotional severance. He owed her something. She tried to compose something profound to say to him, something brave, something about how she had worked so hard, how she had come from nothing, from Queens, and now, now she was something—he didn't know that that something was crumbling. She had put all that at risk because she had loved him and now he was discarding her like some piece of trash, but that was not what came out. What came out was hushed and filled with rage, each word crackling with pain. What came out was "I will not be tossed aside. I will get you. I will use everything I know. I will tell everyone. I will tell Cindy Adams. I will tell Page Six. I will ruin you. You will never ever eat lunch in this town again."

Something about the way she said "get you" made him crack a smile. He was ungettable. Wasn't he? He made millions of dollars, had hundreds of people working for him. He lived at 740, had a daughter at the gray-jumper girls' school. He was a master of the universe. He made Sherman McCoy look like a janitor. There was no way to "get him."

Was there? He looked down Park Avenue. It was the summer of his discontent (and winter, fall, spring), but the problem was the world, not him. He was untouchable. Right? He thought about the world, about the stupid Housing and Recovery Act, the even stupider government of California, the discovery of water on Mars, and then today Ben Bernanke had told Barney Frank's House Financial Services Committee that Fannie Mae and Freddie Mac were "adequately capitalized and in no danger of failing." They weren't, but he was. He was adequately capitalized and in no danger of failing, wasn't he?

She could tell she had lost him. For someone with such a big, big job who made so much money, he seemed to her to be slightly flaky. She attributed this to his big math brain, always busy splitting the atom, unlike her husband, who was busy defrauding investors and trying to keep the whole thing going. What would happen when people found out? It would never happen because no one would ever find out, and besides, she'd be long gone, hitching her wagon to a more legitimate star (she hoped). "Do you hear me? I will not just fade away. I am not some girl."

He wasn't so adequately capitalized. He had been given a mortgage by his employer, a mortgage that was in many ways largely illegal, and there were other things, other problems, tax problems, possible legal complications. There were things Petra knew, things about derivatives, about dealings with Saudi families, about illegal help, and family vacations taken on the company G5. It could look bad put together in the right way (which for him, of course, was the wrong way). He could lose everything he had worked so hard for. But would she possibly believe a change in heart so quickly, or would it look suspicious?

"What do you want?" He was trying to level with her. "What do you really want?"

"That little thing that makes the world go round," she said. And for a minute, she looked defeated, pathetic. Then she lifted her chin haughtily again and tossed back her hair and looked directly into his eyes. "Four million dollars. You owe me. I could have destroyed your family. Isn't your family worth a measly four million dollars?"

Four million dollars? Was she insane? She couldn't possibly need money—Sir Kingly was insanely rich. It was possible that this was a ruse to get him back. Perhaps she just wanted him thinking about numbers. Money was the one thing that would get his quantified right brain going. He had to play her. He had never been good with women, not like that, anyway, but he had to start now. "It's been so hard lately," Petra said softly.

"I know." He was turning around, the way she knew he would. "I know." He put his head in her arms. "The markets are in big trouble, a shit storm is coming like none of us have ever seen before." They were not like his wife's arms; they were hard and filled with sharp pieces of bone.

And so he placated her, he soothed her, he apologized profusely, again and again. They held hands. He told her he'd think about the money, and find a way. He didn't mean it, but he said it. And he kissed her on the cheek and put her in a taxi. And as the taxi sped off he wondered what kind of man he was, what kind of men any of them were. All of them just overpaid hamsters, on giant co-op wheels spinning, spinning, spinning, like his wife did occasionally when she went to Canyon Ranch. And the image of hamsters in suits made him laugh: little furry faces, sticking out of little white collars. Maybe with little paws coming out of cuffs, French cuffs. That was sort of funny.

CHAPTER *Six*

August 11, 2008
Dow closes down 32.12 points to 9,337.95
S&P closes down 3.38 points to 1,007.10

Daisy ran through the hallways. She could hear her red-soled shoes on the stone floor as if someone else were making the sound: *clip clop, clip clop.* Why had she worn high shoes? Because when she had set off that morning to a lovely luncheon for Sloan-Kettering, she didn't think she would be running for her daughter's life. But was she really running for her daughter's life? She didn't know yet, but she was running to find out—running through the Guggenheim Pavilion of Mount Sinai Hospital. For a slip of a second she was struck by the pavilion's grandeur, by its high ceilings and its pink granite. Perhaps someday the Greenbaum family would have a pavilion, would be capable of the kind of immortality that only the very rich can achieve. But even that kind of immortality was fleeting. There was always another donor and more money needed. Soon the

Guggenheim Pavilion would be called the Lady Petra Kingly Pavilion or something.

She hated herself for even thinking about philanthropic ego-stroking at a time when she should be concentrating on her child. Of course she was grateful that Fizzy Tisch had been the one to bring her daughter into the hospital, because the rich always got better medical care than the poor (that was, of course, obvious), but they also got better medical care than the middle class. For the rich there was always a private room, gourmet food from the eleventh-floor kitchen. For the rich the hospital was just a little bit cleaner, friendlier, and better organized.

She despised herself for thinking of private rooms at a time like this, a time when her daughter was possibly hanging between life and death. She should have been thinking about something else, perhaps beating herself up for not being a better mother. There had been times when she had let Nina pick up the girls, when she had wandered off to a yoga class, when she had called Easton difficult . . .

She played the scene back. Had it just been minutes ago? She conjured up the image of herself playing with her salad while the speaker, a gray-looking doctor with a goatee, droned on and on. She usually tried to lose herself in the stale rolls, the wine at lunch, and the rubber chicken, but today she had stayed alert, and after a few minutes she looked down at her phone. And there, hovering over her wallpaper—a picture of her twins hugging—she saw that she had five missed calls, all of them from Fizzy Tisch.

Daisy grabbed her bag and coat, made an apologetic head-nod to her tablemates, and mouthed the words "It's an emergency." And then she raced off into the hallway. It was possibly the only time in her life that Fizzy Tisch had picked up her cell phone on the first ring. She could hear Landon Stone in the background. She hated that Landon was moving in on Fizzy, climbing to the top of the social world, stealing her friend, but there was no time for that. Fizzy was trying to say something to Daisy, but kept tripping on her words.

Daisy couldn't really hear her, couldn't really make out the words. What was Fizzy saying? And what was Landon saying in the background? And why hadn't she gone with them and the driver? She hadn't because Landon had wanted to go alone with Fizzy because then she could have more time to suck up to her, to admire her Birkin bags, to compliment her on some inane skill, to weasel her way in.

But what was she saying? Something about traffic? Daisy distinctly heard the word *chopper*. But why, thought Daisy, did Easton need to go on a chopper? And then she realized. "I don't want you to worry," Fizzy continued.

"What happened? I can't really hear you, Fizzy."

More static, more white noise. Daisy strained her ear to hear. "Meet me at Mount Sinai. We should be there in ten minutes." Then Fizzy rattled off the address of Mount Sinai, which, of course, Daisy knew.

And that was ten minutes ago, before she had peeled out of the Palace Hotel, stole a cab from a little old lady and jumped in, and begged the taxi driver to drive as fast as he possibly could to Mount Sinai. And he had sensed that this was important as he was weaving in and out of traffic.

And there was the hospital smell assaulting her, an unholy mixture of cheap foamy disinfectant and pink plastic sheets. She ran but was pretty sure she was going nowhere. There were arrows painted on the floor pointing in different directions. Clearly at some point in the hospital's venerable history these lines and arrows were useful, but they had long since become irrelevant. She wasn't really sure where she was supposed to be going. The emergency room, the ambulatory care waiting room? Or, was she somewhere else?

"Where is the emergency room?"

A woman wearing a generic black suit pointed down an escalator. Daisy jumped on the escalator. She found herself on the street, on Madison Avenue, across from the projects, staring at a sign for the Martha Stewart Center for Living. Smart move, Martha, Daisy thought.

And then, farther down the street, there it was, black glass doors opening and closing: the emergency room. She raced in. Everyone in the emergency room seemed to be coughing. And there were lines in front of every person who seemed to be of any authority. Lines and coughing—wonderful. Here was the only place on Madison Avenue where no one was white and no one was rich. She hated to be rude but most of these people were actually using this emergency room for routine medical care, whereas she had an actual emergency. She hated herself for thinking that (she understood that most people in the world did not have out-of-network doctors whom they could just put on their platinum cards). But this was her daughter, her beloved daughter, and she had no idea what had happened to her.

She raced to the front of the line. "I'm so sorry but my daughter was just brought in by helicopter, she is CLINGING TO LIFE." Daisy didn't know if this was true, she hoped it wasn't, but she felt it was the only way to possibly get in to see her. Afterward, she would lie next to Easton and worry that this terrible lie would come back, but right now there was no time for worry, no time for anything but force.

The man at the desk pointed to some doors, and Daisy ran.

All of a sudden, Dick was on the other end of her cell phone. She hadn't remembered hearing it ring or picking it up or anything like that. All she heard was him sounding mad. But didn't he understand that this was about Easton? "What the fuck, Daisy? I'm in a huge meeting! What the fuck?"

"It's Easton." She could hear her voice crackling as she got to the nurses' station. "Please, my daughter." And Dick was still screaming into the phone.

THE SOCIAL CLIMBER'S HANDBOOK 109

"What happened, Daisy?"

The fat nurse looked up from her computer.

"My daughter, Easton Greenbaum, was just brought in by helicopter. Fizzy, I mean Fran, I think her real name is Fran Tisch. Do you know Fran Tisch? Landon Stone? She was with Landon Stone."

The nurse gave her a puzzled expression.

Back on the phone, Dick was almost screaming. "What the hell happened to Easton?"

She could hear her voice, brittle to her husband, like she was one of those women, those frail, ghoulishly white women in the ankle-length brown minks who roamed Park Avenue during the winter, walking dogs, commenting on the cold. "Dick, there has been an accident, Easton has had a riding accident, but I can't find her. You have to wait until I find her." There were curtains all around, sick people on stretchers, some of them crying out. Easton must be terrified, Daisy thought. Unless Easton was in no condition to be terrified, which was possible, since Daisy had no idea how Easton was.

"You have to tell me where my daughter is!" Daisy yelled. "She is with Fizzy Tisch. No, wait, that's wrong. Um, Fran. Fran Tisch. She goes by Fizzy."

Just then she saw a bit of Landon Stone's hair, and then Landon herself, looking slightly pleased, as if she knew this bonding time would help her when it came to invitations to the Hamptons.

"Landon?" Daisy called.

Landon looked at Daisy. She didn't really know what to say; it was one of those impossible moments. Landon despised Daisy, but she also knew that letting that show at a moment like this would destroy the very social convention that bonded their world together.

Fizzy finally came through the door to the hallway, like an angel from heaven.

"So, they just took her into surgery." Fizzy took Daisy's arm. But life was still good for Fizzy. Fizzy still had two healthy daughters. Fizzy still had everything. Why was Fizzy making that horrible face?

Daisy realized Dick was still on the phone. "Dick, I think you should get here right now. I think there has been a terrible accident and Easton might not be okay. Dick, come right now, as fast as you can." As she kept talking, she lost track of the things she was saying and Fizzy was hugging her and the clueless-looking nurse was looking at her, and also looking at the naked girl on a stretcher who had been yelling this whole time for pain meds, but someone in the background said something about how no one should listen to her because she was just a junkie and junkies don't know shit, and maybe they should just let the junkies die anyway.

$\mathcal{D}$aisy hated books where the protagonist's child dies. She found them pornographic in the worst possible way. Adversity (however huge) did not (in her mind anyway) make an unlikable character likable.

Waiting in the hospital, she decided that if Easton died, she would kill herself. She would not go on. It was the selfish thing to do, but she had decided it was the only thing to do. It was the only way to handle the pain. She looked at Dick. He could raise Avery. He could remarry some young girl, have more kids, remember his first family and still have a vestige of it with Avery.

"You know, none of this means anything if Easton dies."

"Don't talk like that." Dick was checking his personal portfolio on his BlackBerry.

"No, really, if she dies . . ."

"Don't be so dramatic."

"We don't even know what kind of condition she was in."

Fizzy pressed Daisy's arm. "She fell off the horse and seemed to be in great pain, but she was conscious the whole time. The surgeon is going to come talk to us soon. Don't worry, she is the best pediatric surgeon in the world. New chief pediatric surgeon, a real maverick. We love her. She operated on Finn when she had an abscess on her butt."

"See," Dick said in a vaguely accusatory way.

$\mathcal{D}$aisy had sat, not breathing, not doing anything, watching the clock, watching the black second hand push its way around the white plastic face of the clock. It was strange to her to watch the time pass so slowly, to watch the minutes drip by, like the ants and honey in a Salvador Dalí painting. How had something that normally moved so fast now reverse itself so completely? She looked around; Fizzy Tisch was holding her arm, staring into space. There was an old air conditioner in the wall that turned itself on every fifteen minutes, after the room had gotten stiflingly hot, and then it would embark on a flurry of activity—buzzing, humming, droning, dripping—and then it would turn itself off after the room had gotten meat-locker cold.

Dick sat across from them in one of the plastic 1960s-era armchairs. He kept checking his BlackBerry, but it was long after the American markets were closed. Sure, there were other markets in other places in the world—Australia, Taiwan, Singapore—but there were also other reasons that men check their BlackBerrys constantly: affairs. Still, Daisy wanted to believe in Dick. There were no windows in the waiting room, and no old books or magazines. Hanging off the ceiling was a giant old refrigerator box of a TV that had been tuned to Telemundo long enough for several shows to have begun and ended.

All of a sudden a nurse came in, looked at a clipboard, and called out to them. She looked at the floor and the television and announced, "One parent at a time."

"But can't we both go?"

"No, that's why I said one parent at a time."

"But—" Daisy didn't want to go in. If she didn't see Easton, then maybe it hadn't actually happened. But she knew it had happened, because Fizzy Tisch had been stroking her arm for the last three hours.

Dick looked at Daisy. Dick didn't really want to go either. It had been so many hours, and they had sort of gotten used to not knowing. Now they would have to know the scope of the damage. They would have to face their daughter.

But Easton decided for them, as her scream catapulted them to her bedside. There is nothing more painful for guilty parents than the scream of a child in pain. Every single cell in Daisy's body felt like it might pop. Easton continued to scream, "Nooooo, nooo, I don't care about anything. All I care about is my pony. How is my pony? What happened to my horse?" Of course, Easton didn't actually own a pony. Dick and Daisy rented her a pony from Georgina Bloomberg (a cost-cutting measure that always ended up costing much more than it saved).

Dick and Daisy ran past the nurse, and to Easton's little curtained-off area, which smelled like latex and blood.

"What happened to my horse? What? What? What?" Easton was far from lucid. In fact, she had her eyes closed. "Where is my po-o-o-ny? I need to see my pony."

Easton had a few tubes coming from her nose and some cuts on her cheek—one looked very angry and deep—and Daisy wondered if years later that cut would haunt her, would Marla Hanson her right out of the possibility of being on TV or something. But who wanted their children on TV? Certainly not Daisy or Dick. It was gaudy, or at least they knew they should think it was gaudy. Secretly they would probably have derived some pleasure from it. There were a bunch of more superficial cuts on her face, red marks that looked like they were on their way to becoming bruises, and some dirt still caked in her hair. Daisy was surprised that they hadn't washed her hair or done something to get rid of all the dirt. How would she clean Easton? For a minute Daisy felt panic, pure panic. Could Easton go in the bath like that? Could she go in a shower? Would it be possible to wash Easton off? Would a nurse help her? Could she get Nina to come? She couldn't possibly bathe Easton alone. Half her body was covered in . . . Daisy looked down at the rest of her daughter, and as she did, she saw that one of Easton's arms and one of her legs were in casts.

She looked frantically at the nurse. "Can we get a doctor in here? I want to know what happened to my daughter!"

The nurse sighed and looked at her watch. "Any minute now."

"Where is my pony?" Easton continued to wail.

"Darling, we love you so much," Daisy said, and she looked over at Dick for help. Dick would know what to say. He was smart about these things, smart about getting people to come around to his way of thinking. What a crazy thought. Easton was still out of it, or under it, under the sleep drug, the laughing gas that the doctor had piped into her.

"What happened to my horse? What did they do to my p-p-p-oney?"

Dick ran his fingers through his daughter's hair. Nothing mattered anymore. The stock market, the bond market, the credit market, the end of the world. Let it end, let it end. "Darling, just try to relax."

"But my pony, what happened to my pony?"

"You know she's not going to remember any of this. Let her sleep. Let her sleep it off," the nurse said.

"But she seems so upset," Dick said.

"It's the anesthesia. Just try to get her to go to sleep." The nurse continued, "Whatever you do, don't make her more upset."

She wasn't a pediatric nurse and Daisy realized this later, when she compared her scrubs and level of competence. Easton was being cared for by a surgical nurse. What the nurse suggested seemed to work with adults—adults came out of the anesthesia and sort of looked around, confused, and went back to sleep. Children seemed not to have the same reaction: they popped up out of bed and proceeded to become hysterical.

Eventually a doctor came in—or what Daisy assumed to be a doctor. She was young, and wore lots of gold jewelry under her scrubs. Daisy guessed she was Persian, perhaps second-generation American. She seemed smart and ambitious—not lazy like Daisy was. Fizzy ran up to her and gave her a hug, which made Daisy feel much more comfortable. They were obviously dealing with a pro. The doctor went through an explanation of Easton's injuries—broken leg, broken wrist, concerns about internal bleeding—but the prognosis was good. She said that Easton would be able to leave the hospital the next day, but would need a lot of bed rest after that.

When she left the room, things seemed a little calmer. Daisy and Dick relaxed into the stiff hospital chairs, reassured that the worst was behind them. And Easton had just begun to drift into sleep when she opened her eyes and asked again: "What happened to Heavenly Hash? What happened to my pony?"

Dick looked at Daisy and Daisy at Dick. What had happened to Georgina Bloomberg's pony? What had happened to Heavenly Hash? They thought about what happened to ponies in the movies and frowned at each other; neither had a good feeling about the future of Heavenly Hash. "Don't worry about that just now," Daisy said in her best, most motherly way. She really felt like a mother that day, sitting there with Easton. Easton had been smooshed into a pair of tiny children's hospital pajamas that were covered with pictures of octopuses and little fish. She looked so young and small that day, in her bed, with the tubes coming out of her.

———

$\mathcal{I}$t was dark by the time they were able to move Easton into room 558 in the pediatric building, 1184 Fifth Avenue. Both parents dutifully followed the stretcher in and out of elevators, up and down hallways, through various tunnels, and into the sprawling prewar building, the one children had been saved in and died in.

"I'm in paaain," Easton cried. *"Pain, pain, pain, pain."*

Daisy pleaded with the nurse for more drugs. "Don't you hear her?"

"She has a script for morphine every fifteen minutes through her IV. Morphine is a very serious drug, you know."

Dick frowned. "Well, then give her something less serious. Just make the pain go away because my eight-year-old is crying."

And she was. Tears had sprung from the eyes of Easton. Great, big, round, luscious tears.

"Why doesn't Daddy read you a story?"

Dick picked up a book that Fizzy Tisch had packed for them, *Harriet the Spy.* "I had never set out to be a . . ."

A few minutes later the nurse came back with a needle filled with drugs. She cleaned off the IV and Easton started to doze off.

"Dick, why don't you go home and get some sleep? I can stay here. Nina has made some dinner for you. Look, it's . . ." Daisy looked down at her heavy, expensive watch. Dick had bought it for her because it had bothered him that she still wore a really cheap Timex with glow-in-the-dark hands. It was uncomfortable. But she wore it because she wanted Dick to know that she believed in the power of his objects, of his wealth, of the things that his wealth could buy. Every time she put on the watch she was agreeing, paying homage to the power of his money. "It's ten P.M. It hardly seems possible, but it is. It's ten. Go home, get some sleep."

"No." Dick looked out the window. The park was abandoned. A man was walking a dog down Fifth Avenue, and some people were waiting for the bus. It was so hot that even the windows were sweating with perspiration.

"You have to go to work tomorrow."

"I can work from here."

It seemed so insane it almost made her think that she was dreaming, that she was in one of her husband's ridiculous anxiety dreams. But she couldn't be in his dreams, could she?

That night he slept next to Easton's bed and Daisy slept on the chair on the other side of the room. Mostly he sat on the edge of his daughter's bed watching her, watching her breathe, making sure all the tubes and lights were doing what they were supposed to. Sometimes he would put his hand on his daughter's chest to make sure it was rising and falling with each passing breath. Sometimes his eyes would shut involuntarily, and when they did he would fight them open. Sometimes he would drift off, back onto the plane with the stewardess and his chocolate-coated strawberries and John's toes roasted on the barbecue by his lovely wife. The assistant was in the dream, his moral compass, pointing out numbers that made no sense, saying loudly, "Your bonus is based on you hiding debt, based on how big a yarn you are willing to spin. You realize the moral implications of that, don't you? You realize that you won't have a soul to stand on."

Had she really said that? And was he upset by it? She was after all wearing a fabulous La Perla bra-and-panties thing, fabulous, very chic and distracting.

At one point he opened his eyes to find his wife staring at him. "What the hell is going to happen to us?" she asked. It was as much a statement of her despair as it was a question.

Dick smiled. He was still sort of dreaming, still somewhere between here and there, between awake and asleep, between having sex with his assistant, whom he despised, and reality. And he clung to the unreality of dreams. Just for another second; waking was fluorescent and awful. "Why would anything bad happen to us?"

Maybe he was crazy, she thought to herself, and maybe she was dreaming, but none of them seemed spinning toward a happy ending. "What about Easton? The doctor said . . ."

Dick paused. "Daisy, the kid is going to be fine."

"So what, so our lives can be ruined by Petra?"

"But they aren't going to be . . ."

"She seems to think she's capable of ruining our lives."

"But what do you think?" He was still so uncharacteristically calm. It made her think he might still be sleeping, swimming in the ocean of his subconscious.

"Honestly, sure. Why not? They say hell hath no fury . . ."

He smiled. "I know it firsthand." He frowned.

"Aren't you worried?"

"I'm not running for president, you know." He rubbed his eyes. He was definitely waking up; he took a sip of water from the bottle on Easton's bedside table. The room was as dark as hospital rooms got, still illuminated by a million different machines monitoring their daughter's every function. The park itself was totally, shockingly dark. She was surprised by how deserted and eerie the park was. A good place to murder someone, she thought. She wasn't, after all, stupid.

"You can't possibly mean that?"

"Mean what?"

"People will talk. She'll ruin us socially, if nothing else."

Dick rolled his eyes.

"So you don't care?"

"I'm realistic."

"What does that mean?"

"It means that people are always going to talk."

"Talk? Talk? You think this is about something as minor as gossip?

This woman has the power to ruin us." Daisy felt the rage rise in her. Dick had done this to them. He had found this woman, brought her into their lives.

Dick looked up at his wife. Did she know about Petra's threats? About her demands for money? It crossed his mind that there was a distinct possibility that she had murdered his boss, and there was an even more distinct possibility that she considered murder to be a good way to solve one's problems. But his horror at his wife's possible proclivity was undermined by his profoundly abstract notion of death. If he hadn't experienced it himself, he didn't really believe it was a real thing. Who was to say what happened after one died? No one knew. It was anyone's guess. Anything could happen. Heaven, hell, reincarnation, nothing at all. And maybe this fell into the null set, maybe he could think his wife's bad acts into meaninglessness. Perhaps he could fold her sins the way his mother used to fold egg whites; he could fold this possibility of murder into the nihilism he felt about the crumbling equities markets, about the world in general.

"We are planning to commit twenty million," the voice on the phone said, "and then we'll see how it goes from there."

Kingly didn't want to blow it, but he needed the money yesterday. He knew being overly anxious could blow the whole thing. Would $20 million even be enough? Would it be enough to pay lawyers? Enough to keep things going? For now, perhaps. "Very good. It's too bad such a small amount, but once you see our nice consistent returns, year after year . . ." His voice drifted off and he looked up through the ceiling. Could he see the sky? Not really, but for a minute he imagined he could. What would he have been if he hadn't been this? He couldn't think of a time when he had cared about anything but keeping the scheme going, and now, now, now it would soon be over.

———

She stood in the fluorescent-lit hallway looking at the words NUCLEAR MEDICINE. The words were in that old lettering, the kind that reminded her of the natural history museum in the 1970s, with its still unrenovated nooks and crannies, the obscure halls—like the things pertaining to trees and bizarre 1970s visions of the future. She had, of course, not meant to be down on the MC (the subbasement) level on Sunday morning at six A.M., far too early to be anywhere. She had taken a wrong turn somewhere and now here she was, standing in front of the entrance to the nuclear medicine hall.

She had just wanted a cup of coffee. Daisy kept walking and kept taking wrong turns, and she kept ending up back in front of the nuclear medicine hall. It was like she was in a black hole, a quark that always led to the same place, again and again. She didn't know how it kept happening, but she did think to herself that this would be a great time for Petra to pop up, because this was a place to murder someone if there ever was one. Of course, the whole thing rested on whether the door to the medical examiner's office was left unlocked or not. If it was left unlocked then it could be the crime of the century, the perfect murder. There was no way to know if the door to the medical examiner's office was locked unless she tried it.

And where was the medical examiner's office? She knew it was in the basement, because basements were where they kept everything messy, like nuclear isotopes, crematoriums, and morgues. Crematoriums hid a multitude of sins, both literally and figuratively. Fire was the universal solvent. It could solve all the problems that otherwise posed a threat to the perfect murder: fingerprints, stray fibers, hairs.

But where was the medical examiner's office? As she looked, she found herself more and more lost. Maybe if she tried to look for coffee (as she had been doing before), she might find its opposite, so she started thinking about coffee, the coffee she desperately needed to stay awake after not sleeping all night, and then a few steps later there she was, standing right in front of the medical examiner's office. She turned the doorknob and opened the door and saw that the door was unlocked and all the elements of the most perfect murder were right there, hers for the taking. And, of course, it was empty. Whoever was supposed to be manning the morgue (and it seemed to Daisy that someone was supposed to be sitting behind that brown desk in the corner), whoever this absent security guard was, he had thought the dead could wait.

"You're not supposed to go in there," a voice said from behind her.

Daisy turned, but she didn't need to turn because she recognized that voice, she recognized its various affectations: it was a British accent, no, it was a French accent, no, it was a Queens accent, though Daisy didn't know that. "And what the fuck are you doing here?"

Petra smiled carnivorously. "What the fuck am I doing anywhere? I am following you. Following? No, that isn't the right word. I am stalking you. Stalking you and that husband of yours. Remember Starbucks, the shrink, Exhale. . . . I've been everywhere."

"Why?"

" 'Cause eventually you will give up."

"And then?"

"And then I will take your husband and your daughters, or, better still, have my own."

Petra's breath smelled of vodka. "For God's sake, have you been drinking?"

She put her fingers together. "Just a little."

Daisy put her hands on Petra's bony shoulders. "What the fuck is wrong with you? My husband is not going to leave me for you."

"Fuck you, fatty."

"It doesn't even make any sense, it's been a *year*. Don't you think if he was going to leave me, he would have done it last year? What the fuck is wrong with you?"

Petra was silent.

A few minutes later Daisy had her manicured hands filled with Petra's brains. She had never crushed anyone's skull. She wouldn't do that again—too messy and too labor-intensive. Her arms felt so sore, like she had the flu or had done a double class at Soul Cycle. She looked down at her seven-hundred-dollar shoes. They were ruined; the leather was all smotchy from the blood, which was clotting a dark grayish brown.

But there was no question that Petra was gone because Daisy had done it herself. She had crushed her husband's mistress's skull with a skull-crushing mallet—the kind the medical examiner used before sliding a body into the crematorium.

A few minutes later it was all over. Daisy washed her hands in the gray metal sink. She helped herself to some of the foaming antibacterial soap. There was no more Petra. The weight that they had been carrying for the last five years, the black cloud over their marriage, was gone.

It was so hard to believe that she found herself saying it, whispering it to herself, again and again. "There is no more Petra. No more Petra, no more." She was gone. She had laughed her last laugh, bought her last Birkin, vomited up her last box of cookies, received her last shot of Botox, had her last tennis lesson, went to her last movie screening, fired her last housekeeper, slept with her last trainer, decorated her last Hamptons house.

It was over.

CHAPTER *Seven*

September 25, 2008

Dow closes up 196.89 points to 11,022.06

S&P closes up 23.31 points to 1,209.18

Dick had been personally shorting Washington Mutual on and off for the last five years. Basically, shorting is a way of aggressively betting against a stock. Occasionally the stock had taken off like a rocket and he had been squeezed out of the short, which had made him insanely, well, insane. But Dick was obsessed with his WaMu short. He had always hated the bank. He had always felt it was horribly run, appallingly managed, and ridiculously leveraged. And worst of all, it loaned people money they could never repay and then booked as profits the interest payments that they weren't paying. Of course, tucking decaying assets into level 3 capital, hiding debt or putting it on the balance sheet as an asset, well, that was something Dick had some experience with.

But Dick had never ever believed that the government would let

WaMu fail. After all, Countrywide (ticker symbol CFC), which he liked to think of as the WORST BANK EVER, had been allowed to survive. With a little encouragement from the government, Bank of America bought Countrywide for about $4.1 billion more than it was worth (but that was probably because of the intense-tanning friendship formed between Angelo Mozilo, the orange CEO of Countrywide, and Ken Lewis, the slightly less orange CEO of Bank of America).

Dick was still having the crazy dreams, and that night of September 24, 2008, was no different: same crazy dream. It was dark and he was lying in bed, lying there staring at the ceiling, when he looked over, thinking he might see his lovely and slightly terrifying wife. Instead, though, he looked up to find his mistress and she was decapitated, so it was just her neck talking to him. It was a nice neck but it would have looked infinitely better with a head on it.

"Why don't you have a head?"

"Stupid question," the neck said.

"Okay, so what can you tell me? Since you obviously can't answer the simplest question." Dick wondered why things had taken such a decidedly hostile tone so quickly. "Why have you come, you Ghost of Christmas Past?"

"Oh, witty, witty, witty. Smart and charming, are you single? Wait, I already know the answer to that question. You know, I never would have had an affair with you if I had known your crazy wife was going to stick me into Mount Sinai's crematorium."

"Ain't that the truth, sister? I'm right there with you." Dick was shocked that he used the words *ain't* and *sister*. It was a very dreamlike moment.

"Oh, my God, you are such an asshole."

"Why are you really here?"

"Because I think we have a problem."

"Really? Just one?"

The neck tried to frown. "Sir Kingly is running a Ponzi scheme."

Dick looked at the neck and without flinching said, "Not possible."

"Yes, possible. Have you ever looked at his statements? Have you ever looked at his K-1s? Have you ever looked at his myriad SEC complaints? Have you ever seen the math behind his little fund?"

Dick didn't know much about the fund except it seemed to get pretty solid returns. Nothing spectacular but consistent. He didn't really know how consistent. If he had, he would have had suspicions. But he didn't pay much attention. After all, he was not an investor in Sir Smith Kingly's fund, but he knew a lot of people who were. "Not an investor, so I don't get their letter."

"Two words, asshole."

"That's one."

"No, let me finish. Two words: *feeder fund*. A fund that invests money to Kingly through another entity. So a person might think they were investing with someone reputable like Augustus Malmot and then discover that that person has been funneling the cash to Kingly."

Dick thought and thought and thought, and then he realized that he had put $10 million of his personal moneys in with Augustus Malmot, but Malmot wasn't a feeder fund. "Augustus Malmot?"

"Feeder fund."

"Stop being so needlessly cryptic."

"Okay."

"No, tell me. Malmot?"

"Of course."

"It can't be."

"Hey, be happy. Turns out you own some of a Rothko but most of the cash is with Kingly."

"Motherfucker!"

"Yep. Daisy did the best thing for Kingly. She saved him."

"*Fuck!*"

"Come to think of it, he probably thinks I already did. Oh God. This has become such an enormous mess."

"A mess? What about us? This makes us..." He paused. He couldn't remember if he was awake or asleep. It seemed as if his nightmares were bleeding into his waking life and there was nothing he could do to stop it. "This makes us cash poor. Very, very, very cash poor. What the fuck is wrong with me? Why didn't I have any money in savings, in the bank? Why did we have to spend three weeks last year in Europe? Why did I have to only fly NetJets? Why wasn't I able to live in the black? What kind of person lives like this? What kind of person am I?"

Petra was losing patience with this soul-searching. "You? What about me?"

Dick frowned. "What about you? We are going to get like three cents on the dollar, and this is what I do. This isn't, like, some hobby. I am going to look like such an idiot being mixed up in all of this. I'm not some trustafarian trying to find myself, teaching yoga to Native Americans in the Southwest. This is what I do. And I am supposed to be considered a smart guy. Well. Not anymore."

"But what about me? Now everyone will think that my husband murdered me. No one will know the truth. No one will avenge my murder. No one will look twice at my disappearance, and besides, my husband thinks I've turned state's evidence. The government thinks I've gone into hiding, and the net-net is that your fat wife is going to get away with murder. Hardly seems fair, does it?"

"Fair? I've just lost ten million dollars." Dick felt sick.

"I've been murdered!"

Dick shook his head.

"Go check out the town house. It's like a burned-out crack house behind the forty-thousand-dollar curtains." The neck paused. "But personally I'm not that surprised. I always knew Kingly was up to something. He isn't even a real prince or lord or whatever he claims to be. He bought the title."

"Just like he bought the forty-thousand-dollar curtains." Dick thought about forty-thousand-dollar curtains. How did one find forty-thousand-dollar curtains? Were they made of gold, of copper, of frankincense and myrrh? "Forty-thousand-dollar curtains—it is a pity we never married."

"Well, I obviously didn't have the kind of moral fiber you were looking for in a wife, as I haven't murdered anyone," the neck said.

"Fuck you." He looked at the neck.

The neck paused and started talking in her businesswoman's voice. "Look back at Monday and Tuesday. Did you ever think that the TARP would become a forty-two-page monstrosity of waste?"

Dick looked at his mistress's thin neck and her lovely breasts. He suddenly wondered if she might have sex with him. And suddenly everything had taken on a ghoulish quality, like even he had taken his dreams one step too far. Maybe this wasn't a dream. He looked at her and started trying to wake himself up. Could he do it? Could he force himself to wake up? Could he rip himself from sleep? Was any of this true? What was truth? And what was a lie? Was it true about Paulson? Was it true about the TARP swelling, and the bank holding company status of The Bank and Morgan? It seemed impossible that all the banks would fail, but then they had. It seemed impossible that his wife would be a murderer and not a hapless socialite with just a little bit of a heart, but she was. It seemed impossible that he would just keep spending money, spending, spending, spending. It seemed impossible that Augustus Malmot was running a feeder fund that channeled into a Ponzi scheme and a collection of Rothkos. All these things seemed impossible.

"Just go back to sleep, fatty," the neck said.

"But."

"But what?" the neck said.

"I'm sorry about my wife murdering you. You know that, right? I'm really sorry about that." Dick paused. He felt actual remorse and the slightest bit of shame.

"Thanks," the neck said.

"But I really am sorry."

"I'm a neck now, a decapitated ghost roaming the halls of Mount Sinai. Trying to shake snacks out of the vending machines. But you know what the problem is?"

"No."

"They never have a different flavor of frozen yogurt, and the coffee sucks. They say it's Starbucks but it's some kind of gross burned crap that they put in Starbucks cups. Imagine eating peanut butter frozen yogurt for all of eternity."

Dick finally succeeded in waking himself up.

But the nightmare was far from over; in fact, it had just begun. September 25, 2008, was the day that Paulson made his point, and he did it by letting WaMu fail.

A dead mistress and a murdering wife seemed to be the least of Dick Greenbaum's problems. The events of the morning of September 25, 2008, when WaMu failed, would make everything else seem like conversation.

"Do you see what's happening here?" Dick asked Daisy, sitting slack-jawed at the edge of the bed.

Daisy was trying to find a pair of Lululemon yoga pants that made her look thin. She felt enormous. "No, what's going on, honey?"

"The FDIC is seizing all of WaMu's assets and putting it into receivership."

They hadn't talked about the disappearance of Lady Petra, but both of them knew what had happened. Dick's first clue was when Daisy had returned from her coffee run barefoot and without coffee—and then, of course, there was the dream. They also knew that talking about it would make it real, and somehow make them more guilty. That talking about it might make the crime all the more premeditated. So they stayed silent. "I don't understand what that means."

"The Fed is seizing WaMu. They're taking WaMu down."

Daisy knew this was big, and it was one of those times when the world was so crazy it had almost eclipsed the craziness of their own lives. "Oh." Daisy knew Dick was asking her to bond with him about this, but she had trouble getting too excited. "Okay." Daisy struggled with the yoga pants. She was never ever going to buy anything but black pants ever.

"Oh, my God."

Watching financial television did not really thrill Daisy. She was never really sure what was going on.

"This is big. I've got to get to the office."

"But it's five A.M."

"Doesn't matter. This is a game changer." He started getting dressed. She looked at him. It was still slightly dark outside and the streets were pretty much empty. It was hard to say if they would be together forever, bonded by their children and their murders and their mutual love of stuff. The way he said "game changer" was annoying, slightly patronizing. Even if she was bored by financial television, she was still smart enough to understand basically what was going on. It was, after all, still television.

Sometimes when she couldn't sleep, when she lay in bed staring at the twelve-foot ceiling (which was impressive even to her, despite the fact that its majestic proportions were situated on the second floor), she thought about what it would feel like to take an ice pick and hack him to death while he slept. Of course, the sheets he sweated through every single night were custom sheets made in Italy by little midget monks. They were sheets so expensive and special that one couldn't even buy them, one had to be invited to the factory. Then, at the factory (which was actually a monastery), one was invited to donate to the monks, and this donation (which was expected to be enormous) was your way of showing gratitude, and sometimes the monks would give you sheets in the wrong size and you just had to take them because they all spoke only Italian, and besides, they were a gift. It took three months to craft a single sheet, and this was why often the sheets did not match.

Anyway, it hardly seemed fair to the monks to get blood all over their fancy sheets. Besides, Dick had gotten rid of Petra (not quite as well as Daisy had gotten rid of Petra, but at least he was trying not to philander with his usual zeal). And so, for today she would not murder her husband. Which was lucky, because in a few hours she would need her husband to protect her from the only person that struck fear and dread into the heart of Daisy Greenbaum: her mother.

Trip McAllister watched the events of September 25, 2008, with the same slack-jawed awe as Dick Greenbaum. Suddenly their world, which was usually relegated to the sidelines of the normal news world by its extreme boringness, was the only world. Suddenly the potential bank failure was bigger than the war in Iraq or the heartbreaking rivalry of Paris Hilton and Lindsay Lohan.

This was Trip's moment to, as they say in *The Real Housewives of New York City,* "go big or go home." And Trip had gone to Harvard and so he was smart, and he knew this was his moment. So he was blogging about it as he watched the television, watching the futures turn red at the bottom of the screen, watching the ticker for the European markets, the Brits and the Germans and the French. He found it annoying that he was not on television punditizing, musing about his personal feelings about banks and bank holding companies. Why did no one want him on TV? He needed to be on CNBC schmoozing with Maria Bartiromo.

Across the room, Candy Ross Rose was lying on the bed sprawled on top of the covers, half-naked, drooling on herself, and, of course, snoring loudly. She had fallen asleep Skyping to a friend from college. If she were a character in his novel, the one he had been writing in his head since his sophomore year of college, he would make her OD, maybe not die but definitely get close. He knew he would like her better (and so would potential readers of his nonexistent novel) if she were dead, or almost so. Right now her only addictions were social networking and taking half-naked photos of herself and posting them on the Internet. He was pretty sure that there was no self-help group for that.

Outside, the first rays of sun were screaming across the sky, assaulting the blue, pushing our characters into another day of financial markets in chaos. There were so many opportunities in this brave new world of turmoil, Trip realized. He would either become truly famous on the wings of this, or he would screw himself. He could make a few wrong calls (tell the world to buy Wells Fargo and short gold) and be over forever. He hated the idea of not being famous. Not that he was famous now, but he was known, on the cusp of fame, on the cusp of punditry, and pageantry, and town cars with tinted windows, and people posting spottings of him on the Famous Media Blog. He was on the cusp of Page Six, and free stuff mailed to him every day, like the blond girl from *The Hills*. Who was he kidding? He would never be as famous as the blond girl from *The Hills*. But at least he wouldn't be over the hill at thirty-two.

$\mathcal{D}$aisy was standing in her marble entry foyer. She had not been expecting her mother, and she had been surprised when the doorman had called up saying that she was downstairs. For a minute she toyed with the idea of hanging up the phone and running out the service entrance and hopping on the next plane to Honduras, where she would start her new life as a longshoreman or fisherwoman. But she was pretty sure she didn't have the skills to do either of those things. And besides, she got seasick and hated fish (the smell, the taste). But she was willing to make compromises to get away from her mother. God help her.

Her mother was coming up, her mother was in the elevator, her mother was at the door, her mother was ringing the bell, her mother was standing in front of her with that look she always had on her face, that weird, slightly displeased look. It had been just a few months since she last saw her mother. (There had been a fight between Dick and her father and there had been emails back and forth. She could hardly remember, but what she remembered made her slightly anxious. It was not a good story.) But here her mother was looking . . . shockingly young! What was it? Why did her mother look so disturbingly rested? What made a woman her mother's age look so rested? Was her mother having an affair? Was her mother cheating on her father? No, there must be another reason her mother looked so rested, and then she realized what it was. Her hippie feminist mother had gotten an eye job. "Mom!"

"Darling!"

"*Mom!* Did you get an eye job?"

Daisy was staring at her mother, who was dragging a large wheeled suitcase behind her. Daisy looked at the suitcase in semihorror. It looked too large for a day trip, too large for a weekend, too large for a long weekend. It looked to Daisy Greenbaum as if her mother had sinister plans. "I've come to take care of my granddaughter and you cannot stop me."

"Right, right, yes, yes, of course, but mother, answer me this."

"What?"

"Did you get an eye job?"

Daisy liked to think of herself as talented at telling who had had what plastic surgical procedure. And sometimes it was tricky, but eye jobs were easier to spot than a more subtle tummy tuck or a slightly asymmetrical ski-slope nose that had at one time been beaklike. Of course, the more grotesque molestations of flesh were obvious, like overfilled breast balloons, like tufts of fake hair like brown Astroturf. She had a sixth sense for plastic surgery, and in her old age, i.e. her thirties, this was serving her well.

"And Botox? Are you 'toxing? Mom!"

"Why shouldn't I look good? Would I stop you from looking good?"

"No, not what I was saying at all. I'm just slightly shocked, that's all. I did not think of you as someone who would be 'toxing, that's all!"

"I will not let you oppress me."

"Oh, God, Mom. That was not what I meant."

"First of all, I am not just a baby maker, I am not breeding stock! I am not a product of your capitalist culture!" Daisy's mother wasn't a great listener. She was, however, a very gifted talker.

"You live in Roslyn and shop at the world's largest mall. You are a product of your own capitalist culture."

Her mother was a boomer in the worst way, all sound bites over substance. "We made so many sacrifices for you! I am your mother and I fought for the things that you now take for granted. I burned my bra and marched on Washington so that you could have a better life. I know that I wasn't Alice Walker or Germaine Greer, but I did my part for you and your sister. I made my voice heard. And I did it for you."

Daisy rolled her eyes. Would she be this annoying to her own children one day? It hardly seemed possible. "Mom, I think we may be getting slightly off track here. . . ."

Her mother interrupted sharply, "I know you think you are too good for your parents, but here we are. Or here I am!"

"Oh, God, Mom, not again. This is totally insane. I don't think I am too good for you. I think you are insane, totally, utterly, and completely insane. And that crazy thing at Dad's party? It was totally a misunderstanding." Daisy tried to remember if it was, in fact, a misunderstanding or if they really did have a huge fight about a real thing. She couldn't remember. Everything bled into everything else, like the blood gushing from the head of Lady Petra all over her new fabulous shoes. "I love you. I love Dad. I love Jenny. I don't think I am too good for any of you. I am just busy. I have two kids and all Dick does is work."

Her mother put her head in her hands. It was clearly meant to be a dramatic gesture. Then slowly she pulled her face out of her hands. "But he resents us! He resents our family! He is oppressing you!"

"Mom! He is not oppressing me! Mom, you can't do this. You can't say bad things about Dick, not while you're in his house"—she dropped her voice to a whisper—"and not when his daughters are in the other room." She paused. "Besides which he is just successful and busy, get over it."

"Fine, but I am just saying, and I will never say it again, just this once, only one time."

"God, if only that were true," Daisy mumbled.

"He resents us. He resents your sister because Jennifer is such a strong woman."

Dick had hated her sister, hated. This was because he thought she was a mega-JAP, not because he thought she was some kind of feminist warrior. "He doesn't have time to resent my family. Because he never thinks about anything but work, work, work." And it was true, for the most part, even if it wasn't just his job—it was the crumbling equities market, the bankruptcy of Lehman Brothers, the Emergency Economic Stabilization Act, the pumping of billions of dollars to create quantitative easing to unfreeze the credit markets, all in the hopes of avoiding the biggest economic catastrophe in decades.

"Look, I am over it. But your father is a proud man."

"Mom, this is insane."

"Dick needs to apologize to your father."

"For what?"

"I'm not going to talk about this anymore."

"Mo-o-o-m." She had been in her house for exactly one minute and they were back to the Stein family's particular breed of insanity.

"I'm over it!"

"Great, then let's not talk about it, ever again."

Daisy's mom took off her light green Ralph Lauren jacket. "Now, where is my granddaughter? Because I would like to get to work. I have brought *The Secret Garden* to read to her. You used to love that book, remember?" (She said "you" in a vaguely accusatory way, as if Daisy had murdered the book or made it impossible for her mother to love the book anymore or something.) Sarah Stein paused for a minute and looked uncomfortably at Daisy until Daisy realized that her mother wanted a hug, *ugh,* a hug. Did she have to give her mother a hug? Of course she did. What kind of daughter begrudges her mother a hug? She would hug the homeless, she would hug a leper if she could find one, she would hug a meth addict covered in sores, but she wouldn't hug her own mother? It was insane. She was insane.

Daisy launched herself into her mother, almost toppling the poor woman over. "Mother! I love you! Thank you for coming so soon. Thank you for coming to take care of Easton! Thank you! Beloved mother." It was too much too soon and Daisy realized this, but as she said it she realized that she was relieved to have her mother there, that she did mean it, at least a little bit.

"Well"—her mother was caught slightly off guard by this sudden display of affection—"I love you too, darling, and we are going to have a wonderful couple of . . ."

Days? Weeks? Months? Sarah Stein was not able to finish her sentence (a sentence that needed to be finished) because they were distracted by Avery wandering into the foyer, looking irritated the way only Avery could. "Easton is asleep and I'm bored."

"Look, Grandma's here." Daisy had her fingers crossed that Avery would recognize her.

"Grandma!" And then Daisy remembered which daughter this was. "I missed you so so so so much. I love you so-o-o-o much!!! Can we go and spend some quality time together!? I love you, Granny." Avery then grabbed her grandmother's legs in a hug that would have been appropriate when the girl was five but now seemed horribly wrong, as it had Avery's head very near her grandmother's crotch. But this was typical Avery, typical of the daughter who was always pouring it on, always.

And so three generations of Stein women stood in the foyer of an enormous apartment at 740 Park Avenue, an apartment that had for many years been considered the Jewish apartment in the building, an apartment that was now filled with little knickknacks and mementos of climber-ism: a wooden staircase to nowhere purchased by a decorator at the Nina Griscom store, a giant Damien Hirst spin art painting, a Gucci bench that was covered in pony skin (she told Easton it was faux), and various other artifacts of the wealthy.

Thousands of years from now, when scientists excavate Daisy Greenbaum's lair, they will find all sorts of baffling displays of wealth: huge televisions as flat as pancakes, electronic systems that control music and floor temperature but are far too complicated to ever work the way they are supposed to, fur coats that are sheared to be far too thin to ever keep a person warm, giant sneakers that claim to make one's butt small, and various other oddities that someday will find themselves in a museum as the people of the future puzzle over how the people of the past could have been so incredibly and shockingly and bizarrely vacuous in their own tragic way.

―――――

Candy Ross Rose knew where she and Trip McAllister would some-day marry: Southampton. She was counterculture but she wasn't that counterculture; she did go to the fancy girls' school. She was still a fancy girl, deep down under the Harvard and the tattoos. Since she had been a little girl at the fancy Wasp nursery school, she had always wanted to marry in Southampton, the house of her rich uncle Herm Rose. And maybe for now Trip just thought of her as a piece of ass, as an intellectual pinup (à la Elizabeth Wurtzel), but soon, soon the world would realize her ambition. Soon she would break The Bank and become famous—famous as a financial reporter, which was even more famous than some lame memoirist. She could be really famous, like Maria Bartiromo, the "Money Honey." She might end up on TV. All she had to do was keep working in the office that was right next to her mother's office, where she was hearing every juicy tidbit from the life of the Greenbaums, which both mother and daughter had real-ized (independently of each other, of course) was shockingly sala-cious.

Recently Candy Ross Rose had come to the conclusion that Dick Greenbaum was a sex addict. She had been fascinated by sex addic-tion, had written her senior thesis on the sex lives of nineteenth-century presidents, and had always thought someone's sex addiction might (à la Monica Lewinsky) someday make her career. And as she listened to his annoying wife grapple with the challenge of raising moral children in the face of privilege, she thought about how easy it would be to seduce her husband. She had to do it: it would be fun, it would be great, and, most important, it would work.

Would it be a betrayal of her beloved? Once in high school she had been sent to a shrink because her mother felt that she was really a borderline personality, though her mother had not told her as much. Candy had listened to her mother's phone call to her colleague, whom she would make Candy see for half of her junior year. Her mother had described her as devious and morally questionable, and had ended the conversation by saying in a slightly flirtatious way to the shrink, who was going through a bitter divorce at the time and was totally susceptible to the charms of any woman who would show him the slightest bit of interest, "Sometimes I wonder how you can teach a child empathy."

Even now the words made Candy furious. Of course, she had taught all of them a lesson by sleeping with the shrink, getting pregnant with his baby, and then threatening to tell the world. It could have ruined them all, but instead she had quietly had an abortion and said nothing. She had proved she had power and now she had material for a memoir, or, at the very least, a *Vogue* upfront column. Oh, how she longed for a *Vogue* upfront column.

And so the answer was, for the right piece, for the journalistic score, she would betray anyone.

CHAPTER *Eight*

September 25, 2008
Dow closes down 196.89 points to 11,022.06
S&P closes up 23.31 points to 1,209.18

Nina was cutting vegetables in the kitchen with a knife that cost more than her childhood home. She was staring out the kitchen window, which glumly looked out into a gray air shaft. She was wondering about the secret lives of New York City pigeons and trying to think of a way to quit. She was always trying to think of a way to quit, though she never actually did it. It had been so long that it was hard to think of what it would be like working for anyone else.

They weren't such a bad family. Easton was very smart but spent most of her time riding and complaining. Avery was very dramatic and probably smart but there was no real evidence either way. She didn't go to a particularly hard school, she did not get particularly good grades, but there seemed to Nina to be some spark of smartness there, something, a knowledge about people, a kind of charisma that the rest of the family was, sadly, lacking. Nina actually loved the girls. She had been with them since they were born and she found herself oddly attached to them. Though they were not her daughters (her own daughter would never recognize her now, her own daughter had grown up in Poland with her mother, her own daughter she had not seen in ten years, her own daughter made her eyes well up with tears of regret for missed opportunities, for a life spent in quiet solitude in a room in Queens). So Easton and Avery were the closest things that Nina had to real family and she felt a kind of connection to these little aliens. As they got older, not much about them made sense to Nina. She did not relate to their obsessions with status, or to their insane neuroses, or to their hatred of their bodies, but Nina did feel responsible for how they turned out. She wanted to see what they were like when they grew up. She needed to know the end of the story.

The thing that made it hard to stay, the thing that made it almost impossible to endure, was how unhappy Dick and Daisy were. Nina had never in her fifty years experienced anything like Dick and Daisy Greenbaum.

It was hard to say what it was about them that made them so profoundly hard to like. They were always nice to her, saccharine nice, almost pathetically nice. They overpaid her, gave her raises, tolerated various minor infractions of decorum, but there was something about them that Nina did not trust.

She heard the door open. She was pretty sure. It was Dick's assistant.

"Nina?" She came into the kitchen.

Nina smiled at Raja. "How are you?" Raja had her arms filled with dry cleaning; so much so that Nina could barely make out the tops of her eyes.

"Can I bother you for a drink of water?" They were both acutely aware of the difference in status between the two of them: domestic workers ranked below office workers. Raja was young and beautiful and came from a very upper-middle-class Indian family. She would not return to her homeland to marry the man whom her family had picked out. Raja was capable of something that Nina wasn't—social mobility. She would eventually climb the ranks, but, sadly, remain forever childless, and people would pity her, stating the maxim that you can't have it all.

"Of course."

Raja stared at Nina as she drank her warm glass of tap water. They both wanted to say something to the other, to connect, to commiserate about their lot in life. "So how is it here?" Raja said, finally. It was an open question, the kind that allowed for the other person to say as little or as much as they wanted.

"You know." Nina would need a little pushing if she was going to spill the family secrets.

"Stressed?" Raja asked.

"Yes." Nina turned. She was about to say much more, but she could see the door to the kitchen moving just slightly, making her think that someone might be behind it.

"I've never seen a rich group of people more miserable, and you know Dick . . ." Nina put her finger to her lips. Daisy's mother, Sarah Stein, was behind Raja. Had Sarah heard their conversation? Would Sarah dime them out? Raja paused for a second and then continued. Raja obviously didn't understand what the finger meant. She just kept on going. "I mean, these are wealthy, wealthy people and tormented. Of course, Dick has some . . ."

Nina interrupted. "Hello, Mrs. Stein, can I get you something?"

Raja became flushed. She started stammering, "Oh, I'm sorry. I was talking about . . ."

Sarah Stein had the body of a young person (slightly thinner than her daughter). She had young-looking blow-dried hair, and from behind she looked like she was in her twenties. This made the shock of her profoundly, unnaturally taut face all the more jarring when she turned around.

"No," Sarah stammered. For a minute it could go either way, then Sarah said, "No, I want someone to talk to me honestly. What is wrong with my daughter and her husband? Are they happy? You must know, Nina."

It was such an American question, filled with the kind of intimacy that was both brutally honest and strangely impersonal. Nina didn't totally absorb all the nuances of American honesty and the various flavors of American hypocrisy, but she did understand the not-so-subtle subtext, which was that Sarah Stein absolutely did not really want to know how her daughter was. "Well"—Nina was very gifted at the subtle art of pretending to know less English than she did—"I, how do you say, like . . ." She had also learned the great secret of American life and American media, which was that if you didn't want to answer a question, you could just answer another question, an unasked question that one might have stumbled on an answer for: "I am making the girls mac and cheese for dinner tonight." Nina paused. "It is Easton's favorite."

Sarah Stein grabbed Nina and held her tightly. Nina smelled slightly of the onions she was cutting. Sarah smelled slightly of Chanel No. 5. Both women found the other's smell slightly comforting. "You can trust me not to say anything. I am on your side."

Raja interrupted. "I think it is a complicated time for everyone in the investment world." Dick would have appreciated that.

"But really! Please, both of you, you can trust me not to say anything to Dick and Daisy."

But the rich ladies always said that when they wanted something. Nina had been lulled into trusting one of them at a previous job that had ended in disaster. But she had been pretty then. For Nina, pretty had presented far more problems than it solved. But she wanted to like Sarah Stein, even though she wasn't sure why. Possibly it was Sarah's earnestness, which was oddly out of place on Manhattan's Upper East Side.

Nina wished she liked Daisy more. Daisy wanted Nina to like her, and that was rare, to have a boss so insecure. But there was something about Daisy that Nina didn't trust—she was almost too affectionate. She would often try to hug Nina. Nina tried to answer Sarah. "You know how hard it is for these woman." She paused. She probably shouldn't have called Daisy "these woman"; after all, it showed a certain nuanced English that she had been tacitly claiming not to possess, but it was too late now.

"Yes, yes," Sarah said. Sarah would have said anything to keep Nina talking. Sarah was desperate to figure out what the *fuck* was going on with her daughter, and her bizarre life. She wanted answers, she needed to understand who this person was, this person who once was her daugher, the one with the custom everything, the one who seemed so guilty, who ran from soup kitchen to soup kitchen.

"This world isn't like other places, you know of what I am speaking?" Nina tried to revert back to broken English in the hopes of confusing and distracting Sarah.

"I know." Sarah pretended to follow. "I know."

"And so, we cannot judge too harshly."

"But what is happening with them?"

"What are you speaking of?"

"Are they happy? I have never seen my daughter so unhappy. I understand they have been through a lot with Easton's riding thing, but still, why is she so unhappy? Life is good. She is enormously wealthy, richer than I ever thought people could be. One would *think* that would make a person happy. Tell me, just answer me this one question. Make a mother feel better, help a mother to sleep at night, fix a mother's fear, make it so I don't have to drink my antacid: what the hell is happening with my daughter? Is she happy?" It was the kind of theatrical ranting that Avery might have delivered.

"It is . . ."

"Is she happy? Just, I beg of you! I implore you! Please, my darling Nina, please."

Nina paused. It was an impossible question. And it made her think back to her previous job when her boss had said she just wanted the truth. But then, when she got the truth, well, it had not set anyone in that house free, except perhaps for Nina, who was quickly fired with a small and begrudged severance package, basically because at the end of the day the boss had chosen to believe the claims of her lecherous husband and not the claims of her bright-eyed and naïve employee. Of course, years later that husband finally did succeed in leaving that wife for a nanny, but she was a summer girl who came from Harvard and was studying art history and was a Rockefeller. The wife would have been better off keeping Nina and giving her a raise, and the wife thought about that sometimes in her sad little house, while she cursed herself for ever signing a prenup, but that was millions of years ago, lifetimes ago, on the Upper East Side. "The girls are wonderful, so pretty, and Easton is such a wonderful rider." Nina was not going to make the same mistake twice, she was not going to give it up for Sarah Stein. If Sarah Stein cared so much, she could figure it out herself. Nina had a family to feed, or she had had a family to feed when she left Poland twenty years ago. Now she had a hostile twenty-five-year-old and a hostile ex-husband who both wrote her nasty letters and asked for money. Ah, the great American Dream. But she did have, like, three hundred channels of television and she did live one block from the best doughnut shop in all of Queens. And recently the doctor in the clinic she went to had given her a prescription for Xanax, which had delighted her with profoundly dreamless sleeps.

"So will Easton ever ride again after this?" Sarah asked, trying desperately to spark some connection. Sarah knew very well that Easton was still in a wheelchair, and that her two long, thin, toned legs were stuffed into big, hard white casts. Easton would walk again, the doctors assumed, but riding seemed a long way away.

Nina frowned. "You'll have to ask Ms. Greenbaum about it. I have no idea about such things. Oh, look, hello, Ms. Greenbaum."

Daisy came in. "Hello, Mother. Hello there, Nina."

"We were just talking about Easton."

"Oh, yes," Daisy said brightly.

"Will my granddaughter ever walk again?"

"Mother!" Daisy put her finger to her mouth. "Not so loud!"

"Can't you? Can we just talk about this for a minute, please?" Sarah had gotten desperate. Sarah had gotten hopeless. Sarah had gotten slightly crazy.

Daisy frowned. "What do you want to know?"

"Will she ever walk again?"

"Don't be overdramatic," Daisy snapped. She could be so profoundly cruel with her mother. She would never talk that way to anyone else in the world. "I'm sorry, Mom, that's not what I meant. What I meant to say was yes, she'll walk, and no"—Daisy's voice became very hushed—"no, she will probably not be able to . . ." Daisy looked off into the air shaft. Sun was refracting off the light, making it look like the air shaft was filled with the ghosts of her victims. Only three, not that many. Not like Ted Bundy. Of course, Ted Bundy was a lot better-looking than she was. No, that was crazy. She couldn't compare herself to Ted Bundy. He was a different species. She was not a monster, not a child molester. No, nothing like that. "It's actually worse than that." Her voice became even more hushed. "The horse, we had to kill her horse, well, not her horse, Georgina Bloomberg's horse. But she doesn't know yet." Daisy paused and looked at both women.

"Oh, darling." Her mother hugged her. Nina felt uncomfortable and then went right back to cutting vegetables. Cutting vegetables was safe. It was one of those things they always wanted you to do.

Daisy started to feel herself crying. She started to feel the tears coming out of her eyes, like cleaning fluid on a bloody bathtub. "How can I tell my daughter that the one honest thing about her, the one honest love of hers, is gone?" Daisy looked up at her mother. "Nothing in life prepares you for breaking your child's heart." Sarah held her daughter hard in the hug they had tried to have earlier with less success. "I love you."

Nina looked out at the air shaft, feeling very uncomfortable.

"I love you too, Mom, and, you know, I am really really happy you are here to help me with Easton and Avery. We are all having a rough time with the accident and the credit markets, and Dick is so stressed and . . ." It felt good to try to cry, just a little. Nina wandered off into the maid's room to hide. She couldn't stand to hear it anymore. These women had nothing to cry about, with their seven-thousand-dollar handbags and their lives of leisure.

"Oh, darling. I know." It felt great to be let in. And Sarah knew she had to enjoy it while it lasted. She could be cast out of the Garden of Eden at any time.

$\mathcal{A}$nd so Candy Ross Rose had hatched a plan. She would seduce Dick, she would get inside his mind, she would find out everything, and then she would write the story that would bring down The Bank. How hard could it be? She knew everything about them, everything about Dick, everything about Daisy, and even more than that.

And so Candy Ross Rose went to the Harvard Club, where young, beautiful Ivy women pick up old rich guys (she had also heard Dick musing about his love of slipping in there for a coffee during the workday, just to "clear his head"). And there she sat having coffee in the giant reading room for three long days, and then, like a biblical story, on the morning of the fourth day, God sent down a man, and that man was Dick Greenbaum, and he sat right next to Candy Ross Rose. After all, he knew he could no longer touch, but he could look, couldn't he? There was no rule against talking to the one beautiful, slightly punk twenty-four-year-old in the whole place. He was married but he wasn't dead. He could talk, couldn't he? He had of course forgotten that this was how he got in all that trouble in the first place. Once upon a time Petra Smith Kingly was just a sexy woman with a too short skirt sitting next to him in first class on a British Airways flight from Athens to London. And since she was drinking (quite a lot, now that he thought about it), and since he hadn't had sex with his wife in three weeks, what was the harm in a little . . . anyway, that was ages ago, when he used to fly commercial.

"What are you reading?"

She lifted up the *Crimson* so he could see. She was going to add something about how she had written for it but thought better of it. "I had a boyfriend who wrote for it."

"Oh, yes?" He smiled.

He was sexy. This was fun work. She might have slept with him on her own. He was just her type—small, dark, ethnic-looking, not the kind of man you would want to have children with because your sons would all be five feet two. But in the way rich and powerful men are handsome, he was deliciously handsome. "Yes," she said, smiling.

"I feel this incredible sense that I've met you before," he bullshitted, and then looked around the room to see if anyone would recognize him. The room was almost empty and it was raining, and the rain was beating on the windows, and he was thinking about the rooms upstairs. They weren't grand but they were perfect for something like this.

"I don't think so."

"Did you go to Harvard?" He smiled and let out a positively effeminate giggle.

"Yes, but"—she looked at him and batted her eyelashes softly—"I'm only twenty-one."

Twenty-five minutes later they we having very rough sex in the small square white-tile bathroom of room 22 of the Harvard Club. It turned out that Candy Ross Rose was into slightly masochistic sex. It turned out that Candy Ross Rose was going to let Dick do all the things his wife would not. For a second, life was wonderful. There was no injured daughter who might never walk without a limp, no dead horse, no problems with the Bloomberg family because of that dead horse, no frozen credit markets, no London Interbank Offered Rate at an all-time high of 2.54 percent, no crumbling equities markets. Then there was a promise. They would meet the next day for lunch, a room service lunch in room 22 at the Harvard Club.

And so Candy Ross Rose betrayed her love, her one true love. But she betrayed him for the story, and isn't that what journalists are supposed to do?

That night when Dick got home the parents summoned all their strength to go and talk to their daughter. Daisy looked at him on the long walk to their daughter's room. He looked ashen. She put her hand on his. "Is it really that bad?"

He was, of course, thinking about Candy, not about the markets, about Lehman Brothers, about the credit markets. He tried to snap himself back to normal life, with his normal wife. He looked at her, his lovely wife, his lovely murdering wife, and he was cheating on her again. Was he so stupid? Sure, the last time he had lived, the last time it had been his mistress. But there was nothing to say that this time it wouldn't end up being him. After all, it had for a minute or two looked like she might have decided it was all his fault and stuck him in the freezer or something. He had seen it, the change in her eyes, the way she became a slightly different person, like a drunk in her cups. His wife had several selves.

But she would not kill him, because she needed him, right? She needed him, because he knew how to do things (like make money). And so he had to keep her slightly terrified, which wasn't so hard because the truth was slightly terrifying, or perhaps worse than that. "You know, it's the closest we've come to a depression since 1929. But this has the legs to be so much worse, so so so much worse."

His wife looked appropriately ashen, and he felt sort of relieved. If the last few months had taught him anything, it was that this was not a woman you wanted to piss off. "Oh, dear." She stopped in front of Easton's door. She grabbed his hand. "I feel like I can't do this." She nodded to the door of Easton's room. But they had no choice; it was time for Easton to go back to school, to life. They couldn't keep her forever sequestered in 740 Park Avenue like some kind of postmodern Rapunzel.

The door was slightly open. Easton was lying on her bed watching television. They had gotten her a television after the accident because they felt so bad for her, and so she had spent the last three weeks glued to it, zombified, stupefied, obsessed with the flickering box. The constant stream of images and sounds coming out of their daughter's room unnerved both parents, but they were also so crushed by their guilt over what had happened to her that giving her everything she asked for seemed only natural.

"Darling," Daisy said cautiously. It was odd to Dick, knowing what he knew about his wife, that she should be so frightened of their child. But he was scared too.

Easton just stared at the TV, like she was stoned. Both parents walked over to her twin-sized bed. Her father stood in front of her and her mother sat on the edge of the bed. "Darling," her father said.

But there was no response. Daisy thought about a Bret Easton Ellis novel she had read in college. Was there something about kids being zombies? Or maybe that wasn't it at all: were the kids on drugs? Was it about drugs? Would that happen to Easton?

Daisy put her hands on her daughter's dark, smooth hair. "Darling, we need to have a serious talk."

Dick looked nervously at his wife and his daughter. Daisy knew this was going to fall to her, of course it was. Daisy looked at Dick again. She wondered where he had been when she had called earlier that day. His secretary had said he had been in a meeting, and maybe he had. There was a slightly sheepish look about him, which she (consciously or unconsciously) recognized. She would never trust him again, or maybe eventually she would. Maybe eventually she would forget about Lady Petra and the murder. She doubted that, but modern American life was filled with amnesia for greater crimes than that. "Mom."

Daisy was shocked that Easton was still in there. "Yes, love."

"I don't want to talk."

"I know, but look." She looked at Dick, for a few words, for some parenting, to save her from her child. Dick was actually looking at his BlackBerry. She was angry, but deep down she didn't necessarily want him to be a better parent. This power structure had its advantages for Daisy, and so she continued, "You are going back to school next week and we need to talk about a few things. Would you mind turning off the TV for a little while." It wasn't a question.

Easton flipped off the TV and looked at her parents as if the impetus now fell on them to entertain her. They looked at each other; it had been a long summer, a long August, an endless September. Easton had been a miserable patient. She had been unhappy with everything, and frustrated with her condition. She was stuck either on crutches or in a very small metal wheelchair. The whole thing smacked of a kind of creepy Victorianism—Daisy taking her daughter out every morning in the chair to air her, as one of the Southern nurses put it. Easton had multiple nurses, all of whom preferred to be paid in cash.

Overnight Easton had been transformed from a healthy, strapping figure of youthful athleticism to a cripple. She was still taking all sorts of drugs for pain, but beyond that, Easton had been affected by the experience in a way that neither parent could quite qualify. It seemed to both of them that being sick had made her delicate in a way she had never been. She was not the girl who had started the summer with them; she had become, in a few short weeks, a significantly more complicated individual, containing nuances that her parents never suspected her of. For example, she had started reading books all the time, and not kids' books, not *Gossip Girl* or something age-appropriate like that. She was reading classics—*Little Women* and *The Scarlet Letter.* Daisy had nearly dropped her Diet Coke when Easton had asked for them. She had been shocked, but she was parent enough to know that she should just let this go and see if it amounted to anything. Her daughter, the shallow one, had been quietly reading all of these classic novels, for what purpose she was not sure.

"Doll, we have to talk to you about something," Daisy started. Dick frowned, and Daisy looked up at him. "Would you like to?"

He looked back at his BlackBerry. No, no, he would not. "Go ahead." He said it as if he were giving her permission, and not just totally passing the buck (ironic, though, as he did quite literally pass the buck to his wife all the time, in the form of money).

"Thank you," she said in a way that sounded suspiciously like "fuck you." Then, to her daughter, "Easton, you know, we have never talked about what happened to Heavenly Hash. And I think it might be time to talk about it. And maybe we can talk about some other things too."

"No, Daddy told me. He has been in the North Fork stables since my accident." Daisy looked at Dick with the look of death. He did not want to be murdered, and for a second he paused and studied his wife. She was annoyed but clearly she understood. After all, they had both kind of agreed that they wouldn't really tell her, and he had probably been caught by surprise. "I didn't want him riding in the classic. After all, he is my pony, at least for the year."

"Easton." Daisy took her hand. She wondered if as an adult this moment would be replayed to various shrinks again and again. She could just see Easton in a sensible but overpriced suit musing to some shrink about all the love her mother could never give her. "Easton, you had a very serious accident and it wasn't your fault." As she started to talk, she could feel herself start to cry, tears streaming out of her eyes, lots of tears, big glossy tears. Was she wrong to say that it wasn't Easton's fault? Easton knew it wasn't her fault, and maybe it was worse for Daisy to say it. Maybe by saying it wasn't her fault she was saying it really was her fault. She couldn't worry about that.

"I know, Mommy. I know."

"Well, you don't know all of it." Dick frowned at Daisy. "Well, you do it, then," Daisy said, wiping the tears from the corners of her enormous eyes.

"Heavenly Hash had to be shot and now he is dead." Dick was never a man known for his delivery, and this had never been more true than today.

"Dick!" Then to Easton: "I'm sorry, that wasn't what Daddy was trying to say. What Daddy was trying to say was that it was time for Heavenly Hash to go to heaven."

"Or to hash," Dick whispered.

"Shut up!" Daisy hit him. Both parents paused and looked down at the ground. This was a serious thing, right?

"It's not true, you know it's not true. You told me that he was just at a farm. Mommy, tell Daddy he is lying."

"Sweetie." Daisy looked at Dick. Daisy believed that the medicine had made her daughter more severe, had made her daughter's brown eyes so dark they were almost black now.

Daisy grabbed Easton in her arms. "No, darling. No, darling, Heavenly Hash is dead."

"It's not true." Easton was crying and sniffling and catching her breath in that way that sounded like wailing.

Just then Avery came in. She ran to her sister and put her arms around her. "What's the matter?" Avery looked up at Dick and Daisy in a vaguely accusatory way, as if she were sure they were somehow responsible for this. "What did Mommy say? What happened?" Though Avery and Easton weren't close, they surprised their parents sometimes—in moments when one twin knew intuitively that the other needed her more than usual. For a minute Dick and Daisy were jealous that they would never have someone like a twin, someone who loved them so much as if to be a part of them. Avery looked into Easton's eyes, and for once used all of her dramatic powers on her sister, and started wiping the tears away. "What is the matter, my love?"

"Daddy just told me that they killed my *pony*!"

"Look, you are going back to school next week and back into the world. You are going to have to face some things about the accident." It sounded so cold the way Dick put it. She was eight. She shouldn't have to face anything yet. Daisy looked at Dick, at his mouth, which was slightly contorted into a frown. At that moment she realized, perhaps for the first time ever, that her husband was a cruel person.

"Dick!"

"Daddy." Avery chastised him too.

"Mom-m-m-my, Daddy is lying, Daddy is a liar."

"Easton, please, you can't call your daddy a liar. It's very rude."

"Mommy"—Easton was having trouble talking through the tears—"he told me the pony was okay. He told me so."

Avery had overheard the grown-ups talk about how badly her sister had been hurt during the accident. After all, no one was sure that Easton would be able to walk normally after this. Avery drew in a deep breath, as if she were preparing for a role in her drama lessons, as if she knew that this was her moment to be the sister she always imagined herself to be. "Easton, you are going to be okay. And I am going to help you with everything. I am going to be here for you and help you."

"But it's not true."

Daisy looked at Dick. "No," Dick said. "No, I'm sorry, Easton. But it is true."

"I don't believe anything you say, Daddy, and I never will again because you lied to me." Easton caught her breath between tears and words. "And I would never lie to you like that."

And as she said that, both Daisy and Dick had the same horrible thought. If she was so upset about this, just think what she would do if she knew everything else.

"You think I am just being dramatic, but I'm not." Easton was still fighting with her breath and her tears. "I am not just being dramatic. I will never ever trust you again, Daddy, because I am your daughter and I trusted you and you betrayed me and for that I will never ever forgive you." Easton wasn't the kind of kid who used words lightly, and both parents knew that that day was a turning point for the fancy twin. From that moment on, the world was no longer a place filled with beautiful people and beautiful things devoted to making her happy. No, Easton had been expelled from the garden.

CHAPTER *Nine*

October 2, 2008

Dow closes down 348.22 points to 10,483.85

S&P closes down 46.78 points to 1,114.28

Dick Greenbaum was frantic to get out of Augustus's feeder fund. And every morning since his headless mistress had visited him like the Ghost of Hanukkah Past, he had had his secretary call Malmot's office. Finally, on the fifth day, Malmot called back.

There was almost no small talk, nothing at all. As if both men knew just how dire the situation really was. "I want to redeem my maximum for the quarter, which I am pretty sure as I am looking at the agreement that we signed is five million, as soon as possible."

"But why? We're up two percent for the year. Whereas everyone else in town is blowing up. You shouldn't ever want to redeem from us. You should redeem from the people who are losing money, not making you money." Dick looked out his office window, irritated by Augustus's tone.

"Of course, but . . ."

Malmot laughed. "Of course, I get it. Robbing Peter to pay Paul. I understand completely. You have bills to pay. Who doesn't? Everyone else is down. How much is your desk down anyway?"

That was a base thing to say. The S&P was way down and the prop desk was profoundly leveraged (meaning they were down powers of ten more than the standard long-only mutual fund). It was low of Malmot to bring up his returns, his desk's returns. "Look." What could Dick say? He couldn't very well say he had his doubts, that he was visited by a headless ghost in the middle of the night. That he was looking into it with his friend who worked for the SEC and the friend had said the whole thing seemed like there was something question-able going on and he wasn't sure why there hadn't been more of an investigation but there certainly would be now and the whole thing was certainly flagged. But Dick couldn't say he thought Kingly was a criminal, and that Augustus had misled him by giving all the cash to Kingly and buying those stupid Rothkos. He couldn't say that, could he?

Dick wondered why he didn't just keep the money and buy a Rothko. No, he had to say something else, something that made more sense, that was more in character. "I feel like it's time to buy that house in the Hamptons."

Augustus didn't buy it. "Really?"

"Yes, the market is down and people are panicking. I feel like this is my moment."

"But I just talked to a few of my people and they say. . ." He sighed (it was one of those sighs that was long enough to project an air of re-laxation). "And, you know these are the people to talk to about things like this. Of course, I can't say who they are, but they are the kind of people who could buy and sell people like us many times over."

Dick really didn't like the idea that there were people who could buy and sell him many times over.

"And they say the Hamptons market is going to bottom out in March. It's my professional opinion that you should just wait one more quarter. Can't you wait just one more quarter? One more quarter may save you millions." Both men noticed their palms were wet with sweat.

"I don't think I can. Daisy is really a pain in my ass. She is making me nuts. You know Fizzy is her best friend and she really is pushing her. Wives, can't live with 'em, can't kill 'em."

Malmot didn't laugh.

"Of course, I'm kidding." As opposed to his wife.

Malmot just ignored him. "But we are probably going to be twelve percent next year, or maybe even fourteen."

Both men were panicking, but they expressed it in different ways. "I want to make the redemption."

Realizing that he was not going to convince Dick, Malmot changed his tack and said in a slightly hostile way, "Well, you have to file all the papers before the end of the quarter. You may not make it."

Dick could feel the fear in the pit of his stomach.

One lunch had turned into another and soon into an affair, and though she was in it for the story and he was in it for the sex, the two of them had formed something almost meaningful. Which was not good for any of the parties involved, least of all Candy Ross Rose. Dick enjoyed her, maybe even liked her, though. Poor Candy Ross Rose was a vile tonic—the smugness of youth mixed with an intellect that had been Harvardized within an inch of its life. This was a girl who believed she mattered, who believed she would undoubtedly go on to change the world, to affect the zeitgeist, to land on the cover of *New York* magazine, covered only by her enormous tattoos. This was a girl who had Pop-Tarts in her stomach and pop culture in her blood, and sometimes when Dick was fucking her he was dreaming about stabbing her with an ice pick.

"You are so sexy for an old man. You're like Jerry Stahl."

"Who the fuck is that?" It was six P.M. He had slipped out right after the markets had closed, and slipped into Candy Ross Rose, who was always free for hotel sex, or, as she liked to call it, "research." Of course, Candy was doing research on The Bank, but she was at heart a memoirist and not a reporter. Turned out her décolletage was no assistance with reportage. She wasn't deft at getting people to tell her their life story without making them feel like they were stupidly exposing themselves for all the world to see. She had sort of lost track of what it was that she was trying to expose. Was it Dick? Or was it The Bank? Or was it some larger culture of corporate greed? Also, since Candy was a product of the MTV generation, she had grown up in a refracted world of TV, Game Boy, the Internet, and the subtle art of text messaging. She had been prescribed Ritalin for her ADHD. She had promptly snorted and sold it in the hopes of being like Elizabeth Wurtzel. It hadn't worked.

Despite her growing affection for him, it was so hard for Candy to concentrate on Dick for more than a few minutes at a time. She found herself so much more interesting. Every time she tried to get him to open up, she lost interest. She knew a few things about Dick and his miserable marriage and his anxiety dreams, and if she knew a bit more about the markets (or if she had even known what a derivative was or its dependence on the housing markets not slipping), she might have been able to piece all that stuff together, but she didn't.

"Oh, my God, I can't believe you don't know who Jerry Stahl is. He's, like, the coolest guy. He is, like, the hottest . . ." Dick tuned out. A famous old male writer, a story that wasn't about him in any way, but was instead about someone "as old as he was," was not something Dick was even remotely interested in. In fact, he could not be less interested in Candy's writer blogger world. Brooklyn could detach from Queens and float off into the ocean and be lost forever and it would have no effect on the lives of the Greenbaums, not one element in their lives would change, except that possibly Nina the house-keeper would have a shorter commute. He didn't even know that blogging was a state of being, a verb. It sounded to him like barfing or dieting, something that a person could do, but not for a living.

Dick smiled at Candy. It was a vaguely patronizing smile. He was old and tired enough to no longer believe that infatuation was love, and perhaps there was a bit of tragedy in this realization. He used to fall in love with his affairs; he used to genuinely think of the possibil-ity of living happily ever after with them. Now he mostly thought about the very real possibility of his wife murdering his current fling, and even that didn't elicit much feeling. "Not bad for an old guy," he blustered.

"Hot, very hot." They were lying in a big bed in a big room in the Peninsula Hotel. She had fallen in love with the lifestyle. She was in love with the linen sheets, with the giant comfortable bed, with the car service cars that dropped her off every morning at Trip's loft, where she arrived with coffee and a slightly smug expression on her face. Trip knew she was sleeping with someone else and this made him feel very relieved and perhaps only a tiny bit jealous. He had been giving Candy Ross Rose even less thought than usual, because he was spending every night closing in on the biggest Ponzi scheme ever. It was going to be his *Citizen Kane*.

"I have to get going, but you can stay in the room. I have it for the rest of the night, or I can have the car drop you off, after it drops me." He was worried: worried about the stupid ban on short selling; wor-ried about the fact that it was hard to think of who was worse, Joe Biden or Sarah Palin (who were debating that evening on television); worried about the TARP; worried about breadlines; worried about the fall of capital markets as we know them; worried about the possibility of Weimar Germany part two.

"But you're going all the way uptown."

"I have to get home."

"Right, to the W-I-F-E and K-I-D-S." Candy had slept with married men before. She had had affairs, and she had even broken up marriages. After all, she was very worldly for her age, but it always felt the same way. It always hurt in the same strange way: it was as if she felt rejected by their very existence, even though they preexisted her.

"Well, I have a marriage, you know."

She was very slightly drunk; drunk enough to think she could say anything without there being consequences. "Would you ever leave her and the girls, for someone delicious, someone young and fresh . . . someone who gives the greatest . . ."

"Never." Dick looked away. "Never. And I have been totally honest about this the whole time, you know that. I will never leave Daisy."

"Gee, I was just saying." She sat up and took a slug of her champagne. "You don't have to freak out."

"I think it's time to go. I told you not to fall in love with me. I told you this would never ever work. I am a married man, very happily married." Candy looked at Dick. He was five six, perhaps five seven on a good day, slightly effeminate and slightly simian. It was hardly like he was the catch of the century, and here he was telling her not to fall in love with him. She was a postmodern sex kitten. She should be warning him not to pine away for her when she ran off with Jerry Stahl or one of the many literary luminaries whom she had seen admiring her "body" of work.

"Obviously, very happy." Candy lit a cigarette.

"What are you doing?"

"Smoking."

"You can't smoke in here. This is the Peninsula Hotel. This room is a grand and that's the corporate rate. Look, don't be upset with me. I never lied to you once."

Candy had met men like Dick before, men who believed their bad actions could be forgiven by warning the other party before. But it didn't work like that. "Yes, you are a wonderful person. I am just thrilled. Thrilled that you fucked me and now you are going to discard me. What kind of man fucks a twenty-one-year-old and then just tosses her aside? You know . . ." Of course, Candy was twenty-three.

Dick hated being reminded that cheating on his wife was actually a bad thing. Being told that he was a scumbag didn't jibe with the way he saw himself. He wasn't a bad person. He was a good person. He was a moral person. He had tried to save the banks. He just had a little problem, a little sex problem. That was what it was. It wasn't his fault. He had a very stressful job. Besides, wasn't what he had really an addiction? Was he so different from the alcoholic or the meth addict? He couldn't help it, just like they couldn't.

She interrupted his thoughts. "Do you want to go one more time?"

He looked at her enormous breasts, slightly hidden under the white sheets. He didn't have to be home right away, did he? "Well."

She took him in her hands.

"Oh, okay."

On the other side of polite society, the more polite side, perhaps, Easton Greenbaum was sitting on the classic Billy Baldwin sofa, reading her French textbook and sipping a club soda with lime.

"Is your mommy home?" Landon Stone was wearing crumpled J.Crew chinos and a gauzy white Chanel shirt that her mother had bought her but not before Landon had burst into tears and admitted to her mother that she hated all her clothing and that her husband was a total loser. Her mother was addicted to hearing bad things about her son-in-law, the one with the big, fancy name and not much else. Landon's mom loved buying her things, lots of pretty things. After all, the Stones were rich and this had not always been the case. They had actually been rich and then poor more times than she liked to remember, rich and then poor, poor and then rich, and now finally—with drivers, chefs—rich enough to support her long-suffering daughter. That said, not rich enough to make her daughter rich.

"I think she's still out with Grandma. Why?" Avery said. Since Easton's accident, Landon had been giving Avery a ride to and from school when she took Walker. Today, though, Landon Stone had insisted on escorting Avery up in the elevator, even though the girl had assured Landon (or Mrs. Stone, as she liked to be called by drivers and children) that Nina was upstairs waiting for her.

"Well . . ." Landon panicked. Why was she there? She wanted to look for clues. For years, she hadn't been able to shake the feeling that Daisy had had something to do with her sister's demise. It would make her so happy, so profoundly happy, to bring Daisy Greenbaum down for her sister's murder or for whatever else. Landon hadn't been close with her sister—she had been young enough to not remember things—but certain things were impossible to forget, and they made up a vague, haunting tapestry of her sister's life, like her sister's pink room, the way her mother cried herself to sleep for years after, the times she would peek over her crib at her sister. *Sister:* the word felt almost foreign, like an old Sanskrit prayer or something once written in hieroglyphics.

She was there to save her sister who had died long ago, to bring down someone who had to be stopped. But why did she have to be stopped? And why had it fallen to Landon to stop her? What kind of world was this?

"*Bonjour,* sister. *Bonjour,* Mrs. Stone!"

"Hello, Easton." Landon Stone tried to be friendly.

"*Bon-jour!*" Now that she was back in school, her dark mood had passed and Easton had made the transition to crutches seamlessly, in typical Easton style, and she was now enjoying all the privileges that invalid status granted her at the gray-pinafored school. She got to ride the elevator. She got to skip gym. She got to be the first one to get lunch. She even got dismissed a few minutes early. It was so typical of Easton to be able to make being almost crushed to death by a pony look good.

Avery tried to suppress her feelings of annoyance about her sister's incredibly seamless and irritating recovery. "Are you okay, sister darling?" Avery said dramatically.

"Yes, darling sister." Easton smiled. Avery leaned over to give her a kiss, but moved her hand so that instead of leaning on the sofa, she was leaning on Easton's cast just the slightest bit.

Easton let out a yelp.

"Oh, my gosh. I am so sorry, sister. So sorry!"

Easton smiled. "It's fine, beloved Avery. Fine!" The two sisters kissed on the cheek. They'd been going through a strange phase since the accident—instead of fighting, as they had their whole lives, they suddenly were incredibly affectionate with each other. Dick and Daisy weren't sure what to make of it. Was their affection some kind of ruse to get something from their parents? Or was it just a reflection of the state of twinitude—as close as two humans can be without actually touching? It was an impossible state, the state of twinness—next to each other all the time, touching, breathing the same air, occupying the same small square of space, even when they were miles away from each other. And sometimes this made them want to kill each other; sometimes they felt that there was not enough air for them both, not enough solid ground for both their feet, and not enough space in the four-thousand-square-foot apartment for both of them. But at other times it was just the opposite; they couldn't imagine the pain of a world alone.

"Is your mother around?"

"Non," Easton answered. "But the ever charming Nina is *ensconced* in the kitchen."

"Good vocabulary word there, sister!"

"Merci!"

"When do you think your mother will be back?" Landon found the Greenbaum twins endlessly irritating.

"Do you need to talk to her?" Avery asked.

Landon Stone looked at both girls. They were both little twerps, little brats who had far more than they deserved, and they would get the spots at the Ivies, or they would get the good husbands and the memberships to the good clubs, the Wasp clubs. It wasn't her fault that most Jews were good with money, except her family. It wasn't really fair. It wasn't fair at all. "I just want to leave something for your mother." That seemed plausible. Did it?

"Of course." Easton smiled and pointed to a few doors behind her. How big was this apartment anyway? She had been to other apartments in 740 Park, but this one seemed freakishly large. It wasn't that she had self-pity, it was just that these people were so-o-o-o-o ridiculously rich, and okay, she had self-pity.

"Where is her desk?" Landon kept thinking that the proof that Daisy was a murderer might be lurking on her desk. It didn't make a whole lot of sense, but Landon was not all that smart.

Both girls paused. They were like little Siamese cats, rich Siamese cats. They looked at her in that slightly suspicious way. Landon hated them. She hated that at the tender age of eight they knew they were richer than she was and would always be. She could feel them looking down their hook noses at her. "I think your mother would be very upset if she knew that you both were . . ." Landon paused. Was she going to need to spell it out?

Easton frowned at her sister. Both girls had the same gnawing anxiety that pissing off the mother of the most popular girl in New York City was a bad idea.

Avery hopped to her feet in a move she had clearly learned at Ballet Academy East. "Please excuse my sister's inability to walk! Let me show you to mother dar-r-r-r-ling's desk!" Avery said in a giddy voice. It was easy to be giddy when you lived at 740 Park Avenue, when Daddy was a master of the universe and not some drunk fuck who was out on an ashram trying to find himself. An ashram. Who goes to an ashram? He said he needed to find himself. And here Landon was, stuck alone with four kids in an apartment that looked out at other better apartments, a victim of downward mobility in the worst way.

Easton followed Avery as she leaped and bowed and generally was the pretentious little twerp that Landon felt she was. "Here is my mother's desk. As you can see, she is very neat and tidy." She giggled.

The desk was a total and utter mess, covered in pieces of paper, in paper clips, in little candy wrappers. "Thank you, Avery."

"Mommy doesn't like anyone touching her desk. She is very very very very serious about it. You see, that is why it's so incredibly messy. Even Nina is not allowed to clean her desk, so it stays like that. Daddy calls it an eyesore. Daddy is very neat. Mommy calls Daddy a neat freak." Avery could talk all day, and often did.

"Okay, thanks." Landon didn't mean thanks, though.

"Okkeeeeeeeeeeeee, I am going to check on my sister, my cute cute cute cute cute sister. Being a twin is the greatest greatest greatest greatest thing in the entire world. I love it so much. I love it. I love being a twin!" Avery flitted off.

"Okay." Landon waited half a second and then she started searching, first with her eyes and then with her hands, but there was nothing that even made any sense, just receipts and various notes about various community service projects she was, or wanted to be, involved in. There was a ton of stuff about Obama too. Landon hated Democrats, and she hated politically correct Democratic assholes who had more money than she did. So annoying. Landon was about to give up, she was about to just pack it in and go home and vomit up some cookie dough, when she spotted out of the corner of her eye a little picture of a little girl who was definitely not Easton and definitely not Avery. And the picture was old. It was very old. She reached forward and plucked the picture from the picture frame it was tucked in the corner of. It had to be her sister, it looked like her sister. She thought back to the picture her mother had framed on her dresser. It looked like her. It would have to be her. That was the cornerstone of the whole thing, it had to be the clue she had been searching for—it had to be. For a moment everything rushed back to her. She had been the sister of that girl at one point in her life. They had lived modestly but happily, and Daddy had been unstable and thus unable to work for a long time, so they had been getting poorer and poorer, but then something amazing happened. Hayden had disappeared from summer camp. Daddy had promptly used this as the excuse he had been looking for to kill himself. Then her mother, who had always been one to make lemonade out of lemons, promptly remarried a millionaire. They moved to L.A. and changed their names and became rich, and now there they were, back in L.A., and here she was, tracking down her sister's murderer. And how was it going? Well . . .

"Why are you looking at a picture of me as a child?" Landon felt a hand on her shoulder. It was a cold, sharp hand and it felt like a knife cutting through her bones. Landon wasn't so sharp; she wasn't a rocket scientist, and yet, she knew, knew from the feeling of that hand on her shoulder, that Daisy Greenbaum had in fact murdered her sister. It was just something about the way Daisy's fingers touched her flesh, like she was a vampire or a witch or some kind of slightly overweight Grim Reaper.

Landon dropped the picture. "Not looking . . ."

Daisy moved her hands up to Landon's neck. And Landon wondered if Daisy was going to murder her right there in front of her daughters. But instead she stroked Landon's necklace and said, "Are those Lanvin pearls? I have been dying for a choker."

CHAPTER *Ten*

October 3, 2008

Dow closes down 157.47 points to 10,325.38

S&P closes down 15.05 points to 1,099.23

Trip McAllister was not the only person who was looking for Petra Smith Kingly. But he was the only person to make the connection between her and Dick Greenbaum. On the Upper East Side of Manhattan, far from the genteel intellectual aspirations of Brooklyn Heights, Sir Smith Kingly had been pacing around his giant dilapidated town house all week, finding change for egg sandwiches from the overpriced diner, frantically raising whatever money he could, trying to stonewall all the redemptions (withdrawals) that were coming in.

He had had a sinking feeling about his wife's sudden disappearance. He had toyed with the notion of calling her few relatives in Queens, but had decided against it, because Sir Smith Kingly was unequivocally convinced that his lovely trophy wife had turned state's evidence against him.

He paused and watched himself in the custom-made mirror, one of the few things that they had not been able to cancel delivery of. He adjusted his white hair. He had been so smart for so long, and then he had been so lucky for so long, and then it had been such a bull market for so long, but now, now it was all over.

His mind wandered back to his wife. He had always known deep down that she was a good-time girl, the kind who would be gone at the first hint of trouble. Still, it was one thing to think such a thing and quite another to experience it firsthand. He felt betrayed, but could he really? He had committed any number of bad acts; did he really have any rights anymore?

A city away, that same dark night, in Brooklyn, all the Jehovah's Witnesses had witnessed what they were going to witness for the night and had gone to sleep. It was one of those particularly starless fall nights. The air was unseasonably cold and there was a kind of hazy mist that had fallen on the trees and low buildings. Trip was sitting in his kitchen drinking a cup of cold coffee. He had noticed that Candy had been less interested in marrying him lately and he could only chalk this up to one of two possible reasons. One was that she was playing hard to get (this seemed unlikely but possible); the other was that she had fallen in love with someone else (this seemed much more likely). Her being in love with someone else had made her infinitely more attractive to him.

"Where were you last night?" Trip asked. He had been at a new media party for Wittered Media Consortium Group, a porn website that had just been bought for $12 million by a big German conglomerate. It had been the usual new-media scene: bloggers, urban hipsters, MFA students, a few old weirdos, some advertising guys in suits, a couple of die-hard alcoholics, and painters looking for free drinks and loose underage girls.

"Nowhere."

"You weren't at the party I went to. Thought you'd be there for sure.

It was totally your scene. In fact, everyone cool was there. Moby was there."

"Yah, yah. Moby will go to the opening of an envelope."

"Moby is a genius. Moby is a religion. Moby has dated every smart, hot woman in New York. Few people are smarter and more talented than Moby. He even has his own line of teas."

"Well, perhaps you should make him your girlfriend, then."

"Okay." Trip smiled. "Maybe I will, but only if you tell me where you were last night."

"I was busy."

"Doing?"

"Why does it matter?"

Trip tripped on the words, but he still managed to croak them out. "You're my girlfriend, you know."

"Oh, now I'm your girlfriend."

Trip frowned.

"Why do you want me now, all out of nowhere and everything?"

"I don't want to . . ." Trip paused. This conversation was about to go in the wrong direction. "Not the question. The question is . . . where were you last night?"

"And the answer is . . . why do you care?"

Trip stopped. "Okay, fine. Do whatever you like. I don't care. In fact, you can fuck whoever you want. After all, you already fucked my whole house in college. Why stop now?"

"Stop it." Candy burst into tears. It was just one of those things. She couldn't hold it in anymore. She had been getting tons of mean comments on her blog, plus less traffic (which meant less money from click-through ad sales). She was very hurt by what had happened with Dick, and now here she was being yelled at by the one man she had ever truly loved. Plus there was a rumor that the *New York Observer* was working on a fictionalized diary by her that was supposed to be horrendous.

"Don't cry." Trip hated it when women cried. His little sister had been a huge crier and it had made him nuts. Of course, she was becoming a neurosurgeon now, which was even more annoying. In the novel version of his life she would be a meth addict—wait, he couldn't make both the girlfriend and the sister meth addicts. That wouldn't work. He could, however, put the sister in a cult. He loved books where people were in cults. Maybe the sister would be a vampire. No, that would be a bit much.

Candy perked right up, still crying but suspiciously less, as if perhaps her tears were a theatrical affectation of someone who wasn't actually upset. "You know, everything I'm doing I'm doing for you."

"And what exactly are you doing?" Trip sat down at the small table next to the kitchen island in his huge loft.

"I can't tell you yet but it's something that is going to blow you away. You are going to be impressed. Very, very impressed by what I am doing."

Trip could feel something stir in him. He was working on something even bigger, and he felt slightly annoyed that Candy thought she was going to put *him* on the map. *He* was going to put *him* on the map. Trip thought about what he was doing, what he was working on. The Kingly drama, and all the feeder funds. This thing would rock all their lives. But he needed a way in. He needed more proof. He had a hunch but he needed to be sure. He knew that Petra was a loose cannon, a crazy, a girl who would tell all the family secrets. If only he could find her, which so far he could not. And he had looked. He had hung out outside the town house but no one had come out or gone in, except his lordship. This struck Trip as odd. Most people of Kingly's enormous wealth had multiple maids and drivers and dressers and hairdressers and cooks and butlers, and here was the town house on Seventy-eighth Street with almost no one coming and going. It made no sense, unless things were already unraveling, unless the scheme had already started running out of money.

Which was why he had to start getting frantic. He might be running out of time and he knew he had to get to Petra before the authorities did. He had to find her. The city had never felt so enormous. He had gone to her hairdresser, to her nail salon, to the European coffee place five blocks from her house. No one had seen Petra Smith Kingly. He had gotten desperate.

It was unlikely that Candy would know her. But Candy and her mother were the kind of Manhattan people who knew everyone. Walking down the street with them was incredibly annoying, as people were always stopping them to say hello or hanging out of black SUVs waving. Trip joked that she was like the mayor. Maybe Candy knew someone who knew Petra, or maybe Candy had at least heard something.

"Have you ever heard of Petra Smith Kingly?" He had to be smart about the way he talked about it with Candy. He didn't want to tell her why he was asking. He didn't want to give away the amazing story that was going to make him famous. He knew that Candy was ruthless enough to scoop him if given half a chance, and even though she was pretty incompetent when it came to journalism, she was viciously competitive, so much so that she could possibly scoop him just to show she could.

"Where have I heard that name before?" Candy thought for a minute. Had she gone to Harvard with her? Had she been friends with her mother? Then she realized that Dick had been saying the name in his sleep, murmuring it frantically, as if it were his Rosebud, his sled. She hated sleds.

She gave him a puzzled look.

"What?"

"Why do you want to know?" She had the power again and it felt good.

"Do you know her?"

"I want to know why. Why do you want to know if I know her?"

"Forget it."

Candy didn't want to lose that power. "I will tell you one name of a person who I think knows Petra Smith Kingly but then I want immunity."

"Immunity?" Trip tried not to roll his eyes. Sometimes Candy really seemed like a moron to him.

"Yes, immunity."

"What, pray tell, does immunity entail?" Was he being patronizing? She suspected so.

"Immunity means that you can't ask me any questions, none at all. You can't ask me how I know the person I am about to mention or why I know him or anything. You get the name but you aren't allowed to ask me any more questions, okay?"

Trip nodded. He assumed this was all bullshit that would lead up to nothing, but you never ever knew. And the Roses did know everyone. Besides, he was getting sick of waiting on Seventy-eighth Street staring at the town house trying to look like he was doing something that wasn't spying. "Fine."

"Nothing. You promise? You can't ask me anything about how I know him or why I know him, or who also knows him, nothing at all. I need you to promise me that you will ask me nothing."

"I swear."

"Dick Greenbaum."

Trip dropped his mug on the floor, where it shattered, but Trip was too shocked to lean over and pick it up. Instead he just sat there dumbfounded, silent.

A minute passed. It was probably only a few seconds but the silence of it, the absolute emptiness of it, totally enveloped both of them. Candy looked down to see that her hands were shaking. She realized that she had done absolutely the wrong thing. If she could have just untold the secret. . . . But it was too late, the mug had been shattered.

Trip looked right into Candy's ferret-esque brown eyes. Candy could have been a great beauty if she had a slightly shorter forehead and a slightly thinner nose. He had to ask the question quickly before she had time to cook up a good story. That was the thing with Candy. If you gave her too much time she would cook something up, something plausible enough to make Trip doubt himself instead of her. Trip looked at her. He realized he was slightly afraid of her; there was something about the way she looked at him. She was ruthless in the way he was ruthless. She was all prose over people, all fame over family. She was a sellout in the deep recesses of her soul. "Okay, so you're having an affair with Dick Greenbaum, is that what it is?"

Candy looked away.

"So I'm right. You're having an affair with Dick Greenbaum."

It was Candy's turn to panic. "I said I wouldn't talk about it. You said you wouldn't ask." Candy started to get indignant, but Trip and Candy knew that Candy's indignation was a sign that she was trying to hide something. "Do you remember what we just said about immunity? Remember that?"

"So how long have you been sleeping with him?"

"I don't know what you mean. Dick Greenbaum's daughter is a patient of my mother's and I do not screw her patients."

"Your mother told you that?"

"Of course."

"That is appalling. She isn't supposed to tell you who she sees. It is disgusting. She should lose her license for that."

Realizing that she had done something wrong that might endanger her one source of designer handbags, she backpedaled. "Of course my mother didn't tell me. I just saw him coming out of her office sometime. That's all. She never told me anything. After all, my mother is on the ethics committee. She is very, very, very ethical. Very."

"So when did you start sleeping with him? And why? Are you into money now?" It seemed amazing to her that she had once turned her nose up at town cars and fabulous hotel rooms that rented for thousands of dollars a day. "Are you all about money over fame? You know he is never going to leave his wife for you. He is famous for his affairs but he never leaves his wife for them. They will be together forever. They have one of the most famous, most dysfunctional marriages in all of The Bank's history."

Candy frowned. "I love you."

"So you sleep with Dick Greenbaum. Nice way of showing it. It's like me saying I love you so I am going to sleep with Condoleezza Rice. Actually, Condi is much hotter than Dick Greenbaum, but not my point. No, wait, fucking Dick Greenbaum is like me sleeping with Madeleine Albright or Golda Meir."

"Who is Golda my . . . what?"

"Oh, my God." Trip got up to get a broom. "I think you should move out."

Candy wasn't sure if he was kidding or not. The seriousness of his mood, of his rage and his utter betrayal, had not hit her yet. "What?"

"I want you to move out."

"What?"

"I need to work. I can't do this. I'm busy with the blog, I need to focus."

"But!"

"It's obvious that you are not in this relationship."

"But I do love you."

"But you're sleeping with Dick Greenbaum!"

"But I'm doing it for you, for the story, for your blog. I wanted to find out all the secrets of The Bank. I wanted to bring down The Bank. I wanted to do it for you."

Trip didn't believe her. In his own way, Trip was a very wounded person.

"I think you should get out."

"But I did this for you."

"I want you to move out."

"But you never said you wanted me to not sleep with other people. In fact, when I would ask you for a commitment you would say no. Don't you remember? You would say you weren't ready, you didn't want to, you weren't sure. And now here we are and you want me to move out. You're my soul mate. I did this for you. This is your story, this is for you." She started crying. She looked into his eyes. "Please, I love you. I will die without you. You are everything to me. Please. Please!"

"No, and I don't want to talk about it anymore. You make me sick. He is, like, a hundred years old. And you are a whore. You know that, right? You can call yourself anything you want—postmodern sex kitten, my ass. You are a whore and I hope I never see you ever again."

Trip McAllister was actually a man of very few bad acts. And so not many things haunted him. When he died many decades later as a man with many children and grandchildren, few things would weigh on him the way this tirade would. And until he died, until that moment all those many years later, Trip would replay his unkindness again and again. Had he really said he never wanted to see her again? Had he really called her a whore? Had he really said that she made him sick? Was he really the kind of person who was capable of that kind of cruelty, of words that were that awful? He didn't think of himself as that kind of person, but who does?

For a serial killer, Daisy wasn't particularly sneaky and she wasn't particularly stealthy. She was (of course) afraid of getting caught, but she had an oddly fatalistic attitude about it. So much of her life had sort of happened to her. She also fancied herself as a slightly less awful murderer because she operated under a kind of moral code. She was, after all, a mother, and she knew that part of being a mother was modeling behavior for her daughters to follow. She didn't want them growing up to be people with bad morals and values, vapid girls who married rich men and spent their days shopping and abusing their staff.

So when Daisy happened on Dick's BlackBerry, she paused. Should she read it or not? Aside from the moral issues, she was very worried about what she might find in his emails. It was exponentially less painful to just not know.

On the other hand, there were her mother's words drilling a hole in her brain. Daisy had been spending a lot of time with her mother, which had been surprisingly good for both of them. Her mother had said again and again that it was Daisy's responsibility to keep an eye on Dick. After all, now Daisy knew the score. She knew that Dick had a wandering eye. Daisy's mother had confessed to her that her father had also had a wandering eye and that Daisy's mother had had to take extraordinary measures to keep him from straying. Daisy had inquired no further, because she doubted her mother's extraordinary measures were the same as hers. That said, she hoped not to find out.

And so, standing there in the bedroom that night, as Dick bathed his hard-earned hemorrhoids (he had gotten them the way all rich Jewish men got them, from a nasty, totally uncontrollable case of irritable bowel syndrome that sent him into fits of pain whenever the S&P plunged more than fifty points) in a warm salt bath, Daisy Greenbaum crossed into spying and read his emails and text messages from Candy Ross Rose. And when she went off to her office to Google this Candy Ross Rose, there she discovered that her husband was cheating on her yet again, with a twenty-one-year-old half-naked girl who was actually writing a blog about the affair, and the name that she had given her husband, the blog name that Candy Ross Rose had given Dick Greenbaum, was Mr. Big Money. Mr. Big Money, how derivative. But perhaps it was fitting for Mr. Big Money to have a derivative pseudonym when he did in fact write derivatives.

$\mathcal{I}$t wasn't such an unusual occurrence for Raja to stop by after she left the office. This time she was carrying several huge boxes of stuff that Dick had left and felt he needed to skim that night, stuff that "absolutely could not wait." So she had schlepped in a car service car, through massive traffic, to the Upper East Side. Raja lived in the West Village, like all the other wealthy, fashionable single girls. Ah, the Upper East Side, convenient to nothing but one's shrink. Not that she was supposed to have a shrink. Her parents would have died if they had known that she saw a shrink. She was supposed to have certain things—a gazillion-dollar weeklong Indian wedding, a degree (or two) from Harvard, a few Chanel suits, a serious work ethic. A shrink was not one of those things.

And now here she was standing in the kitchen of her rich and slightly insane boss, staring at his wife as she jumped from her computer to greet her.

"I'm sorry, I didn't mean to frighten you," Raja said. She could barely see Daisy over the stack of boxes she was holding.

Daisy jumped up from the kitchen table and slammed the lid of her laptop shut. "No, you didn't frighten me. I was just wasting time. The Internet, what a time suck."

"I didn't mean to interrupt." Raja was one of those people who was always apologizing.

"No, I was just spacing out." Daisy happened to also be one of those people who was always apologizing.

"I was just dropping off some things for Dick."

Daisy was staring at Raja's face. She wondered if Raja had ever slept with her husband. It seemed like everyone had. Had she as well? But Raja seemed not capable of doing something so amoral as sleeping with another woman's husband.

Raja noticed that Daisy was just standing there staring at her, so she interrupted. "Are you okay?"

Daisy paused. Could she trust Raja? No, she could not trust Raja. "How is life at The Bank?"

"Fine. You know how busy he's been. He's been working such long hours." Raja looked away. Daisy decided to ignore whatever that look might have meant. "Not that I'm complaining, but right now it's been a little crazy."

Daisy looked absently at Raja. "Will you have a drink with me? Dick is in the bath and he probably won't be done for a few minutes."

Raja obliged. She was feeling so friendless, so lonely, so isolated, and so uncomfortable in the world. She longed to be home. She longed to be anywhere but friendless Manhattan, soulless The Bank. "Absolutely."

And so the two ladies sat with each other and drank a glass of scotch. Neither of them loved scotch but Raja didn't want to offend her host and Daisy didn't have the energy to walk into the study to get the vodka. "I am so worried about this economy. What's going to happen? Dick doesn't really want to talk about it but I know it's looking really, really bad."

And here it was, Raja's opening to tell Daisy Greenbaum her biggest secret, the thing that had been tormenting her since she had first noticed it, the crime that Dick Greenbaum was committing. Perhaps if she told it to Daisy, then Daisy could stop Dick, could stop this culture of corruption, this culture of dishonesty. "You know what I am worried about?"

"No, what?"

"Well, we have this system where we write off the debt." She didn't want to out Dick right away. She was going to build up to it. But she also wanted Daisy to know the truth, the horrible secret that she would otherwise go to her grave with.

"Oh, yes, writing off level three capital. Is that what you are talking about?" Daisy said casually.

Raja paused, digesting the possibility that her deep, dark secret was something that was fodder for dinner table conversation at the Greenbaum house. To say she had been a mess would be the understatement of the global economic slowdown; Raja hadn't slept in a week. She kept running the numbers. She kept examining the scenarios, one worse than the next. That was, in fact, what she was talking about. "How do you know about that?"

"Dick talks about it all the time. He doesn't like to do it but he feels he must. After all, there will be major consequences if he lets the balance sheet explode. Everyone does it but it's really, quote, questionable math, unquote. But what are you going to do?" Daisy said casually.

Raja was totally shocked and for a second or two she just sat there speechless. And then she realized that perhaps Daisy Greenbaum had a different sense of morality than she did. Perhaps this whole insane world had a different sense of morality than she did.

Daisy sighed. "Dick says they do it big-time over at Morgan."

Candy was shocked at how little she had brought to his house: a few books, a few magazines (those she would leave), a toothbrush, fancy European toothpaste that cost eleven dollars, some underwear, a silver bikini that she had posed in for photos once long ago. She loved that bikini. She might leave it so he could find it one day and remember how much he missed her, how hot she was. She looked at herself in the long mirror in the closet. She had it all, body and brains. She didn't have to worry. She could trust in her magnificent body and her enormous intellect—she would find someone better than Trip. And Trip would be an anecdote, relegated to the world of people she had at one time had feelings for, or perhaps for no apparent reason loved.

He would see her on the cover of a magazine, on the cover of *Vogue*. Maybe not *Vogue* but some fabulous magazine, and he would feel sorry, very sorry.

She was going somewhere, and looking at herself in that mirror, she knew she would someday be famous. It wasn't a question; it was her truth, it was what her inner child screamed for. Even the creepy psychic she had seen when she was on a dumb family vacation, even that woman had said she would someday be famous, and she would. And when she was famous and married and rich, she would call Trip and let him know how she had made it and he had not, and now who was sorry?

She left the shiny bikini folded on the bed, and below it she left her notes for the Dick Greenbaum story. Those notes were useless now. She certainly wasn't going to write a story about him now. She might marry him, she might steal him away from his wife, but she certainly wasn't going to sell him down the river. So why leave the notes if she needed him, if she was going to run off with him? Because she wanted Trip to see what she could do, what she was, what he was losing. Besides, he would never be able to finish the story. There were too many loose ends, too much that was just conjecture, libelous. In fact, in the whole time she had known Dick Greenbaum the relationship had produced more questions than answers. She knew that he had more of a conscience than most of his colleagues, but she wasn't sure that relative morality was quite enough to qualify him as a good guy. Ultimately the story was sordid enough to taint all who came in contact with it. There was enough damaging information to make even the good guys look pretty questionable.

She heard her phone buzz, and she looked down at her BlackBerry with glee: three new messages from Dick Greenbaum. It was all going to be okay. She was overcome by the familiar feeling of getting what she wanted, even as she was convinced that the outcome would be otherwise. It was all going to work out for her, just like things always worked out for her. As she looked at the text messages, she started to get giddy, because they were implying that perhaps Dick was too hasty when he said he would never leave Daisy. Maybe he might, maybe he had to talk things over with her, maybe they could figure something out. And as Candy left Trip's loft for the last time, she thought, Fuck you, you asshole. Soon I'll be living on Park Avenue, soon I'll be covered in jewels, soon I'll have blowouts every single day.

𝒥t was getting late on Park Avenue. Maids were fighting with frying pans, cooks were struggling with sauces, nannies were battling spoiled children. Raja left without waiting for Dick. She was pretty tipsy at that point and she figured she might be better off not waiting for Dick to get out of the bath. Daisy had thought little about Raja declining her invitation to stay for dinner. She didn't have time to worry about the nuanced moods of Dick's employees.

Easton and Avery and Grandma were all snuggling on the sofa watching a movie in the den. As Daisy walked into her den, her feet enjoyed the feel of the lush Stark carpeting beneath them, and she looked with shame at all the beautiful material possessions about her. She didn't deserve this carpet, this flat-screen TV, this square of Park Avenue. The twins and Grandma seemed happy, proving that material possessions worked for some members of the Greenbaum household; perhaps not for its matriarch, but other things worked for her—things more expensive than Stark carpeting.

She was surprised to see Dick sitting on the floor next to the girls. He was working on his computer but he was home, and with the girls, and for a second her brain flooded with serotonin. Ah, domestic bliss, life was good . . . and she remembered her errands.

"Hi, darlings, can I borrow Daddy for just two seconds?"

The girls looked up, and Easton answered cheerfully, "Of course, Mummy!"

Dick frowned. "Does this have to be done this minute? Does everything have to be done the minute you want or need it to be done?"

"Darling?" Daisy frowned in a way that reminded him just how much power she actually wielded.

Dick looked at his computer then back at his wife. He took a deep breath. And then he got up and walked into her study.

She had the website up already. It wasn't Zero Hedge, the one site that Dick actually read. He didn't recognize the font, the color, the little icons on the screen; he wasn't able to make out the face on the head of the bikini-clad body, but if he had . . .

"Sit down."

"Listen, Daisy, I am totally crazed, things are totally . . ."

Loudly but calmly, Daisy ordered, *"Sit down."*

Dick sat. She pushed the chair in so it was right next to the desk and then she said, "She calls you Mr. Big Money."

Dick started looking at the words on the screen. Many of them were erotic, but he still had trouble focusing, then he scrolled up to look at the half-naked photo that served as a backdrop for the blog and he turned as white as a sheet. The room started spinning. He could feel his palms wet with perspiration. She was going to murder him. He could protect himself, couldn't he? Wasn't there something he could do, something to save himself? He didn't want to die, and besides, he earned lots of money. What would she do without him? What would happen to her, to the children, to their grandchildren? What kind of legacy was that? Could he say that to her? Would it flip her out, drive her into rage? What could he do? What should he do? He was smart, smart with numbers anyway, not really so smart with people, but he was charming . . . Oh, my God, she was going to mur-

der him! He was, for someone of his advanced age, still totally and utterly and completely afraid of death. Death filled him with panic. The
idea of no longer filling his custom-made suits, of no longer hailing
taxis, of no longer sitting at his table at the Four Seasons, of no longer
overtipping the doormen at Christmas—the idea of him no longer
being, of ceasing to exist—filled him with so much panic that it made
him actually see stars. Well, if not stars, then little flecks of colored
light around his eyes.

"So." Dick looked at Daisy. He had to be smart about this. He had
to play this right, because now he was playing for something big. He
was playing for his life. Dick let out a breath. "So, I think you know
how sorry I am. How terribly, totally, and utterly sorry I am."

Daisy looked at him. He could take her. He was stronger than she
was. But he would not be able to keep his guard up for the rest of their
lives. Sooner or later, she would find him sleeping and wrap a plastic
bag around his head or shoot him with a .45 or push him off someone's terrace. Sooner or later, she'd get him: that he was sure of. So he
threw himself on her mercy.

"I am weak and stupid. I am totally, utterly, completely sorry. This
will never ever ever ever . . ."

Daisy put her hand on his arm. "Listen to me. I will say this once
and once only. I am going to take care of this for you, and then that is
it." She turned to walk out of the room. Dick stared at the computer,
dumbfounded.

"But wait."

"What?" Daisy frowned at him.

"I'm sorry."

Daisy opened the door of her office to leave.

"I am sorry, though."

"So am I. I'm sorry too." Dick didn't like the sound of that. That
didn't sound promising. Why was she sorry? Daisy turned the hand-
hammered brass doorknob. She had found them in a little shop that

was owned by an aging socialite whom Daisy was pretty sure had been sleeping with Dick. But she had bought the doorknobs anyway.

"Wait, Daisy, wait." It was a rare dynamic, something that had up until a few months ago never happened in their marriage, something that was happening more and more, as Daisy continued to take back the night. All of a sudden he was begging her to wait for him.

"What?"

"What about . . ." He couldn't ask her if she was going to murder him. People didn't ask questions like that, and besides, he didn't really want to know the answer if, God forbid, it was yes. And how could he really trust a no anyway? She changed her mind all the time. Today's must-have became tomorrow's castoff, today's best friend was tomorrow's worst enemy. She looked unsettled. Black hair matted around her face, slight rings under her eyes as if she had been crying and rubbing them (which she undoubtedly had).

"What, Dick?" She sounded so tired and for a moment he realized that he had made her that way and it made him slightly sad. This marriage thing had been hard on her; and it had been harder on her than on him, and he had been really cruel to her. And he could see it in the way she had started to wear slightly around the seams, the eyes, the mouth, the places that used to be soft and smooth and young-looking.

"Daisy?"

"What is it?" The money had taken its toll on her in a way that it had not on him. He still had a soul. It was deteriorating rapidly but it was still there. But Daisy had that hollowed look to her, as if her soul had been sucked out the window the last time the G5 hit forty thousand feet. The sheer facts of her life, the murders, the constant status anxiety, all of it had made her a sliver of the person she had once been. He was suddenly flooded with compassion for her. She was just doing what she could do to survive the best way she knew how.

"Can I please hold you?" And one time Daisy might have thought that was a stupid ploy, but not today. She nodded and he took her in his hands and started to stroke her hair and he whispered to her, "I will make up for this, you will see. I will make up for this. I will make up for this. I will never ever do this to you, never again." But it was easy to say that, she thought. It might have even been easy to do that, but he didn't have to go and end a life over it, and she did. As she left the room her heart felt heavy with the thought that that night there would be one less breathing blogger in the borough of Manhattan.

$\mathcal{T}$rip was sure that Candy would come back, would come home, even though he had told her not to. He was sure she would come back anyway because she was just that kind of girl, the kind that comes back even when you tell her not to, because you think you don't want her to come back. He sat in his leather armchair looking out the window into the skyscraper-filled sky, the area of lower Manhattan that was, at that hour, totally deserted. He choked on a cigar and drank a scotch. It was yellowish and bitter and tasted nothing like butterscotch. He thought back to his teens and wondered intermittently if possibly he had started drinking scotch with the hopes that it actually tasted like butterscotch. And that perhaps there was a piece of him that was always profoundly disappointed when he took a sip of scotch and it didn't taste like butterscotch.

But she didn't come back, not at midnight, not at one, not at two. He watched TV. He looked at the string bikini she had left him. It was actually made of surprisingly cheap material, and this kind of shocked him; he always thought of her as such a spender. He drank more. He thought about looking at the papers under the bikini. But he didn't.

He watched the night janitors work at the *Watchtower,* he watched the mops move silently over the floors.

He watched more TV.

He drank more.

He thought about calling his mother, but it was four in the morning.

He looked at the papers under the bikini. He was sure there was something profoundly awful in those pages, like a suicide note or some kind of awful, badly written letter, the kind that was filled with clichés and revealed just how shallow the author's emotions really were.

But he looked at them. He opened up the pages and was surprised at how compelling they were. There were pages and pages of notes on Dick Greenbaum. Sure, she had been fucking him and there were notes about that: intriguing sexual peccadillos, etc. But more than that, there were just pages and pages of details, of various mishandlings of business deals, of the prop desk doing slightly illegal things, things that were not okay. And while there was nothing that was so bad on its own, the package together could have brought down the house of The Bank in a large and profound way. It was perhaps the first time that Trip was really surprised by Candy.

He lay there reading, and eventually he slid into slumber. It was one of those hot, alcohol-induced sleeps. He found himself vacillating between sweating and freezing. He could feel himself slipping in and out of sleep, in and out of waking. And in his dreams, in the pictures that flashed before his eyes, he saw Candy, with her brown hair down her back, wearing the metallic bikini, and she looked beautiful with her large, round breasts. He even thought in the dream that this was the kind of girl he could bring home with him, the kind he could marry, the kind he could end up with forever and ever. And he was going to tell her all these things about how he had been cruel and wrong and how now everything would be different and wonderful. But he didn't have time, because just a few seconds later he found her unconscious on the floor of the bathroom, covered in blood. And he took her in his arms and became covered in her sticky, sticky blood, the kind that was viscous and thick, the kind that was filled with white cells and red cells and cells of every kind and description.

And then a few hours later he was woken by the sound of what he thought was his alarm but was really his phone ringing again and again. It was her mother, the mad shrink, the consummate social climber, the money-hungry sellout who might one day publish her memoirs, and she said, "What the hell have you done to my daughter?"

"She's gone. She left me." At that moment he realized he absolutely knew where she was. If she wasn't with her mother, then she had to be with Dick Greenbaum in some hotel.

"She told me she would be right back, but that was ten hours ago." She sounded frantic and Trip wondered why. Candy was a big girl, and she had pulled all-nighters since she was in middle school, fucking her parents' friends, even her own shrink, in the hopes of showing them all.

"I am sure she is totally . . ." Trip cleared his throat. He took the tone he usually used with hysterical parents, the tone he almost always talked to his mother in. ". . . totally fine. You know, your daughter is a big girl. She's probably just at a friend's house."

Dr. Rose didn't care much for Trip. He came from a family of morons—rich morons, but morons just the same. That said, she felt a certain warmth in her heart for him today. He was kind and she hadn't particularly been nice to him. He was just a young kid, trying to make it in a world filled with masters of the universe. She couldn't help but feel for these little adults with their smooth skin and their endless ambition. It was not necessarily going to be a happy ending for these kids. They were up against an impossible dream. They would never be as successful as their parents. They were destined to be footnotes, anecdotes, perhaps dinner party fodder, but they would never have their ambition realized, they would never be able to afford to live the way their parents lived, they would live in prefab houses, they would move to the lesser suburbs on the edge of Westchester. They would be driven from the land of the superrich with matzoth on their backs. "But Trip, I just have a feeling. I have this bad feeling. I've never had a feeling like this." Trip wanted to interrupt her, because he also had that same feeling, the feeling that the life had already been snuffed out.

Trip wondered if every family of every missing girl had that feeling, that sense that it was in fact over, that there was no need to look, that whatever they would find would be too horrible to comprehend. He knew where she was, he knew she was in some hotel, the Palace or some place downtown maybe. Right? But there was some feeling he had somewhere deep down that Dick Greenbaum would not let Candy bring down the house of The Bank, or perhaps someone higher up than he was or perhaps something else, but he did have a feeling, deep down, below the jealousy, that there was a distinct possibility that he would read about Candy in the paper tomorrow.

Trip hated himself for lying but he did it anyway. "I'm sure she's fine. I'm sure she's just at a friend's house. Go back to your patients." He paused. If he was going to lie, he might as well go for it. "They need you, they need all of you." He felt like he was going to throw up. What kind of person talked like this? He felt disgusted. He wasn't a bad person. Or at the very least he didn't consider himself to be a bad person. But what he absolutely was not was a liar, and so in some ways this was the worst day of his life, and it had only gotten started and he sensed that it was only going to go downhill from there. "Please, Dr. Rose, please do one thing."

"What?" Dr. Rose felt sad for a minute that she was too old for Trip. There was something so profound and sensitive about this young man. This was a man that her daughter should marry.

"Please throw yourself into your work. Be there for those children and please, please, call me as soon as you hear from her."

"Of course."

As Trip hung up the phone he could not have felt worse if he had actually murdered her. He could not believe that he had become the one thing in the world he hated more than all others, the thing that he had promised himself upon first reading *The Catcher in the Rye* at Choate he would never be, the one thing that made him want to throw up green bile. And here he was, looking at the receiver, listening to the dial tone loud and clear and thinking to himself, How could I have become such a phony?

CHAPTER *Eleven*

October 3, 2008

Dow closes down 157.47 points to 10,325.38

S&P closes down 15.05 points to 1,099.23

The night that her mother murdered her shrink's daughter, Avery Greenbaum could not sleep. She had had sleep problems since she was old enough to formulate worries. For a long time she would run into her parents' bedroom and wake them up and then demand either to have one of them sleep in her bed or to join them in the marital bed (which had become far less marital since their daughter had started sleeping in it), but then Daisy had gotten smart and she had started paying (yes, paying) Avery not to wake her up, and, fortunately for Daisy, it worked. Unfortunately for Easton, Avery now woke Easton up.

"I can't sleep, Easton."

Easton was a deep sleeper. And that night was no exception. She was dreaming about what she dreamed about every single night: riding. She was dreaming about that feeling when the horse takes off, when you stand, your legs gripping the belly of the enormous beast, when you hold your hands in its glorious mane, when the noise stops and all there is is the sound of air screaming past your ears and then hoofbeats and the rhythm of an animal and the earth.

"Can you sleep?"

And the horse she was riding that day in the glorious dream was a massive horse, one of those giant seventeen-hand beasts, all white with only a brown muzzle. She had seen the horse around the stable. She had been told it was an Arabian that belonged to the Saudi royal family. She had never seen anyone but the people who worked at the barn ride the horse, though she had been told by another little girl that the horse was the favorite of a young prince who might come to America to go to school. The story seemed improbable, too Disney.

"Easton, are you awake? I can't sleep." Avery looked over to her sister's bed. It was a big room, but even from all the way across it, Avery could tell her sister was sleeping peacefully.

Easton was trying to hold on to the horse, to the dream, to the sound of the hoofbeats on the sand, but Avery was ripping her away.

"I think you are awake."

Easton looked dreamily at her sister. "I am now."

Avery leaped onto her sister's bed. "I am sorry to wake you but I was getting lonely. And scared."

Easton rolled her eyes. "There's nothing to be scared of."

"Did you feel something weird tonight?" Avery believed that she and Easton had magical powers because they were twins and special.

Easton rolled her eyes again.

"You know, I felt something."

Easton looked at Avery. "I'm tired. You can sleep in my bed if you want, but no talking!"

Avery frowned at her sister. "Don't you think Mom and Dad have been weird lately?"

"No. Go to sleep. You're so dramatic."

"Dad sat with us and watched *iCarly*. Dad watched *iCarly*. Our dad watched a show on Nick."

Easton shook her head. "Maybe Mom told him to."

"Or maybe..." Avery paused. She hated to upset her twin, her perfect twin. "Or maybe they are getting divorced!"

Easton was more vulnerable than usual. She was still in a soft blue cast, she was still using crutches, and she was worried about the winter and the ice and snow, and the fact that her feet still couldn't really fit into shoes. And Easton was devastated about losing the one thing she loved, the one thing that made her feel like a real person and not a paper doll dressed in a gray uniform. "They can't possibly be."

"Why not?"

Easton looked at her sister. Easton was not stupid. Just because she was happy and good at school, that did not make her stupid. It did make her sister and mother think she was stupid—well, not stupid, not exactly, she couldn't really put her finger on what it was, but they thought there was something slightly weird about her. It was as if the thing that made her normal in the eyes of everyone else in the world made her totally and utterly freakish at home, and that frustrated her and made her slightly more apt to antagonize Avery. "Because..." Easton looked at the walls of their room. They had been done in a very subtle, very chic wallpaper that had been printed in France. Their carpet was silk and felt like heaven under their feet. Everything around them was beautiful and perfect. Well, not everything. "Mom has seemed sadder."

Avery was annoyed by this comment. Avery was the one who was supposed to be closer to their mom; Easton was closer to their dad. "I think they are definitely getting divorced, and you know what I bet is going to happen?"

Easton paused. "No, what?"

Avery looked at Easton. "They are going to split us up and you are going to go with Dad and I am going to go with Mom."

"No."

"Yes." Avery paused. "After all, you are Daddy's favorite. And as his favorite . . . he'll obviously want you."

"Not true."

"Truth!" Avery smiled.

Easton started crying. "I don't want them to get divorced and I don't want to move and I don't want to go and live with Dad and never see you or Mom again. What is going to happen to me? I don't think I can do it."

"Don't worry, honey, you'll grow to love living with Dad," Avery said in mock compassion.

Easton kept sobbing.

"It'll be fun, except for all the long hours that Daddy works. But otherwise. Nina will come with Mom, of course; the nanny always goes with the mother."

"No!"

"Don't worry, darling sister, Mom and I will come and visit you, unless . . ." Easton looked panicked. "Unless Daddy moves you somewhere. Unless Daddy moves you to some weird place. You know, it's possible that Daddy will take you to go and live somewhere like Saudi Arabia. You know they hate Jews there." Now Easton was really crying. Meanwhile, Dick Greenbaum was walking to the kitchen feeling as if cancer were eating away at his stomach. He thought about death. If he died, who would take care of the girls? Who would fix the prop desk? Who would fix the system? He thought back to his discovery about writing off the level 3 debt. How he had been so incredibly dismayed, horrified even, by the possibility that his people, his glorious bank, would mislead their shareholders. He thought back to himself just a few months back, so indignant, so convinced that the financial system needed to be healed and that he was the man to do it.

Now he laughed at that man, so utterly hapless, riding high on his moral high horse. Dick Greenbaum had been thrown from his moral high horse, and could not be clearer as he was waiting for his wife to come home from murdering his girlfriend. At least that's what he suspected. Of course, Candy hadn't even ever quite risen to the rank of girlfriend. Perhaps she could have, had she stayed alive. Easton's crying cut through all his musings about the horrible things that grown-ups do to one another.

Dick opened the door to the girls' room. They had put two enormous bedrooms together to make a giant lair, which they'd tastefully decorated, only to have it filled with tacky bubble-gum-pink things that Miley Cyrus had been hawking on the Disney Channel. "What is going on here?" Dick Greenbaum said, as if it were not three o'clock in the morning.

Easton sat up. She hoped her father hadn't heard her say that she didn't want to live with him, because the truth was, she loved her father very much and she did not want to be cruel.

"Nothing," Avery said. She was the more guilty one. She was the one who could get in trouble for this whole thing if there was one person who could get in trouble.

Dick was wearing blue pajamas. They were the pajamas that movie star dads wore in 1950s movies, ironed and fresh and creased in all the right places. "Then, why is Easton crying?"

Avery was silent. Dick knew she had done something to cause this.

"I love you, Daddy, but I do not want to live in Saudi Arabia."

"Who is living in Saudi Arabia?"

Easton pointed to Avery. Avery was annoyed. Easton was always good for diming her out. "Well, when you get divorced."

A shock wave went down Dick's spine. Had the girls seen something? Had their mother said something to them? Had someone told them about the website? About Mr. Big Money? Had they caught on to his many affairs? Or did they know that their mother was a murderer? Was that what happened? Dick felt himself turning ashen. He had to strike out against this rumor, he had to present them as a united front, even though they might not necessarily be united. He needed to present them as such, he needed to make a strong stance. "Why on earth would you think something like that?" And then just for good measure he added a fatherly chuckle. It was the kind of chuckle a father who slept in movie star pajamas made. It was filled with fatherly confidence.

Easton looked at her sister. "Avery said . . ."

"Not true! *Not true!*"

"Look—" Dick paused. He didn't want to get mad at Avery. He didn't have the time for, or the interest in, chastising her. "No one is getting divorced. Your mother and I are very happy." He sat down on the bed with the girls. "Your mother and I love each other very much." Almost too much, he thought to himself. After all, Mommy was off murdering anyone who had ever made eyes at Daddy, and Daddy was, well, Daddy seemed to have a problem loving too much as well.

"I was worried," Easton said through the tears.

Avery looked annoyed. Then, seeing which way the tides were turning, she decided to participate. She had to get on this train before it left the station. After all, she was not going to let Easton get all the pity. "I was worried too," Avery said, with infinitely more tears and infinitely more wailing.

Dick looked at his perfect little twins. He had so much to lose, and it was much more than money. He had to keep his family together. Suddenly it was the most important thing in his life: he had to keep together the family that he had been doing his best to destroy for the last few years.

"So you are not going to get divorced?" Easton asked.

"No!" Dick said, hugging both girls in his arms.

"And you are not going to move to Saudi Arabia?" Easton asked.

Avery felt slightly sheepish.

"Why would I move to Saudi Arabia? I don't work in oil. I've never even been to Saudi Arabia. Where did you get that?"

"Nowhere," Easton said, winking at Avery. Avery owed her, and both girls made a mental note of this.

"You know what this is making me think?"

The girls both looked at him. Easton knew what he was going to say but Avery had no idea.

"It's making me think that it is time for you guys to come down to the office and see what it is that I actually do."

Easton frowned. "Dad!"

"No, really, I don't work with oil at all." The idea that their dad worked with something that was an actual existing thing, and not just an amorphous debt product, caught the girls off guard. Easton smiled. Maybe she could get Avery stuck there, ha-ha, that would be funny.

"Daddy, you should take Avery to work with you. Avery is very interested in what it is you do."

Dick smiled. He didn't want to take Avery with him. Avery was the flake. Easton was the one who went to the fancy girls' school; she was the one being bred for the life of excellence. Besides, Easton was the one who wanted to grow up to be just like Daddy. "Okay, great! But Easton wants to work at the prop desk when she grows up."

She had forgotten that she had told that to her mother. Why had she told her mother that? That was dumb. She should have quit while she was ahead. It was because India's dad had been an anti-Semite. She hated that she had said that. She hated it most because it seemed like now her parents wanted her to be interested in whatever it was that their dad did.

Meanwhile, Avery was a little offended that her dad had brushed her off like that. "What about me?"

"Of course I want you to come with me. But more important than that, I want you both to know just how much I love you both and how happy your mother and I are, and how we are never ever ever ever ever going to get divorced. I promise you!"

Easton looked at Avery, as if to say, "Fuck you." Avery looked at Easton as if to say, "I'm sorry." Both girls looked at their father. And their father looked at them, eyes filled with fatherly pride for his two daughters, who were braving the brave new world of extreme afflu- ence without becoming too twittish. Of course, they were only eight. They still had time for eating disorders and drug addiction, not to mention teen pregnancy and mental illness. But today Dick Green- baum had only one mentally ill person to worry about, and that was his wife—his wife who was at that moment murdering the daughter of Avery's shrink, which seemed like profoundly bad timing, after all, right now. Avery needed a shrink, and perhaps more now than ever.

The next day, the sun rose as if nothing had happened, and Daisy got on with it as if she hadn't murdered a twenty-one-year-old girl the night before. Her youngest victim since Hayden, and the earth didn't care. Everything kept going, CNN droning on, pundits punditizing about Sarah Palin and the upcoming election and moose-hunting jokes, and it all kept going. That morning as she brushed her hair she wanted to scream and throw the hairbrush against the mirror. She wanted the mirror to crack in two (the way she had long ago), but she didn't want to wake the kids.

She brushed her teeth with the minty Italian toothpaste that didn't cause cancer. She watched herself brush her teeth. She thought about the night before. It had been one of those nights, dark and cold, filled with the spirits of old northeastern witches. As a child she had believed in God and in witches, and in vampires, and in monsters. She didn't believe in those things anymore. She was as close to a witch as there could ever be; she was as close to a monster as the earth could hold. What was there to be afraid of when you were the scariest thing you could think of?

When she read the *New York Post*, something had been wrong, something had not made sense. For a few seconds Daisy was not sure what it was as she looked over the pictures and SAT scores. They had put together a lot of information in a short period of time and Daisy was surprised, but what she didn't know was that a childhood friend of Candy's worked at the *Post*, and in fact this had quickly become her big break.

But why did she still have this feeling that something was wrong with the facts? And then Daisy realized the *Post* said Candy had been dumped in the river. She hadn't dumped Candy's body in the Hudson. Daisy could not have lifted Candy over the enormous guardrails, could not have deposited her into the swishing river. And yet somehow Candy had gotten stuck in a tugboat's rudder. There was a picture of the boat's captain looking horrified. The caption under his photo said, "Reminds him of 1987."

She tried to remember last night. She closed her eyes and pretended she was back there, so many lifetimes ago. She had never before beaten someone to death, never punched them so many times that the life drained out of them. She didn't think she was actually strong enough to do such a thing but she had been, and now she knew it. She looked at the woman in the mirror, the woman who was capable of shutting off a life before it had even started. Her knuckles were slightly swollen and bruised from the experience. There were cuts, little red marks, places where Candy's nails had dug into her flesh.

She had left Candy in the park, her body slumped over, soft, round and lifeless. She had not dumped her in the river. In fact, the thought had never occurred to her. She had never ever even considered dumping Candy's body in the river. For a minute, her mind wandered, exploring the possibility that maybe someone followed her, that perhaps there was someone out there who knew about her evil deeds. But for some reason Daisy shut her mind tight to this possibility. Instead she assumed that a homeless man or someone else had come and attached another crime to hers, perhaps raping the dead girl or stealing her Cartier watch.

The streets had been empty and dark and for a minute she had worried about her own safety, but the odds were slim that she would encounter someone more dangerous than herself.

$\mathcal{L}$andon Stone was sitting next to her mother, but neither woman was speaking. The sound of hair dryers made the possibility of conversation, even idle chitchat, nil. That said, at any pause in the hurricane of hair dryers the ladies would look at each other and try to communicate—often with mixed results. They were sitting where they sat every Saturday early morning in the winter months, side by side on the second floor of the Valery Joseph Salon on Madison Avenue.

"Mother—" Landon looked around to make sure Daisy wasn't behind her. But there were just a few other women at the salon that day, two little old grannies getting outdated helmet-head bouffants and a racehorse-looking Wasp with enormous teeth. Landon assumed Daisy was not friends with the Wasp with enormous teeth because Daisy was a Jew and the two did not meet often (the Wasps stuck to their bunny hops for Sloan-Kettering and the Jews bathed in the glory of all things UJA). What Landon didn't bank on was the unifying factor of extreme wealth—Daisy was rich enough to no longer be considered Jewish. In fact, that racehorse was none other than the current wife of Bowdy Lodge, the mother of Ryland Lodge—the girl, not the motel. "Mother, I just can't get this thought out of my mind."

"Are you still prattling on about that Chopard Happy Watch with the Happy Diamonds? Do you understand how much tuition your father and I pay a year?" Both mother and daughter had stopped calling him "stepdad," with the hopes that it might lead him to leaving all his money to her and not to the clinic for obesity, which had cured him of his fatness.

Landon was embarrassed. "Shush!"

Her mother frowned. She was embarrassed too. She always did that, said too much, was too much. "I'm sorry, darling."

"It's fine." Landon paused, hoping this infraction might be worth the watch, but it was unlikely. "Do you remember Daisy Greenbaum?"

"Who?"

"You remember her. Used to be friends with . . ."

"Oh, yes. I saw her on the street last week. Do you know her husband is the head of some big thing in The Bank? She married well. My God, considering how odd-looking she was, how positively not attractive she is compared to you." Landon's mother was doing it again. She was making Landon feel small, making her feel awful about her inability to marry a millionaire.

"Mom!"

"You know, they live at 740 Park."

"Mom!"

"What? What?"

"Shush. Besides, she's not so great."

"Really? Because I see her picture everywhere. And look at this." Her mother held up a copy of the *New York Post* that she had been idly reading, and pointed out a picture of Daisy with Dick at a benefit on Page Six.

"Didn't you ever think it was weird that she was the last person to see Hayden alive? Don't you think it is a little strange?"

Holly Lodge leaned in. She was watching the ladies in the mirror as she pretended to read *InStyle* magazine. "Why?"

"Well, here's the girl who last saw my sister and . . ." Landon didn't have much else to add. She had been convinced for so long, but now that she thought about it, she didn't even have a single solid fact. She tried to think. She just didn't have a scrap of evidence. She just sort of had a feeling. Could she say that without seeming insane? What could she say? She glanced in her mirror and saw Holly Lodge studying her face, as if she were getting ready to report her facial features to Daisy Greenbaum. Nothing good could come of this.

"Yes, and now she is one of the most powerful girls in New York. You should become her friend."

Holly had trouble controlling her laughter. Landon looked at Holly in horror. *"Mom!"* Landon turned totally red. "Mom! Shush!!!!"

The conversation had only made her madder—maybe she wouldn't be able to prove that Daisy had killed her sister. But she would get back at her anyway. She would find a way. She snatched the *New York Post* off her mother's lap and thought.

$\mathcal{T}$rip McAllister was not totally sure what to do with the *New York Post* that morning. He looked at it and then set it down, picked it up again, and then set it down again, and then he did the very same thing again. It was hard for him to look at the picture, which was a picture of Candy clad head to foot in white ridiculousness from her deb days. It was not a picture that a serious person would allow herself to pose for. They had come from that same dying Wasp world, both of them, and now another one of them was gone.

The cover was its usual screaming red and black, like a nun on fire. The headline proclaimed, MURDERED DEB FOUND FLOATING IN THE HUDSON, then on the second page it showed pictures of Candy in the bikini and said, "Murdered Deb Had Secret Life Writing Sex Blog."

"It was hardly secret," he said aloud in the empty apartment. Just because no one was interested, that didn't mean it was secret.

He put the newspaper down again, and he picked up the *New York Times*. The story was above the fold. God, above the fold in the *New York Times*, that was famous. He went to his computer and typed her name in Google and got pages and pages and pages of hits. Her name alone had gotten two thousand hits in the last ten hours. The story had legs. Candy Ross Rose had legs. Now she could sell that memoir she had been wanting to write—about twenty-four hours too late.

A college friend had called him, a bunch of them actually, all the old gang from Adams House. They were no strangers to death. One of their brethren had ODed at Harvard, another had died suspiciously in Moscow while working for *Forbes* magazine, and one had frozen to death hiking Everest. These kids were bred for speed but, sadly, not for life expectancy. They had encouraged him to solve the mystery. One friend had remarked that the story could be a cover for *The New York Times Magazine;* another had said to aim higher. What about *Vanity Fair?* This was the kind of story that *Vanity Fair* loved. This was his moment to really shine. Of course, the friends offered condolences, but none of them had liked Candy all that much, and this was clear even when she had slipped from this world to the world of the past tense. It was remarked on by one female friend that "she was competitive with the girls, merciless with them, and seductive with the boys, in a cold, calculating way."

One friend, a poet/SAT tutor who lived on the Upper East Side in his parents' maid's room, had mused, "It could not have happened to someone who had deserved it more for seemingly no reason." That cut pretty hard considering that the girl was saying it to Candy Ross Rose's boyfriend, but everyone assumed that he had had the same handful of mixed feelings. Meanwhile, the truth was not that simple.

But it was random violence—right? It wasn't a murder. There wasn't a mystery. She was in the park, in Riverside Park. Maybe buying drugs, nothing hard, maybe pot, it was something that they did all the time, big deal. He would probably buy pot later that day, in Brooklyn.

So perhaps it was just another act of random violence in a city filled with violence. He was surprised there wasn't more violence, with all these people mashed together in such a small space.

And he tried to explain this to his friends who called. He told them that this kind of thing happened. Sure, it wasn't common, but it did happen. People got killed randomly. Wrong time, wrong place. It was a hazard of living in a big city.

And then one friend, Gabe from Adams House, said, "Really? Really, this kind of thing happens all the time?"

Trip looked out the window. "Well, maybe not all the time, but some of the time."

"Some of the time in the eighties . . ." Gabe waited for a laugh. There was none, so he continued, "Do you know anyone who has gotten murdered in the last decade?"

"No, but . . ."

"Pretty young girl from prominent family murdered, turns out she's writing about having an affair with a guy called Mr. Big Money."

Trip could feel the rage rip through him. "Great, right?"

"You know what we call that? Motive."

"You write for a police show, Gabe. The world isn't really like *CSI*, you know."

"First of all, I do not write for a show. I am the show runner for one of the longest-running procedurals of all time."

Trip rolled his eyes. "Yeah, right. Of course."

"I'm just saying there might be a case here." The way Gabe said "case," it was clear that the only interest Gabe had, the only interest anyone seemed to have, in Candy Ross Rose was in her demise. "I wouldn't let this story slip through your fingers."

"Um."

"Look, I'm just saying, maybe I'm being paranoid, but this definitely merits further investigation. Don't you think?"

Trip paused.

"Just find out who Mr. Big Money is, at the very least. My God, man, you used to be a journalist."

Trip flushed with anger. "I am a journalist, a financial journalist."

"Wonderful. You should be very proud. How much money did you make last year, because I made almost a million dollars."

"Yes, but you're a sellout."

"A sellout who beds a different model every night of the week. A sellout who flies NetJets. A sellout who . . ."

"I get your point, thanks." Trip was about to hang up on his friend, though this kind of good-natured teasing was pretty much par for the course, and then, out of nowhere—an epiphany. "I am pretty sure that I know who the guy is."

"Really?" Gabe leaned in. He was housewife-esque in his love of gossip. "Who?"

"She left notes for a story on my bed with a silver bikini. Remember that silver bikini from her photo in *New York* magazine?"

"That was hot. She was hot, in spite of her horrible personality."

"And the notes." Trip started to panic. What had he done with the notes? He had been very drunk last night. So drunk he might have tossed them into the trash. But he found them lying on his bedside table. He must have left them there before he passed out. "Who?" Gabe howled.

"You're not going to know who he is. He's not famous. Or he is only famous in finance. . . ."

"I know finance," Gabe said. He was a touch insulted by the implication of his ignorance.

"Dick Greenbaum."

"Never heard of him."

"Shocking. Look, I gotta go." And it was then that he put it together—the murder, the affair, the story, the fall of the Greenbaums. Trip believed that this all tied in to Dick Greenbaum. And maybe it didn't, maybe he was wrong, but either way it gave him an entrée into the world of the Greenbaums, back into the Garden of Eden. He wanted back in. He was happy. So maybe Candy Ross Rose had died another faceless victim of a violent city, or maybe, maybe, maybe something smelled rotten in Denmark.

And just then, just as the wheels were starting to churn, his phone rang, and on the other end was an Upper East Side socialite named Landon Stone.

CHAPTER *Twelve*

October 6, 2008

Dow closes down 369.88 points to 9,955.50

S&P closes down 42.34 points to 1,056.89

Sir Smith Kingly was pacing back and forth in what he had once hoped would be his grand living room. Of course, that had not happened and his dilapidated town house on East Seventy-eighth Street had remained exactly that—a gutted mess, spilling wires and insulation everywhere. He remembered when he had bought the house, filled with the intention of restoring it to its former glory. Buying the house had been one of those moments in Manhattan life, one of those triumphant moments of dreams and ambitions realized. He remembered the feeling of handing over that check for $15 million. It had been money he was supposed to manage and not spend; the money itself had belonged to a pension fund for retired ambulance workers. But that somehow did not make the moment any less triumphant.

This house was supposed to be his legacy, the place where he could die surrounded by all his pretty things—his wife (now gone), his hand-painted ceiling (the artist was never commissioned), his custom Turkish carpets (who knew what happened to those).

And now everything had changed. Now he was thinking about dying as a way to get out of what was coming.

He was, after all, seventy-five years old. He wasn't greedy. If he could just keep the scheme going a little longer, say, another five or ten years, then he would give it all up and die.

He looked at the big hole in the floor. Through it he could see the exposed beams and, beyond that, the basement. There had been just enough construction to make the place dangerous to live in.

He looked up through the second floor, up to what might have been the children's rooms. He was pretty sure Lady Petra didn't want children, but what if she had changed her mind? What if he had missed his only chance at forever?

He knew it was crazy to think about children at a time like this. Maybe it meant he was slowly losing his mind. Maybe it was all the loose lead paint or all the asbestos. He had always harbored a fear of losing his mind. It had developed as a child after visiting a particularly senile old uncle who had been taken advantage of by his young wife and left with nothing but his title, which he could not sell, as hard as he tried, because the young wife had robbed him of the mineral rights that went along with the title and without which the title was unsellable. He shouldn't be worried about kids. He should be worried about his investors.

At that exact same moment, someone else was thinking about that exact same thing: less than half a mile away, Jacob Friedrich Behrend, the head of the Special Prosecutions Bureau, was holding the elevator for a rather large fellow who was dressed like a gangbanger but with a gut hanging over his waistband. Jacob sighed—few places were as gloomy as 100 Centre Street. From the graying ceiling to the musty smell, from the ancient bathrooms with the rickety stall doors to the building's inhabitants, a graying army of overweight people and their crying children, few places made a person want to give up and die like 100 Centre Street.

Of course, he had tended toward the morose since kindergarten, and perhaps that was his Germanic-Jewish roots growing through the dirt and exposing themselves to the sun. Even though his family had been in this country quietly buying up buildings and eventually entire blocks since the 1850s, his German ancestry seemed to affect him in strange and profound ways. In fact, some of his minions in the Special Prosecutions Bureau called him (behind his back, of course) "Der Führer." He knew he was far from beloved, but he didn't care. Jacob Friedrich Behrend had one agenda. He told people it was protecting the little guy, but really it was becoming more famous and successful than his father. And he had succeeded, in a sense. He was as famous as anyone in the investigative division, but that still wasn't too famous compared to, say, a real celebrity, like Britney Spears. Recently business had been good. He was fresh off the rush of the Dennis Kozlowski and Mark Swartz case. He had put more than $50 million into the state's pocket, which would cover the city's toilet paper budget for a week. But it didn't matter. He had won, and everyone from his little world of the Fifth Avenue Synagogue had seen his glory.

But none of this glory placated his rage toward his white whale, which is what he secretly called the man who he believed was running one of the largest and most profound Ponzi schemes ever.

The problem was that he had had someone on the inside, an accountant, who was now gone. And then he had had someone else on the inside, a secretary who no longer returned his calls. And then he had hit the jackpot when he had met Petra Smith Kingly through one of his wife's crazy charities. And she had been willing to tell him everything. Perhaps a little too willing. She had also disappeared. Perhaps her husband had murdered her. He had never in his career seen someone murder a witness, but that didn't mean it didn't happen, did it?

$\mathcal{B}$ack uptown a few hours later, a brokenhearted mother and a destroyed father sat in their lonely bedroom, fighting. "You understand that this kind of thing is normal when you are processing a loss of this magnitude," Dr. Rose said to her husband.

"Stop shrinking me! I'm not some teenage girl who hijacked her mother's black American Express card."

"I'm not shrinking you."

"Oh, yes, you fucking are, and none of it works in distracting me from the reality, which is that you don't want to have a real funeral for our daughter," her husband said. "And the detectives, we need to put pressure on the detectives. That's the only way things get solved in this city. Didn't you treat Giuliani's son? You have to call him. We need to put pressure on them, we need to make things happen, that is how things get done in this city." They were sitting in the dark, with just the TV flashing blue light across the wall behind it. It was a dark and unremarkable bedroom in a dark and unremarkable brownstone that they had bought for $100,000 in the 1970s. It was a very narrow brownstone, and though their bedroom was on the third floor and faced the garden, it was a very dark garden, surrounded on all sides by skyscrapers. "Do you hear me? We have to put pressure on the police, we have to fight for our daughter." Mr. Rose was not from the city. He had left Oklahoma for Harvard when he was seventeen, but he still believed that the city was a small exclusive club that he would never be able to fully join, and he believed that nothing in New York City happened unless you had connections. He wasn't actually sure what those connections were, but he had a pretty good feeling that everyone else but him had them.

She sighed her best shrink sigh. "I am not going to talk about this anymore."

"But . . . this is not your choice to make. I am her father. I am fifty percent of this. I am sick of you pulling rank on me."

"Pulling rank?" Dr. Rose was exhausted. She didn't want justice. She didn't have time for justice. "Listen to me, I have already lost my daughter. Our son has lost his sister. I just want this whole nightmare over. No more!" She put up her hands as if to shield her face; from what, Mr. Rose had no idea. "No more us being dragged through the cover of the *New York Post* every single day. My daughter's death has already ruined my life. Does it need to ruin my career too?"

He snapped, "I knew this was what this was about. I fucking knew it. This is about all the fancy people that you want as clients and not scaring them off. This has nothing to do with what matters in life— our family." It was more than a little ironic that someone who was so interested in using his wife's connections was chastising his wife for trying to keep them intact.

"Our family matters, but I have worked hard to build my practice."

"Right, and God forbid your daughter's murder scares off one of the Tisches."

Dr. Rose paused. She could feel the rage, and in some small way it made her feel alive. "Look," she stammered. "Look." She paused. Of course he was saying family first. It was easy to say family first. Easy to say it after years of working till midnight, of skiing trips in Vail with the other associates, all to make partner at his white-shoe firm. But it was different for men. Men could be fathers and lawyers. He was expected to have a career. No one held him back, no one chastised him for missing school conferences. Meanwhile, she had gone off and become something her mother could never in her wildest dreams fathom. She had become a famous shrink: a shrink who treated everyone who was anyone's kids, and who wrote books.

Maybe not *New York Times* bestselling books, but regional bestsellers. "I have worked hard for my patients, for my practice, and I am not going to let it go up in smoke because my daughter allowed herself to buy drugs in Riverside Park."

"How can you be so . . ." He had always suspected that deep down she possessed a cold and clammy center, like the inside of an oyster. But something about the way she said what she said made him know this fact, and he was surprised that this felt like a revelation, but it did.

"I gave her everything I could give her and she still became a drug addict. That's on her, not on me." There was something about the way she spoke that smacked of a kind of overtherapized selfishness. She really felt like a member of the me generation. "I make no apologies for the woman I am."

He turned to walk down the creaky stairs of his town house and then he turned back. "We're a terrible match."

It had been five solid days of alliteration-filled *New York Post* covers, each more amusingly grotesque than the last. Five solid days of local coverage devoted to the fall of America's favorite sex-blogging deb, and Trip McAllister couldn't help but feel he was missing his moment. He wasn't a bad person. He had loved her more than anyone else could have due to her rather unpalatable personality. He did not want to besmirch her memory, but he also realized that she would have felt more besmirched by being ignored.

He needed to break the story—Candy's story. But he didn't have enough evidence yet. He needed someone in The Bank to cooperate, to give him the last missing piece. If he could just talk to Dick Greenbaum, he'd have enough leverage. Maybe. But he had no idea how to get inside, though, no idea of where to start; as he had never really been an outsider, he had never had to make an introduction himself or had to cold-call someone. He had never had to do anything that there wasn't an obvious way into. He was very much not a salesman. He had been an analyst, which was basically a person who wrote term paper–like blurbs about companies, and then he had become a blogger, which had made him even less of a "people person."

And he had never had to make an introduction for himself. Sure, he had interviewed for his job at The Bank, but it was an economic boom and he had a good name and a Harvard degree, and he and the guy across the desk both knew that the interview was really a formality. And even after he had lost that job, when those stupid fuckheads at the SEC had unceremoniously censured him, that same day, a mere half hour later, he had received a phone call from an old college friend who invited him to start a blog on his platform. Things had always been that way for Trip: rejected from Princeton, got into Harvard; rejected from medical school, got a great job at The Bank that would eventually pay a million times what being a pimple popper would. So Trip didn't have any idea how to cold-call Dick Greenbaum.

Also, Trip believed (though he knew enough to hide this belief) that everyone in the world hung on every word of his blog, and since he believed this to be true, he was very worried that Dick would harbor hostility toward him because of all the various assaults he had lobbed at his predecessor over the last few years.

So he had gone crying to Daddy. His father was a graying old Boston Brahman who collected maps and sailed and never did a damn thing in his entire life except rise to the level of president at their beach club in Nantucket, which was no great feat as nobody else from a family of "long-standing members" could be bothered to show up for the three meetings a year that took place off season during the times when getting to Nantucket was like being the star in one's own Dickensian drama. But Trip's father had a name—it was one of those melodious names that sounded like beach houses, family compounds, trust funds, private planes, and private clubs, and all sorts of things that even money couldn't buy.

Trip made a real point of never asking his father for anything. He was already filled with resentment toward the man because his father controlled all of his great-grandfather's hard-earned cash. Trip's father had managed to not squander the money, but this was not exactly a huge testament to his brilliance. It also annoyed him that everyone in the family believed his father to be a great genius for getting bank account–like returns while the rest of the world was catching up by getting more aggressive with huge commitments to hedge funds.

Trip had no respect for his father, but he also had no choice; he had to ask his dad to make the call, and of course after some back and forth with his charming young assistant, Trip's dad began a long and seemingly meaningless conversation with Dick Greenbaum, a long and seemingly meaningless conversation in a life filled with long and seemingly meaningless conversations.

Ultimately Dick Greenbaum answered. He answered that he was happy to meet with one of the heirs to such a venerable fortune, a fortune that The Bank had always been sad it had never been able to collect its 15 to 20 percent from.

And a few days later, Dick Greenbaum's assistant met Trip as he got off the elevator, an efficient-looking Indian girl who made almost no chitchat but did offer some water.

He paused to stare at her for a few seconds. What did she know? What secrets did she possess? Did she know about the various bad acts that the rest of the world knew? About writing up the value of trashy securities and handing them over to the Federal Reserve in exchange for treasuries and essentially screwing the American people? What did she know? "I think I would like some water."

When she came back he saw her eyes wander over to the stack of notes that sat on his lap, and maybe she even saw Dick's name. But that was Dick's problem, not Trip's. After all, Trip had not asked to be brought into this whole thing. In fact, Trip had just been minding his own business when his girlfriend had disappeared.

A few seconds later Dick Greenbaum entered. He was shorter than Trip had imagined. Trip wasn't really thinking about Dick, though. He was thinking about the big story he had been trying to break since this Candy thing fell in his lap. He was thinking about his only witness, Petra Smith. He had seen pictures of her on different wire services, and also on Cityfile.com and in the Famous Media Blog. He had even talked to her once on the phone. She had promised that there would be more phone calls. She had alluded to the possibility that she might answer some of his questions about missing K-1s, about financial hanky-panky (not to mention Hanky and Bernanke). And then she had disappeared into the night, never to return—no more sightings, no more pictures, no more anything, just gone.

Trip had wondered where she had gone. Perhaps she had turned in state's evidence. That was possible. It was also possible that the husband had sent her away somewhere where there were no phones, a place like Harbor Island, somewhere she could shop and not concern herself with the coming storm.

And then there was his dead girlfriend. Was there some connection? There couldn't be. Dick Greenbaum probably didn't even know the Kinglys. There were, after all, so many rich people in Manhattan and many did not mix. From just a quick look around Dick's office, Trip could tell that Dick was a rich nonreligious Jew. This meant he went to the fancy Reform temple on Fifth Avenue. His kids probably went to coed schools with high academic standards. And likely he lived in one of about fifty buildings on Park or Fifth.

But enough sociology; he didn't care where Dick Greenbaum's children went to religious school. He did, however, care passionately about Sir Smith Kingly—his demise, that is. God, that was a story he wanted, that was a story that could make him. It was a story that was in a million ways better than the dead girlfriend story. Because in the dead girlfriend story, he figured quite prominently. After all, there would be much talk of drug buying and underage drinking and perhaps a hint of sadomasochism—who could even remember? Also, he was the "boyfriend," which made him seem like he had a vested interest in the story (not classy), and she had a sex blog (also not classy).

Dick Greenbaum was not really sure what Lansing McAllister had wanted with him, and after speaking to him (or listening while Lansing lectured him about all of his relatives who had signed the Constitution) he was even more confused than before. It was like talking to someone underwater. He could hear the ice in Lansing's drink clinking. He could hear the long words and even longer sentences. He wondered if Lansing was drunk or just very boring.

Ultimately this was a man who had lots of time (too much time to be deemed powerful or important), whose wealth betrayed him, made him seem lost, made him seem stupid and aimless. From what Dick could glean, Lansing wanted him to meet with his son. Dick assumed that Trip wanted a job (they all wanted jobs), and of course The Bank wanted to manage the McAllister family fortune, so perhaps the two interests could dovetail. And even if they didn't get the money, Lansing had other good qualities, connections that could get Dick into any private golf club, for example. It was worth it for Dick to waste a few minutes of his day. After all, what was the worst thing that could happen? The prop desk getting another not so smart but very socially connected peon was not going to knock the earth off its axis.

Dick sat down at his desk. He took a breath, inhaling the smell of leather, of his delicious office air, of all the money that floated through it each day. He smoothed the papers on it, as he often did, and then he looked up to study the young man sitting across from him.

To say that Trip McAllister felt uncomfortable was the understatement of the year. Being back at the old office building was haunting.

It was horrible. He felt like a failure, a loser. He had worn sunglasses in the elevator with the hopes that no one would recognize him. Of course no one did. He had been an analyst a few years ago, low man on the totem pole in a world of unrecognizable celebrities too numerous to count.

"So." Dick looked at Trip. It was nice to have power over someone so much better-looking and taller than he was. It was lovely to have the power to crush the dreams of someone who could have quite literally crushed him had they been in the same high school. Yes, Dick might be only five feet six inches, but he was for the purpose of this conversation six feet tall.

Trip felt slightly embarrassed. He hadn't really figured out how he was going to start this delicate conversation. He didn't want to alienate Dick. He didn't want to take a combative tone. "So?"

"Well, I spoke to your father last night and he said . . ." Dick paused. He had no idea what the father had said. As far as he knew the father had clinked the ice in his drink a couple of times and then laughed and then lectured him about the lost art of cartography. Dick looked down and tried a trick he had recently seen a bank president do. He just stopped talking, with the hopes that the other person would become nervous enough to fill in the silence.

Of course, Trip was more nervous than Dick, and so he tripped on himself right away. "First of all, let me just say that anything I might have felt about your predecessor . . . none of that holds true for you."

Dick looked confused.

"I really do want you to know that."

"Of course." Dick was the kind of guy who could not admit when he was confused. He had been taught not to, because it was bad form to look like you didn't understand.

"And anything I may have written . . . about John."

Wait, this guy was a writer? This wasn't totally making sense—not even a little sense—and the phones were starting to ring, people were sending him IMs, emails. He needed to finish with this. He wanted to go for lunch, for lunch in bed, but all his mistresses were dead. It was a morbid thought. He could have a quickie with his wife, he guessed. It seemed slightly disgusting, and also somewhat pointless. He was already paying thousands of dollars a month to keep his wife in that apartment of his. Did he really need to pay more to give her a place to go for lunch? Dick interrupted Trip. "Look, I thought your dad wanted to get you a job here. You can be an analyst but you can't expect special treatment."

Trip looked at Dick with eyes filled with rage. He was not used to being confused with other people. He was not happy. "I worked here! I was fired! I am now a financial blogger. My blog is called Cluster-cash Nation."

It all came back to Dick. That's right, but it had happened awhile back and not on his floor, and what the hell was this guy doing in his office anyway? "Well, we have very strict policies about talking to the media, so I am sorry to say that I am going to have to . . ."

Trip could see he had worn out what little goodwill his father's birth entitled him to. He had to think fast. He remembered the phone call from Landon Stone—that haughty Upper East Side bitch. Maybe she hadn't had concrete evidence. But she knew, just as he did. "My girlfriend . . ." He hated to say "girlfriend," it clogged his throat, made him feel slightly disgusting. He had never felt that she was a girlfriend before, and now that she was gone, now that there was a story there, now that she had ended up on the cover of the *New York Post*, now he was going to milk that story for everything it was worth. He hated the disgusting self-pornography of being a writer; it was like being a rapist and a victim in one. ". . . was Candy Ross Rose."

Dick's face turned cancer white.

Dick was Mr. Big Money; he had thought as much all along. How Candy had gotten to him in the first place, Trip didn't know. Rich people found a way of happening into journalists, into the people who knew how to betray them. He felt sick, the same sick feeling he felt when he thought about his father sitting in his huge old house with all his maps—he felt like the world was laughing at him, the way it did at his father.

"So . . ." Trip paused. "So, you were Mr. Big. . . ." It was a bold move, but American life was filled with bold moves, filled with second acts that were based on being the spokesperson for diet products.

Dick audibly gasped. He then put his head in his hands, which shocked both men. It was an expression of weakness that neither party saw coming. For about ninety seconds Dick left his face in his hands. During that time Trip thought about how uncomfortable he was, how unprepared he was for unexpected things like this. "You can't prove it. It's just speculation." But as Dick was speaking tears were streaming down his face. The tears were so shocking to Trip that they stopped both of them cold. Both men simmered in the unreality of the moment—how had they fallen down this rabbit hole together. So much of their lives were like that, about crossing the threshold of disbelief, but somehow this seemed far worse. This seemed more untrue than all the other untruths of the Affluenza they both suffered from.

"And you had something to do with her disappearance." Landon had been right. He knew it.

More tears. For such a tough guy, the man was crying a lot.

And then Trip took out all the notes, all of Candy's notes, and he put them on the table.

"What is that?" Dick said.

At that moment Raja was lurking by the door to Dick's office, which was just the slightest bit ajar. She pretended to be filing.

Trip looked up. "That is . . ." Trip pointed to the notes in a kind of coy way. "That is twenty-seven pages of notes. Detailed notes, about you, about the things that you've done, the mortgage that The Bank gave you, all the . . ."

The phone was ringing. Then the second line started ringing, then the third, then the fourth. "What do you want?"

Trip paused. What did he want? He guessed that ultimately he wanted fame, but he couldn't say that, could he? And the fame wasn't for himself, it was for his blog. That was much more admirable, right? To have his blog be famous; he wanted many more unique hits—who didn't? It was all about unique visitors, a phrase that sounded like it referred to extraterrestrials. No, this was about more than fame. He wanted to be right, he wanted the moral high ground, and he wanted to avenge the death of his beloved girlfriend. If he even cared about that. He felt fuzzy when he thought about her, about how he would feel about her ten years out. Would she be nothing but a green light on a dock years from now or would his memory far exaggerate her nubile qualities? Trip panicked; he had to say something. "I want justice." It was the first thing that came into his mind. It did in fact sound totally hollow and meaningless. What did that even mean?

Dick rolled his eyes. "What if I trade you?" He didn't want to look desperate, especially in front of such an idiot.

"For what?" Trip immediately got where Dick was going with this, because they were the same in their shared thirst for blood.

Dick paused. He didn't have to be so desperate. After all, it seemed from Trip's speedy response that he might take whatever was on the table. And so Dick slipped back into his usual self. "You're not even going to feign moral indignation?" He also hated himself for baiting Trip, but there was something so profoundly ruthless about this shakedown.

Trip smiled at Dick. These two men had more in common than not. "Make the offer, then we'll see what I feign."

"The idea is a deal. I will trade you the notes, that stack of notes, and of course your silence, so eventually I am trading you that story for an even bigger story."

"A bigger story than the murdered deb sex blogger and her last story?" It was hard for Trip to imagine Dick Greenbaum murdering anyone; for one thing, he had the smallest, roundest little fingers. They were not fingers that could handle manual labor, let alone mauling someone and chucking them in the river. And he was small, five two, maybe five three. He was at least half a foot shorter than Candy Ross Rose. It had to have been his wife.

"What if I give you the biggest financial story in history? What if I give you the biggest Ponzi scheme in history?"

Trip looked down at the paper on Dick's desk. "Sir Smith Kingly." Dick nodded. Trip was a worthy adversary. "What makes you think I don't already have that story?"

Dick smiled. He was also a worthy adversary, perhaps too much so. Dick had to fake it. "I'm sure. You're smart. You have your suspicions. But you don't have actual proof. I have proof. I have the name and the address of a guy who works out of a strip mall in northern New Jersey. Kingly claims he's an auditor but really he's just some guy who sits in an office eating Cinnabons, and he would be willing to talk to you. Unless you can find Petra." Dick thought about Petra, about her pure, white skin. Trip looked at Dick in slack-jawed awe. "But it's my belief that you won't find Petra no matter how hard you look. Because . . ." Dick had never framed anyone before. He liked to think of himself as not really the type. Modern life did not present lots of opportunities for framing, but this was definitely one of them, and why not? He paused coyly. "Because she is not alive anymore."

"Not possible." Trip was shocked. For a second Dick's own guilt betrayed him. Was it possible that Trip didn't believe him, that Trip saw Dick as complicit in the murder in some way? No, not possible, was

it? Trip didn't know about Dick and Petra. No one did. Of course not. Why was he so nervous? "Okay," Trip said tentatively, looking at Dick's tight little mouth all puckered up.

"How do I know? Is that what you want to ask me? It looks like you want to ask me how I know."

"Sure, that's a fine place to start." Trip got out his steno pad, and uncapped his pen.

Dick put his fat fingers to his mouth. "But first a deal."

"A deal?"

"The Kinglys for silence."

Trip paused. It was sleazy, but that wasn't unusual for financial journalism. All kinds of fast news like this was a trade, a war between two evils, one always slightly less evil than the other. "If it checks out. If it's all correct, then yes, then okay."

Dick had ire in his small bloodshot eyes. "No, not okay. Look, I understand honor among thieves but I want you to know . . ." Dick was thinking about the right way to say it, in a way that was still believable but not too threatening. After all, he didn't want Trip thinking he murdered Petra. "I have friends, powerful friends."

Trip paused. He was only half listening. He was depressed enough to find death threats more amusing than scary. He did smoke three packs of cigarettes per day. It seemed to him impossible that someone else would kill him before he did it himself. "Look, you're more used to me as a friend than as an enemy. I can burn you for whatever happened between you and Candy, which would be fun. But let's be honest. We are thieves, so let's honor that. Screwing you now: why? It makes no sense. It's cooking the golden goose, it's killing the beginning of a beautiful friendship."

Dick nodded. He got it. He was on the hook forever and ever. It was fine. Or not fine, but it beat the other choices, the other options. "I got it."

"So." Trip looked down at his blank pad of paper. Soon it would be filled with secrets, secrets that would make him famous, maybe make him worthy of the family name.

"I know this goes without saying, but you have to remove any references to me. I don't want anyone putting this together."

Trip nodded. "So . . . where should we start?" Trip was on the edge of greatness and it felt so amazing, so profoundly powerful. How had he ever doubted himself? "She was murdered?"

"Well"—Dick smiled sheepishly—"she was talking about the scheme. She was meeting with the ADA. Everyone knows they are putting together a case." Dick wasn't sure that this was true but he felt it was definitely a possibility.

Trip nodded. "Well, she called me and wanted to talk. I spoke to her for a few minutes but she clearly wanted to say more."

Dick could not help but feel slightly betrayed. He had to hold himself back from saying what he was thinking, which was something along the lines of, Why didn't she tell me she was already making plans to whore the story around? Also, Trip's revelation confirmed what he had long since suspected, which was that Petra was working as many angles as possible.

And so for hours the two men talked, looked at websites, made lists of feeder funds, of definite, potential, and possible investors. They pored through dummied documents, through investor letters, through all the stuff Dick had been collecting since his headless mistress had visited him oh so long ago. Dick was careful not to reveal how closely he knew Petra, and Trip was careful not to seem too grateful. But both men came away from the meeting filled with respect for the other. Each man found the other smarter than he had anticipated. And at two A.M. when they staggered out of the office, they could call each other friends, and why shouldn't they? After all, they were the good guys, the heroes. They were taking down someone bad, someone who really deserved it, right? No boundaries were being crossed. And that slightly uncomfortable feeling that both men had, what of that? Should they just push that feeling down?

When it was all over, long into the graying autumn night, as Dick was leaving, he spotted Raja still at her desk staring at the window. "Don't you think it's time to go home?"

"I want you to find me another job."

Dick felt a shock run down his spine. "Why? You're great."

"I can't stay here, knowing what I know now. Do you understand what I am saying? I cannot stay at this job, I need you to find me another job." Raja paused as if to ask if that were possible. It was of course possible. "I know this is an unusual request but I want you to know that if you do that, you will have me forever, and my silence will be yours. We'll never talk of any of this, not ever again."

Dick studied the furrows between her eyebrows. She was a young woman, in her early twenties, and yet she looked tormented already. She obviously knew what had transpired that afternoon in his office. He was actually somewhat relieved by the request. Dick nodded. He was quite sick of her moral indignation. He was not the bad guy; the system was. Or, to put it another way, soon she would find herself the caretaker of an irrevocably broken system. "I have a friend at Fortress, or would you rather be somewhere like Bessemer? Do you think you might be interested in being an analyst? I know that it's a huge jump but you have learned a lot of information at this job and I think the discretion with which you treat that information might be worth a job adjustment, don't you?"

She smiled.

And he went home and had a scotch.

This most sordid tale could have ended with Trip posting the story at six A.M. the following morning. With him watching the number of unique hits: first a few, then a hundred, then a thousand, then ten thousand, then a hundred thousand hits. And then there was the phone, ringing and ringing. It rang so much that he would pick it up and it would just be the busy signal. So many people wanted him.

Our story could have ended that afternoon with Sir Kingly arrested at Teterboro trying to board a friend's G4 to Mali because it had no extradition treaty with the United States. It could have ended with a photo of him on the cover of the *New York Post*, hands in handcuffs, the headline saying ROT IN HELL (it turned out he had managed money for News Corporation head Rupert Murdoch).

It could have ended with Trip that night on CNN, or him the next day on *The Daily Show with Jon Stewart,* and the night after that back on CNN to talk to Larry King. It could have ended with Trip signing a seven-figure book deal, with a William Morris literary agent, and a lecture agent, and a TV agent, and a segment (and later a series) on the *Today* show about stopping financial fraud. It could have ended with him coming home to his father to show off his ill-gotten gains.

It could have ended with Dick Greenbaum quietly slipping back into the office the next day. Could have ended with him sitting in Via Quadronno sipping a five-dollar cappuccino with his wife, eating a twelve-dollar fruit salad. It could have ended there on Seventy-third Street, looking out at the Maybachs and the trees. It could have ended with his eyes fixed on the swaying Japanese maple across the street.

It could have ended with both of them sitting there. It could have ended with Daisy promising herself that she would not let herself indulge in her most hideous character defect ever again. Besides, there was no need. Life was perfect now that she had fixed everything. She was convinced that it would, in fact, be that simple. And perhaps it would be.

SPRING 2009

Spring had sprung and the trees in the median on Park Avenue were more lovely than they had ever been. He had walked through the patches of golden sunlight down Park Avenue with a slight spring in his step. It was one of those memoir-worthy nights. Trip found himself the guest of honor at a dinner party that was being thrown at 740 Park Avenue. Here he was, being feted by real people, not some crusty swamp Yankees (like his parents) who considered deviled eggs a fine delicacy. It was all too much, too tempting. He asked the doorman if the Greenbaums were upstairs. Perhaps he was also trying to show off to the doorman, to his friends who were having the party for him, showing that he did, in fact, belong even though the intimidating lobby made him feel otherwise.

The doorman had asked his name more than once, but finally sent him off to the front, to the Park Avenue elevator bank.

And so he went upstairs, just to say hello. After all, Dick Greenbaum had continued to be a useful source. They had chatted on the phone a few weeks ago about a deal The Bank was doing. And of course there was the question of his dead girlfriend. He had basically traded the affair story for the Ponzi story and that was done; too late to renege on that. Besides which, that Ponzi story had put him on the map. He would always love the Kinglys (and Dick) for that. But Trip had wondered if he had sold Candy too cheap. Besides, he was early for the dinner. As for Daisy, she wasn't quite sure who he was but told the doorman to send him up anyway. She didn't want some kind of lobby scene like she had read about in the prior week's *New York* magazine. She didn't want her neighbors thinking she had problems. Of course, in the last few months she had witnessed more than a few neighborly meltdowns. She had found the husband from 3D sleeping on a treadmill one morning when she had gone down for her morning workout. And then there was the cross-dressing son in 2A—twice she had seen him walking the family Pomeranian in full drag. The bear market had made them all crazy, and now a year of breathtaking rallies for seemingly no reason had not eased anyone's anxiety.

Dick was home. He was never home so early in his life, but his back had been giving him problems, so he had been working in the study lying on the wood floor, hoping the hardness of the wood would somehow cure the enormous pain he was feeling. It was at the very least worth a shot. "Someone's here, darling!"

Dick couldn't really hear her. He had been trying to work but now he was just lying there staring at the ceiling, questioning his own existence.

"Someone's here!" she screamed.

Again he had no idea what she was saying but he didn't much care. Perhaps that was the secret of marriage, not having to physically hear what the other person said. Odds were she had come up with another expensive item that she must have—a new sofa or a Birkin or a ridiculously expensive window treatment that she could not and would not live without.

The doorbell rang and Daisy wandered over to the door to open it. She smiled at Trip McAllister, who was handsome with his blondish hair and his big, slightly goofy smile.

"And you must be the beloved wife!" Trip was slightly too pleased with himself. After all, he was famous now. It was the American Dream: born to wealth and power, yet able to parlay that into fame!

"All but the beloved . . ." She laughed and pushed her thick black hair out of her eyes. She was young too. Though the fact that she had pushed children out of orifices made it hard for him to focus.

"I'm Trip."

"Trip, nice to meet you. I'm Daisy." She presented him a tiny white manicured hand that smelled slightly of rose petals. The air was fizzy with the sparks from their chemistry, slightly frenetic.

She was prettier than he thought she would be, with thick black hair and large hollow eyes. He felt immediately that there was a slight edge to her, something nuanced, something slightly sour, something that made all of his suspicions from the year before flood back.

They were walking through the hall, feet treading softly on the wide plank floors, when Dick heard them, his wife and the one person who could destroy her, talking about the moldings. "Yes, these are about three feet high, I guess. We tried to stay faithful to the original. . . . But you know, that's all anyone talks about here, renovations and vacations. . . ." he heard her say. He jumped up from the floor and rushed into the hallway. They were standing there, slightly surprised to see him vertical. "Honey, you shouldn't be standing up like that. Aren't you in utter agony?" He stood in front of the two of them.

Because he loved his wife, and ultimately her crime was as much for him as it was for herself, he felt that it was his job to protect her from the world and, more aptly, from herself. And so, flinching through the enormous pain of all his vertebrae grinding against one another like a car with a gas tank full of sand, he pushed out the words: "Darling"—his back really hurt—"what are you two talking about?"

Trip had never seen Dick in such a state before, and they had been through more than a few subjects that might have caused Dick to appear agitated. Trip watched him curiously. Perhaps Dick was worried about his wife falling in love with Trip. He was a charmer. But that wasn't what this was about. No, Dick was hanging all over Daisy like he was worried, worried about something she might do. Dick had his hands on her shoulders—no small feat, as they were almost the same height.

"Your back, you must be in agony."

"No-o-o-o-o-o." He smiled; his eyes were tearing a little from the pain. "Not at all, but you, my love"—he kissed her on the forehead, slightly for effect—"you must be tired. You should go rest."

"Not right now, darling. I am giving your friend Trip a tour." Daisy paused and looked at both men. It had also occurred to Daisy how oddly Dick was acting. Why was Dick so uncomfortable? "How do you know each other anyway?"

Dick started stammering, "Well, um, uh."

"Work." Trip smiled.

Daisy looked at him, her wild blue eyes locking in on his, the corners of her jagged lips quivering, as if she were in pain. Something was definitely askew.

Landon Stone's voice on the phone echoed in his ear as he remembered that harrowing morning last year: "There is something so not right there. That family, that Daisy, that Dick. People don't just disappear. How many dead people have to turn up before people put it together? She's the one who killed my sister, who killed your girlfriend."

He'd never been positive, since she had no evidence—though it had been great leverage with Dick. But now, looking into her eyes, he knew that it was true: Dick's wife had a secret, a terrible secret. She had murdered Candy because she had discovered that Dick was having an affair with Candy, and then Dick, in an effort to keep his wife from getting caught or himself from being implicated, had figured out a way to get away with it, and that was to blame it on Sir Smith Kingly, who was now going down for the murders of both Candy Ross Rose *and* his wife, who was missing and presumed dead. But that was impossible . . . that would never happen—right? Rich ladies on the Upper East Side don't murder people. It had never ever happened, so how could it possibly start now?

He stopped and he looked at this woman. Without the crazy eyes and the half-cocked expression on her face, he realized that no one would ever believe in a million years that Daisy Greenbaum was a killer. But in a novel, they might buy it in a novel. This whole crazy story would make an amusing novel. And that was when Trip McAllister realized that he had the story of a lifetime and he was going to run with it, all the way to the bank.

Unless she got to him first.

ACKNOWLEDGMENTS

Thank you:
Andy McNicol, Suzanne Gluck, Jill Schwartzman, Caitlin Alexander, Joy Gorman, Lauren Heller Whitney, Bruce Tracy, Mollie Doyle, Sandi Mendelson, and Rebecca Shapiro.

My family:
Erica Jong, Jonathan Fast, Barbara Fast, Ken Burrows, Connie Greenfield, Steward Greenfield, Jo Greenfield, Ben Fast, Dan Fast. All my wonderful cousins and aunts and uncles and stepfamily and, of course, Harold and Linda Koplewicz.

My friends:
Daphne Merkin, Susan Cheever, Alice Kotzen, Alison Cody, Dr. Laura Popper, Amy Wilensky, Hannah Griswold McFarland, Dori Cooperman, Debbie Peltz, Amanda Benchley, Amanda Brainerd,

Amanda Foreman and Jonathan Barton, Tanner Freeman, Alexia Jervis, Jill and Darious Bikoff, Neena Beber, Cee Cee Belford, Deb Kogan, Caitlin Macy, David Patrick Columbia, Bettina Decker, Lauren Santo Domingo, Sharon and Richard Hurowitz, Jill Swid, Marci Klein, Jennifer Saul, Jenn Bandier, Jennifer Rudick, Kenneth Gross, Alex Kuczynski, Andy and Mary Louise Perlman, Madeleine Sackler, Jon Sackler, Mary Corson, Brooke and Burn Nadell, Gretchen Rubin, Ruth Altchek, Gigi Levangie, Billy Norwich, Jen Friedland, Stacy Eisenberg, Jennifer Rubenstein, Jenny Belle, Sue Shapiro, Sherry Fixelle, Ross Brower, Paula Froelich, Melissa C. Morris, Dana Dickey, Anna Holmes, Samantha Stein, Lindsey Glass, Rebecca Mead, Rebecca Traister, Julie Klam, Ellen Davis, Judy Collins, Alex Glass, Glenn Horowitz and Tracey Jackson, James McGinniss, Jennifer Rubenstein, Linda Weil, Ron Hogan, Karah Preiss, Pamela Paul, David Brauschvig, Mary Mobley.

Molly Jong-Fast is the author of the novel *Normal Girl* and the memoir *Girl [Maladjusted]*. Her essays and articles have appeared in numerous magazines and newspapers. She lives in New York City with her husband and her three children.

Read on for an excerpt from

Normal Girl
by Molly Jong-Fast

Published by Villard Books

$\mathcal{I}$ *think* it was Donna Rice or Donna Reed or maybe it was Diana Ross who said Andy Warhol's funeral was like a night at Studio 54. In that vein, Jeff's funeral is the equivalent of a night at Planet Hollywood. But it's all the same really: fast food, cocaine, and disco music. Nothing ever really changes, not around here anyway. Maybe disco has become techno, promiscuous sex has morphed into cautious promiscuous sex, and cell phones have replaced religion as the opiate of the masses, but our relentless obsession with The Next Best Thing–ism (T.N.B.T.-ism) remains the same.

If only it was as simple as me, the out-of-it-never-really-It girl, trying to snort a bump in a speeding taxi. Brushing the cigarette ash off my black tunic, I catch sight of a buttoned-down grandmother and her wiry granddaughter in her school kilt. Flying past them on

Park Avenue, I have a brief moment of that there-is-something-really-wrong-with-my-life feeling. It passes before it can take me. The driver and I argue about which park crossing to take. Ignoring me, he turns abruptly, knocking my little pile of cocaine onto my suede boots. I run my fingers up and down my boots until I've wiped, sucked, and licked every particle of cocaine from within the grains of suede.

Call me an antisocial socialite, but this is my fifth funeral in September and I can't even keep my shoes clean. My grandmother, my aunt, three friends, and a distant cousin have died in the same ninety-one days, making funeral attendance my new profession. I have worn black more in the last three months than I did during my entire Pablo Neruda reading phase. But all this goes with the territory, or so I assume—it's not exactly as if they tell you how to behave when you've murdered your boyfriend. And there's certainly no chapter in Emily Post's etiquette book on the how-to's of attending your victim's funeral.

The temple grows out of the sidewalk on Fifth Avenue, a giant monument to rich Jews. The face of the building is slick, built with white bomb-shelter brick strong enough to withstand the Nazis. There is nothing that could ever affect its structure, not the multitude of deaths mourned here, not the anorexia that wastes the female congregation, not the Prozac that makes them comfortable, not even acid rain. I've been to lots of funerals at this temple; this is the first for someone I've murdered, though.

It's one of those rare hot, sticky, overcast days in September. The kind of day where your thighs stick to the vinyl taxi seats. It's been an exhausting week of hangovers, clumpy mascara, and working at the dreaded gallery. But it's over because it's Thursday and that's when my workweek ends. My plan is this: make an appearance at the funeral; mourn; spend no more than seven minutes alone with my mother; leave; go to Greenwich with some people I find at the funeral; when in Greenwich stay in mother's shrine to herself, raise my liver count, suppress my red-blood-cell count, deaden some nerve endings, and try to have a good time in the process. But I'm flex, except for the seven-minutes part.

Funerals are the cotillions of the nineties, where the young people meet and mingle. All this might seem abnormal to you—the fact that this congregation mourns the teenage sons of bankers every day.

Filling the sidewalk with chatter from their cell phones, these glossy blow-dried mourners shine like they've never had a problem in their perfectly choreographed lives. They aren't like us. The difficulties we normal people suffer slide right off their publicists' backs. Never having had an awkward phase, they live busy lives, adjusting their sunglasses and making sure their unborn children have a place on the waiting list for the Dayton School. Some of them half turn to look at me (maybe it's my dirty fingernails that make me not merit a full turn). I am the living embodiment of an awkward phase. But I must seem vaguely familiar to them—after all, I've been mentioned on Page Six sixteen times, and I'm only nineteen.

I barely have room to move at this movie premiere masquerading as a funeral. There's a paparazzi line and everything, leaving me to wonder who they got to cater the shiva. I really like chocolate rugelach. I noncalorically enjoy the smell of it.

My mother waits for me outside. She is clad in a high-waisted vintage Halston pants suit that's a little too tight for someone of her advanced age, somewhere in the ballpark of forty-five to sixty. Her almost invisible cellulite bubbles in a little bump around her waist. I love her small, doll-like features and her soft voice. I love her littleness. She is thin, in that willowy, dehydrated way all socialites are thin. Her short brown hair may have seen one too many hair dryers, but it still does the job of covering the scars behind her ears. She got her work done in Brazil, early eighties, hence the scars behind her ears. I lean down and kiss her forehead. Because both of us were calculating on the other's lateness, we have nearly missed each other.

"Are those my black burned-velvet pants?" Holding up the back of my shirt, she inspects my butt for a confirmation that they are indeed her pants. "Just making sure you've taken my favorite pants, the only pants that fit me, the ones with the green metallic lining and the feather attached to the back pocket."

"No, hello. No, how are you doing at this tragic time?"

"Sorry, sweetie." She takes my shoulders in a forced hug. I step back, choking on her sickly sweet perfume.

"Where did you get that perfume? It smells . . . hum . . . more dead cat than flower." She frowns and I realize I've hurt her feelings. "I'm sorry. It's nice, very nice and floral. Very floral." I'm trying to behave like nothing is wrong, but the chatter in my head about Jeff, perfume, and the fact that I'd love another bump makes me feel otherwise. A family tree that reads like other people's résumés should guarantee some peace of mind. But I have this feeling where the peace of mind should be, and when I get this feeling . . .

"Miranda, go like this." She points a rounded pink nail in my direction.

"What? Could you not stick your finger in my face?"

"You have something in your teeth."

"Oh, where?" She points to my two front teeth.

"Right there." She sticks her fingernail into my teeth.

"Is it gone?" I look around to make sure that no one's looking at me, the tooth-picker. I have porcelain fronts on all my teeth, making it a challenge to extract things from in between them.

"Here." She pulls the piece of green foliage out. God knows how it got there. I haven't eaten solid food since the advent of Kate Moss, at least I think I haven't. "There." She smiles proudly. She's done with me, finished with her motherly moment. "Let's go."

We walk down the paparazzi line, like sad people at a funeral. Cameras flash but promptly stop when we pass in front of them—

after all, an old socialite and her daughter, there's hardly a scandal in that. If they only knew.

"Should I smile?" I whisper. I just want to look normal. There is nothing wrong with me, no internal crisis that a Xanax couldn't reconcile.

"No, people don't smile at funerals. Keep your head down and look sad."

Mom vogues for the cameras. Like someone who knows how to stick out her neck so her jowls, the jowls of an aging socialite, are stretched out, obscured by her damaged brown hair.

"Right, yeah, sad." I'm not a shrink or anything, but I can say with some authority that it's been a long time since I've had a feeling that hasn't been a direct result of some drug I've taken. So the word sad just seems like another word that rolls down my tongue and out of my mouth.

"Come on, Miranda." She sounds agitated, fidgety; she needs a nice stiff vodka tonic. "I'd think you'd be good at this by now."

"I'd think so too, but . . ."

"Yeah."

"Miraaandaaa!" I feel a shock run through my hair follicles from a voice that could make me bald. I turn, pulling my arm away from Mom's.

James Wool looks like a newspaper reporter but isn't. He talks like he's smart, which he also isn't. And he's natty, like his tweed jacket. His lips are so far from my cheek when he air-kisses me, he's still in the 718 area code.

"Well, well. How is everybody's little vixen?"

"Hi, James."

"Wasn't he young? Isn't this sad? Horrible really? Didn't you see this coming? I didn't, but you must have. Didn't you? Can you believe he was so young?" James doesn't engage in normal conversation; instead he shoots questions in the general direction of the person he's talking at. Doesn't he know I was trained as a charming dinner companion, not as an intellectual?

"No, yes, yes, yes . . . yes, no, well, twenty-nine isn't that young, but it's young to die. I guess." Personally, I can't imagine why anyone would want to live past twenty-one; after all, doctors recommend standard colonoscopies every year after turning fifty—blah. Gastroenterology aside, most people don't die three months after turning twenty-nine. I almost reach for his hand, but then I remember we Wokes don't do that kind of thing. People push past us. James doesn't move. I need him to go away.

"So, Miranda. Tell me, what are we up to these days?" James lived in England for one semester in college. Ever since then his speech has been plagued with annoying Euroisms.

"Nothing. I'm working at the gallery two days a week now, which is really interfering with my martini schedule . . . and I'm supposed to be involved in this group show for women. But I just can't get inspired. So I've decided to go to parties until the inspiration hits me."

"Brilliant, brilliant." Even his chuckle is patronizing as he plays with his glasses, as if to say he finds inanimate objects more interesting than me. "I mean, how many times does one get to be nineteen?"

"Right. But James, most people here think I'm twenty-two, so don't tell them I'm nineteen." He looks at me as if to say this is exactly what he expects from someone like me. "Do you swear?"

"I wonder why everyone doesn't just drop out of college and paint. I wonder why everyone doesn't do exactly what they want to."

"Gee. I don't know. They should. Come out of the closet much?"

"I must find my wife. *Ciao. Ciao.*" He walks away, thank God. I watch his feet until I can no longer differentiate his baby-blue Hush Puppies from anyone else's.

People file in—socialites, models, and various uptowners. You know this is either a funeral or a fashion show, because there aren't enough seats. I slide onto the wooden bench, wedging myself between Mom and the armrest that ends the bench. Mom sits next to Jeff's leathery mother, who clocks enough hours at Capri Tanning Center to be considered more handbag than woman.

I survey the population, like the social scientist I am—behind me is the Southampton, Upper East Side crowd, on my right is the rich and old, Upper West Side communist-turned-capitalist contingent. To my left is the "I want to be an editor, so buy me a magazine" group. Eurotrash is in the back left corner, defrocked royalty in the back right. The group has sorted and divided itself in minutes.

"Miranda." Someone's hand is on my shoulder, invading that invisible barrier of what is mine versus what is yours. I flinch; there are two people who can touch me. One of them is dead, and the other is not Whit. I know it's Whit because I can hear the drag of his umbrella on the tile and I can smell him—even from thirty feet away the subtle mixture of Halston cologne, cigars, and vodka permeates the membrane. Since I've known him, he's always carried an umbrella. It's possible that even if it were to never rain again, he'd still carry an umbrella. I brush his hand off my shoulder as if it were dandruff.

"Whit, what are you doing here?" I whisper, "You didn't even know him."

"We can't all be friends with the A-list. But it's a free country; I can surely attend anyone's funeral." Whit and I met through Crown Princess Marie of Kona (before she died of a mysterious form of pneumonia, aka AIDS). He felt familiar to me, something Harvard in the way he lectured me, something impressive in his vast knowledge of all those books longer than a thousand pages that I hadn't even started. I had a rare moment of good judgment and didn't let him seduce me. I think that won his respect.

"Whit, you look so handsome," I say, flirting, lying.

"You think? How's life in the art world treating you?"

"Use the word *life* lightly."

"Well, how is it?" he says, fishing for a problem to solve.

"You know, the usual. Answering the phone, staring into space, checking my voice mail, keeping one eye out for the future Mr. Woke." I look around trying to find someone cute to make eye contact with to rescue me from this conversation. "So, tell me about how busy you are?"

"What do you mean?" He's so obnoxious.

"I'm sure you're very busy, right?" Something busy that will never materialize into a paycheck or even a mention.

"Hiiiiiiiii. Whit, you look so handsome." Clearly Mom and I have reviewed the same social manual, *The Woke Way for Wakes, Shiva, and Funerals.*

"Hello, Diana." Whit hates my mother, for a number of reasons. Reason number one: He is appalled by her fifty-by-fifty-foot closet filled with enough Manolo Blahnik shoes to bring a Third World country out of famine.

She puts her arm around my shoulder, and I shake her off. "Mom." She senses my annoyance. Maybe I could get high from smoking my boots—there's probably enough cocaine in the suede, but I can't imagine smoking suede is that much fun.

"Well—" Her cell phone rings, and with this she descends into the level of hell reserved only for dermatologists who advertise on subways and socialites who talk on cell phones at funerals. "I'm sorry, darling."

"What are you sorry for?" I snap at her.

A few manicured nails dismiss me with the "I'm talking on my cell phone at a funeral" sign. And yet another mortifying mommy moment has taken place.

"What is she saying?" Whit leans a little too close to me. I shake my head as if to say I don't know.

Lucy Sunningdale winks at Mom as if to say, "Hey, comrade of the mutual admiration society . . ." That should make Mom happy, if she notices. Whit is dressed in layers—blue shirt under gray vest, under brown jacket, under plaid scarf, all under a bowler hat. I wonder how long it takes him to pile on all that clothing in the morning.

"So, Whit, what are you working on these days?"

"I'm working on a project with Mary Westheimer. You must know who she is?"

I do. "No."

"Miranda." He looks at me like I've never had a thought in my life. "She's *the* pinnacle, *the most* famous, *most* important female artist in the world, and I am doing her next piece."

"But you're not an artist."

"Miranda, you need to listen, that's your problem. I didn't say that, I said I was doing her next piece. You're cripplingly literal. That's your problem: black-and-white, literal thinking. You kill me."

I hope not. I can only handle being responsible for one person's death.

He looks at my shaking left hand. I try to hold it still with my right hand. "What?" He looks at me with that I-know-what-your-problem-is-because-I-took-psychology-in-college look. "What?"

"You have been seeming the tiniest bit odd lately. I mean, not that odd but a little . . . a little bit off."

I try to move away from him. "Is it hot in here or what?"

He moves his face closer to mine. "Really. I just think you might . . . I don't know . . . be taking too many sleeping pills. That might be your problem."

"Ah. No."

"You seem, I don't know . . ." Seem like a murderer? I'd go with that. After all, I think I just killed my boyfriend. He inhales deeply and looks at me. ". . . thinner."

"New diet." I smile.

"Yeah."

"I've lost fifteen pounds. I needed to lose the weight. You remember how blubberous I was when I came back from London."

"Yeah. You were huge. Massive. Now, that was bloat, my God, that was bloat." He plays with the handle of his umbrella.

"Thanks."

"But I know the diet you're on." He smiles.

"What? You mean the eighties diet: all cocaine and grapefruit, all the time."

"Not funny."

"Whit, save the value judgments. New topic. I really don't think any of this is your business anyway."

He nods. "It's all my business. Always. Everything's my business."

"What are you, a gangster? You sound like a gangster . . . or a gossip columnist."

"Maybe I am. A gangster, that is."

"Sure, whatever. Maybe . . ." I look around. This conversation is droning on, so I interject the universal sign for "Let's end this conversation": "Anyway." I sigh.

And right on cue: "Oh, there's my dear friend Alex." A mass of golden-brown curly hair walks by us. Whit waves furiously. Those tresses can claim responsibility for seducing every woman under thirty-five in the art world.

"Whit."

"What?" he says as he turns toward Alex and his hair.

"I don't know how you can say Alex is your dearest friend," I whisper. "I was at a party with him, and when I dropped your name, there was no recognition. No flicker that he ever knew what I was talking about. It was like I was speaking Portuguese."

"Your problem is you need to see a doctor. Get help." Whit leaves me to chase after Alex.

I turn back to Mom, who has somehow started talking to Sloane Billbinder. It's lifeboats on the *Titanic*, cocktail-party syndrome. "So, Sloane, what's the new hair color for fall?" Mom asks as if she's discussing Kierkegaard.

"White-gray on the under-twenty set, black for over thirty. I just love the new fall cut, too. It's sooo cute. It's going to look beyond superperfect on Miranda. Marcus—you know Marcus, my husband? Anyway, he thinks Miranda would look great in a sort of modified Paula Jones look. I like to think of the cut as a P.J.—modern yet functional yet political." Sloane never fidgets. Her hands are attached to skinny arms, which are attached to tiny shoulders. Her other bones stick out at fashionable right angles. Her white-blond hair sits in a loose knot at the nape of her neck, and she is wispy the way soap opera stars are when engaged in conversation. She is the kind of woman who stuffs her dead cats and displays them lovingly on the coffee table. I don't even have a coffee table.

"Yeah?" I look at both of them. Is this normal funeral conversation?

"Miranda, you look so cute, darling. Really thin." Sloane squeezes my shoulder to articulate her point. I'm gonna bet Ms. Billbinder never murdered any of *her* boyfriends or ex-husbands.

"Well, if it seems like it'll look good on her, then I want her to have that haircut. I think she needs a new look. In fact, I'm buying her a whole new fall wardrobe. She's been somewhat depressed. I think this will perk her up. Don't you, Sloane?"

"Mom. God. Don't waste your time. I'll just have Dr. Berkenstein up my Prozac."

"Excuse me." Mom takes a tone that sounds suspiciously authority-figure. Sloane seems a little taken aback.

"What? It's the nineties, I can't talk about psychopharmacology at a funeral? At least give me that."

Janice taps me hard on the shoulder. She is seated on the pew behind me. "Hey, kiddo," she quietly mouths. I am kiddo because for all practical purposes I am all of ten years old in the mind of fashion aficionado, former model, former and current junkie, current wife of James, and former stripper Janice.

"Hey, Janice, we were just talking about Prozac. Want to join in? What are your thoughts on the subject of psychopharmacology?" She smiles at me as if to say shut up. She hugs me, and I can feel her ribs through her sheer silk designer blouse. She turns her back to us to go rub ribs with some girl who looks like a refugee but is actually the bearer of the new calf for Calvin clam diggers. She leaves and the smell of Chanel No. 5 lingers, almost blocking out the formaldehyde smell of funeral, which is a taste thousands of grams of cocaine can't cover.

The noise starts to subside. The rabbi enters. For a moment there is silence, just breath. Maybe for a half second I have the feeling everything might be okay. The pressure falls from my shoulders and the silence makes my ears ring. Then the rabbi starts to speak, and so does everybody else.

The rabbi introduces Jeff's plasticky sister and hobbles off the stage. What little of Jeff's sister's body is naturally hers is draped in a gray suit and ice-blue shirt. I sweat a lot; I'd sweat right through that kind of soft chambray. Her smart blond Waspy hair and blue eyes promise her at the very least marriage to a money guy and the fifteen rooms on Fifth Avenue that follow suit. Jeff's sister waxes Upper East Side *Melrose Place.* She had a Porsche in high school and used it, or more accurately the backseat of it, to give all the popular boys blow jobs while Billy Joel whined out "Piano Man." At the time, her tendency toward Billy Joel seemed more offensive than her sluttiness. She gets up and starts to lose herself in her sentences. In a disconcerting muddle she looks at me harshly, like I murdered her brother, which I did.

Jeff only wore black and gray. I'm sure he's wearing a black suit even now. I wonder what he smells like. Probably like formaldehyde. Better than his usual smell of burnt Tums (aka crack), sex, and cigarettes.

Jeff and I never quite worked as lovers. It seemed the harder I tried, the meaner he got. I should have pulled up stakes a long time ago. But as with everything else in my life, there came a point when I didn't have a choice anymore, a time when, like the drugs, he was as much me as I was.

I turn back and look at Janice. She's flirting with the new and soon-to-be-ex editor of *Mavda Magazine*. *Mavda Magazine* vibing with hipness, oozing from every well-formatted, contrived, embellished story about the men who live dangerously in high-end retail stores around Manhattan. Typical, she can't quite pick the winners. The row behind them is filled with journalists like David Faxem, a notorious *Speak Magazine* hit man defined by his love of hotel rooms that rent by the hour and my personal brainchild, the seventeen-martini lunch. David earns his frequent-flyer miles with trips to Hazelden. He rubs leather-padded shoulders with Janice's gay husband, James Wool. James Wool is an artistic genius, or so says *Upper East Side Jewish Socialite Magazine*, which is always wrong about everything, but maybe he's a genius baby-sitter (having cut his teeth on the Schnabel kids).

"Are those pants last season's?" David whispers at me.

"Fuck off."

"I thought I saw them on the rack at Loehmann's." I turn around and smile at David, who in turn smiles at James. Mom, who has radar for anything about herself, tunes in and whispers, "Those pants look fab on you; don't listen to them."

Jeff's sister has left the podium, and now Brett settles in and gazes across the room. The law of cocaine physics dictates that he'll never make eye contact with a single congregation member; the tear of sweat on his forehead further assures this. He struggles with the microphone as if he has something urgent to say. I can see his face try to muster the right brand of emotion.

"He's Mafia," I whisper in Mom's ear.

"Prove it."

"Isn't the suit proof enough?"

Printed in the United States
by Baker & Taylor Publisher Services